THE

The glittering French Riviera.

THE ACTION

A giant jewel heist, an artistic theft of great paintings, a cunning kidnapping, a savage duel to the death against a sinister drug-smuggling syndicate.

THE HERO

A man named Roquebrun, otherwise known as the Fox, the leader of—

THE ZOO GANG

THE
ZOO
GANG

PAUL
GALLICO

A DELL BOOK

TO VIRGINIA

Published by
DELL PUBLISHING CO., INC.
1 Dag Hammarskjold Plaza
New York, New York 10017

Contents

The Picture Thieves

COLONEL Pierre Roquebrun emerged from his villa at nine o'clock on a certain bright, sunshine-filled Riviera morning, and walked down the path to his antique shop which was located one kilometre before the village of La Tourette on the road between Vence and Grasse.

His thoughts were stray, diverse and contented as he let himself into the back door of the elegant shop: a pair of Sèvres vases he hoped to coax out of a widow who lived in St. Paul; the Louis XIII salt cellar that must be sent off to London; some doubts as to the authenticity of a 13th century carved Christ that had been offered him.

Unlocking the front door, he picked up his copy of the *Nice-Matin* and thereafter his thoughts were no longer scattered. For the first page was black with headlines heralding the story of the latest picture robbery, the third apparently in a series of assaults upon world famous canvases owned by the rich.

In the earlier burglaries an El Greco and a Van Dyke had been stolen from the villa of a Swiss industrialist on the Cap d'Antibes, a man with a young wife who had displayed a strange reluctance to discuss the theft. From another mansion on Cap Ferrat, this time belonging to the widow of an Argentine cattle baron, canvases by Picasso, Matisse, Gauguin and Modigliani had vanished. This burglary was accompanied by murder. An aged caretaker who had apparently struggled to protect the property had been shot.

The theft during the past night, confirmed in large black type in the paper before him, of twelve famous Renoirs to the value of two and a half million dollars from the *Musée des Maîtres Modernes* in Cannes, was by far the most sensational and likewise one somehow brought closest to home to the Colonel, since the American millionaire, Joel Howard, to whom the pictures belonged, was a personal friend and client.

The *Musée des Maîtres Modernes* was just concluding a brilliant exhibition of Renoirs. The nightwatchman on duty had been bound and gagged. The burglary alarms and other security precautions had been rendered useless. All of the twelve pictures stolen were on loan from the collection of Mr Joel Howard, the textile magnate, housed in his opulent villa overlooking Cannes. Amongst them was the famous Blue Renoir for which the French Government had just completed negotiations with the American to purchase for the Louvre for half a million dollars.

There were two things that puzzled the Colonel. One was that the third and most startling burglary did not match the other two. The second was that he had heard nothing; no hint of any kind. Not so much as a mouse had squeaked. Not that a respectable antiquarian, who in addition to the usual clutter of French Honours held a number of important foreign decorations, could be expected to be a repository of burglars' timetables. But the fact was that the Colonel had a past. All kinds of strange bits of information, gossip and rumours came bubbling up out of the Riviera underworld, passed inside Colonel Roquebrun's bald, polished skull and there remained sealed.

Now in his sixties, the Colonel tended his antique shop, bought, sold and minded his own business.

A car crunched to a halt in the gravel of his driveway. Colonel Roquebrun looked from his newspaper to the window and saw the gleaming cream and chrome Jaguar of Sarah Howard, Joel Howard's daughter. She was alone.

He went to meet her and stood framed in the doorway, a stocky, indomitable figure whose still young, bright blue and clever eyes showed from a battered countenance that had practically been re-built, for he had suffered unspeakable tortures in the cellars of the Gestapo.

The girl ran towards him from the car so swiftly that her auburn hair streamed out behind her for an instant, and as the Colonel looked into her small, piquant face he saw that she was deathly pale and her hazel eyes dilated.

'Oh, Colonel Roquebrun,' she gasped, and then,

quite suddenly, burst into tears.

'Sarah, my dear Sarah,' said the Colonel, and putting his arm about her shoulder led her into the shop, for although she was barely twenty they were old friends.

When her tears had finished, she looked up and said, 'Isn't it silly of me?'

'Theft is always a shock,' the Colonel replied.

The shouting newsprint caught her attention for an instant and she half whispered, 'They've Daddy's pictures.'

The Colonel nodded. 'I was wondering who *they* were.' He had not directed the question at her and therefore was the more surprised at her reply.

'I don't know! People! Anyone, I suppose.' Then Sarah gave him a despairing look and whispered, 'I'm frightened. Supposing it were all my fault?'

'My dear Sarah, your fault?' But as soon as he put the direct question to her it appeared momentarily to dissipate her panic, or whatever was causing it, and plunge her into a sea of doubts and evasions.

'It's so utterly absurd,' she said. 'I'm sure they're quite all right. They must be, mustn't they?' And since the Colonel did not reply, being unable to, she continued, 'I mean, that's why I have come. You know everyone, don't you—I mean *about* everyone?' Sarah concluded with sudden passion, as though this would solve all her problems.

The Colonel replied cautiously, 'Sometimes.

Who are these friends who are troubling you so?'

Sarah replied, 'I feel like such a fool. You see, Diana has been staying with me at the villa. Daddy has been in New York. I telephoned him. He's flying over tomorrow.'

'Diana who?'

'Oh,' said Sarah, 'there's nothing wrong with Diana. She's English. Diana Finley. Her father has cotton mills. Daddy does business with him. She has a boyfriend.'

The Colonel said nothing and Sarah continued, somewhat too quickly, 'He's very nice and knows an awful lot about things. Diana's quite mad about Kip.'

'Kip?'

'Kip Trenchley. He's really very sweet to Diana.'

A faint bell tinkled in the Colonel's well stocked attic of names and places and people. Ever since a grateful British Government had bestowed the Order of the British Empire upon him he had considered himself a kind of continuing partner of that country and therefore read the English newspapers assiduously. The name Kip Trenchley brought up an association he could not place beyond being aware that it was disagreeable. 'Yes,' he said, 'and the others?'

Sarah blinked at him for a moment, looking as though she wished she had not come, and replied hesitantly, 'Well, there are really eight of us, two more girls and the four men. We've been going places together. The girls Nicole and Elena are very nice—I think. I mean, Harry says they come from very good French families.'

'Harry?' said the Colonel, as though fastening him to a board with a pin.

Doubt again crept into Sarah's voice and gave it something of a little girl quality. 'Harry's the one I'm attracted to. He's sort of fascinating.'

The Colonel nodded but withheld comment.

Sarah continued, 'Well, there's Marcel Dufour who runs the Blue Grotto restaurant. Everyone knows he's all right. He even looks rather like a saint I always think. He's an old friend of Kip's.'

For the first time during the interview the Colonel concealed definite alarm. He did know Marcel Dufour and knew likewise that he was not at all 'all right.' As proprietor of the fashionable Blue Grotto restaurant just outside Théoul, patronised by the international set, he was provided with a cover of firm respectability. The snow-white hair and the thin, tanned face that gave him the look of an Indian ascetic cloaked a wicked man.

'And Count Andrea,' Sarah continued. 'Paolo Andrea. He's Italian. He's a friend of Harry's.'

'Ah yes,' said the Colonel, 'Harry. Harry who?'

The colour that flushed Sarah's face gave away her embarrassment and her voice fell almost to a whisper again. 'Isn't it just too utterly ridiculous? I don't know. Just Harry.'

And then quickly the words came tumbling forth in a rush of self-reassurance. 'He's an American. He's terribly handsome and has been everywhere. Everyone knows him.'

The Colonel had reservations as to who 'everyone' might be, but he merely asked, 'Then what are you frightened of?'

This time the direct question turned Sarah from a fluttering young girl into her father's daughter. She thought hard and deeply, trying to marshal her feelings into coherence. She said finally, her eyes narrowed with the intensity of her concentration, 'I don't really know. I couldn't write it down on paper if I tried and I can hardly tell it to you. I never really knew that I ever felt anything before, but this morning when the police came to the house and told me about Daddy's pictures being stolen and began asking me questions, there it was.'

'There what was?'

Sarah's eyes narrowed again and she blinked once more as though to keep out the light of what she was seeing. 'Well, the four of them,' she said. 'Marcel, Kip, Paolo and Harry. The girls don't count—Nicole and Elena I mean—they're too stupid. Don't you see, when something has been stolen and the police are about, everything somehow begins to look different.'

The Colonel said, 'Yes, I understand very well.'

'I mean,' said Sarah, 'Count Andrea is very nice but he could be awful too, couldn't he?'

'Quite,' replied the Colonel, suppressing an internal shudder. The very word 'Count' was suspect on the Riviera. Then he asked, 'And Harry? Harry and you?'

Sarah replied quickly with a kind of breathless-

ness, 'Oh, nothing has *happened*.' And then she
added, 'I like him terribly, even though sometimes he worries me. Nothing has happened—but
don't you see—it could.'

The Colonel now regarded the young girl gravely and asked, 'And just what is it you wish me to
do, Sarah?'

Sarah folded her hands with the earnestness of
her plea. 'Come and look, would you? We're dining tonight at the Society Club in Cannes. Just
come and sit somewhere and see. You know so
much about everyone. You might be able to tell
whether I am just being silly and childish, or
whether'—and here she gave a quick little shudder—'I'm right to be utterly terrified.'

'Very well,' said the Colonel, 'I'll come. You
will, of course, not recognize me.'

Sarah nodded her head vigorously. She said,
'Oh, thank you. It's the kind of thing I couldn't
even tell Daddy.'

The Colonel accompanied her to the door and
stood watching her as she walked across to her car.
But half-way there she turned and stood uncertainly for a moment.

'You see,' she cried then, 'the utterly stupid, absurd and ridiculous thing is that they couldn't
possibly have done it. Harry and I were together
last night. He didn't leave me until five o'clock
this morning.' And then with a kind of wail, as
though expecting to be disbelieved, she repeated,
'But nothing happened, I promise you, we just
danced. But he couldn't have done it.'

They stood there for a moment facing one another, the inescapable alibi between them like a living thing. The Colonel's heart was torn by the terror behind Sarah's cry that nothing had happened. But one day it would. This was the game of the Harrys who prowled the Riviera. But he said only, 'I see.' And then asked, 'When were the pictures to be returned to your father from the museum?'

Sarah replied, 'Monday. The exhibition ends on Saturday. Why?'

The Colonel merely grunted and said, 'I'll be there this evening. After I have left pay a little visit to the powder room.' He watched her as she got into her car and drove off. At least something seemed to have been lifted from her shoulders by his promise.

The noise of Sarah's departing vehicle had hardly died away when the car of the second early caller that morning ground to a halt outside the shop. The Colonel did not know whether he was pleased or angry at the visit, but in view of the tidings in the newspaper he was certainly not surprised to see Captain Claude Scoubide, Chief of the Detective Force of the important *Service Régionale de Police Judiciaire.*

The Colonel and Captain Scoubide exchanged 'Good Mornings' and Roquebrun thought that the small, clever eyes of the detective were darting about his shop almost as though he had expected to find the stolen pictures hanging on the walls and was frankly disappointed when he failed to see them.

Captain Scoubide did not look like a policeman

or even a detective, but rather like any of the thousands of tourists swarming the south of France that summer. He was a small, slightly built man with a narrow face and a neat moustache over thin lips but his eyes were dark and luminously intelligent. The disguise he affected was simply to dress like every other tourist; slacks, sandals and short-sleeved open-neck shirts in bright colours. Added to this he usually carried the ubiquitous camera and light meter slung about his neck.

But he was nobody's fool and ideal for his job since he was capable and not entirely honest, but his dishonesty was on the side of the angels, so to speak, and had to do with some of his methods, an almost essential quality in a detective operating on the Riviera.

That which had drawn Captain Scoubide to Colonel Roquebrun's antique shop that morning had been one of those policeman's hunches that come from nowhere and every so often pay off most astonishingly. The question that was agitating Captain Scoubide was how to tackle the subject and still remain 'correct'.

The Colonel, well aware of Scoubide's difficulty, was at first inclined to let him wriggle, but then took pity and said, 'Can I help you, Captain?'

Scoubide was instantly into the breach, his head cocked to one side, as he replied, 'Well, can you?'

Such abruptness was verging upon 'incorrectness' and the Colonel felt compelled to challenge him. 'My dear Scoubide!' he said.

But the Captain's roving eyes were now unmistakably halted upon the *Nice-Matin* with its black headlines and strings of zeros denoting the millions worth of the robbery. 'Have you heard anything?' he asked.

'And why, my friend, should you think that I would have heard something?'

Captain Scoubide made a deprecating gesture. 'Your formidable reputation has not diminished, Colonel. Everyone knows you. Everyone trusts you. Everyone is your friend, from the highest to the lowest here on the Riviera. I am not the only one who remembers your services to your country as the leader of the Resistance here, during the war.' Indeed, anyone with half an eye would have noted that the Colonel had been through the wars, though not how he had come by the scars whose white lines ran counter to the furrows made by time on his countenance. Half his left ear was missing. His bald head was a crisscross of scars and he had an extraordinary way when making a sale, taking cash or a cheque, or giving change, of manipulating his hands so nimbly and expeditiously, that the ordinary client would not notice the total absence of finger-nails. But Captain Scoubide knew that the Gestapo had removed these one by one during interrogation and that an American surgeon had rebuilt his face for him when the advancing forces of the Allies had plucked the Colonel from the cellars of his German torturers, outside Cannes, before it was too late. He was still a commanding and powerful figure and one to be reckoned with behind the scenes of the playground known as the Côte d'Azur.

The Colonel remained silent at this and Scoubide continued. 'During the days of the German occupation as the leader of the Resistance this entire area was under your command. There was every kind enrolled in your secret army—perhaps someone might have talked to you.'

The Colonel thought to himself, *what the devil is he driving at?* 'Now who do you think might have talked to me?' he asked.

Captain Scoubide shrugged and replied merely, '—One meets so many people.' He looked about the antique shop again, scratching his head, and said, 'The question which puzzles me is how they will market them.'

The Colonel nodded. 'That is indeed a problem.'

'How would *you* dispose of them?' Captain Scoubide asked. 'After all, you are in the business so to speak.'

The Colonel's face flushed red, colouring all but the long white scar. He said, 'Are you not somewhat wanting in tact, my dear Captain?'

Captain Scoubide threw up his hands, horrified at being misunderstood. 'No, no, no!' he protested. 'A thousand pardons! The question was purely hypothetical. If one had such valuable pictures to sell—'

'—one would realize if one were not a congenital lunatic that the market is extremely limited and the transaction likely to be accompanied by considerable publicity,' the Colonel concluded for him.

Captain Scoubide looked thoughtful and repeated, 'Congenital lunatic! That's a good one. I have just been sniffing about the scene of the crime, and do you know what struck me? The amateur professionalism of it.'

Colonel Roquebrun lifted an eyebrow to distract Captain Scoubide from what might otherwise have been taken as a startled reaction. 'How could that be?' he asked.

'A professional job done by amateurs, perhaps?'

The drift was now unmistakable to Colonel Roquebrun and he thought it high time to bring the conversation to an end. He said, 'I never heard of burglaries and paradoxes mixing. Why not enquire of Marcel Dufour at the Blue Grotto? He would give you an excellent meal during which you could make up your mind whether his restaurant was a professional or an amateur activity.'

Captain Scoubide laughed, and then made a grimace. 'He has too many connections,' he said. 'One could get one's nose pinched in the door there. A large reward has been offered.'

The Colonel wondered where this was leading, but merely commented, 'Yes, 250,000 Francs. The insurance company, I suppose?'

'500,000,' Captain Scoubide corrected, 'the Government has doubled it. A matter of national pride. The Blue Renoir was destined for the Louvre, you know.' And then he added, with what struck the Colonel as almost a curious and pathetic kind of wistfulness, "I would not wish for myself any part of it. For me, the glory of recovering the pictures undamaged would be sufficient.'

The Colonel commented gravely, 'I sincerely

hope your distinguished career will be crowned
by this achievement.'

The Captain acknowledged the compliment and
prepared to leave. 'Should anything reach your
ears—' he said.

'—naturally,' Roquebrun concluded, and
watched seriously reflecting through the window
as the Captain marched to his black Citroën and departed. The Colonel was feeling not at all comfortable.

The four picture thieves sat gloomy and sweating at the back of a dark and scruffy little bar
known as *Le Perroquet Rouge,* off the Place de la
République in Antibes. Their names were Gaston
Rive, Antoine Petitpierre, Jean Soleau and Alphonse Cousin. Some thirty years before, they had
each had a cover name and were known respec-
tively as *Le Léopard, Le Tigre, L'Elephánt* and
Le Loup, and naturally when one of their operations was discussed they were referred to as the
Zoological Gang.

None of this menagerie resembled the *noms de
guerre* they had chosen for themselves. Jean
Soleau, the Elephant, was a wry, dried-up shrimp
of a man, now a wholesale dealer in onions, but
his speciality during the days of resistance had
been sabotage. Gaston Rive, the Leopard, was
enormous, fat and slothful. He had been corpulent
even in his youth, which worked in his favour
since the Germans were inclined to consider him
useless. Now fatter than ever, he was the proprie-

tor of a small electrical contracting business in Cannes. He had been invaluable to the Zoo Gang during the war in eavesdropping communications or anything to do with electricity.

And no one could have been less like his namesake than Antoine Petitpierre, the Tiger, a tall, cadaverous, mild-mannered, gentle, melancholy man. And yet, perhaps 'Tiger' fitted him very well, for he had been the executioner when it was necessary, for whatever purpose, to kill. The Tiger did it quietly, efficiently and unemotionally, with whatever weapon circumstances dictated, but his preference was for a long, thin bladed knife.

The last of the group, *Le Loup,* or the Wolf, as Alphonse Cousin had been known, was the owner of the bar. He did have something lupine about him, dark and lean, with glowing eyes and a sardonic mouth. Before he had acquired his café, he had been a locksmith, and thus his natural method for making life difficult for occupying Germans had been breaking and entering. He also had an avocation which he cultivated as an aid to the group. He could fly anything that had wings.

The door to the back room was shut so that their desultory murmur of conversation could not be overheard. A radio, turned off, stood on the sideboard. The copy of the *Nice-Matin* lay on the table. The Tiger said, 'Dear God, whoever would have thought there would have been such a fuss over a few pictures?'

The Wolf gave a snort. 'You call a millionaire's Renoir collection a few pictures?'

The Leopard had asthma as well as too much blubber, and his breath whistled through his nostrils as he exclaimed, '500,000 francs reward!' He nodded his head in the direction of the radio. 'You heard it!'

The Elephant said, 'Every stool-pigeon in the neighbourhood will be trying to earn it.'

The Leopard sighed like an engine discharging steam. 'And the police setting up road blocks. We shall never be able to move them now.'

The Elephant eyed him coldly. 'Are you proposing, then, to leave them in my warehouse amongst my onions 'til the *flics* descend upon us?'

The Wolf leaned darkly across the table, poking a long finger at the Elephant. 'Can you suggest an alternative, old friend?'

No one had anything to offer.

The Tiger leaned back in his chair and examined his fingernails. 'Perhaps we were a little too hasty.'

'I said we should have consulted *Le Renard*,' put in the Elephant.

The Wolf laughed silently. 'The Fox would have vetoed it.'

The Leopard said, 'He was always our leader—'

'—and the only one of us with any brains,' concluded the Elephant.

The Tiger completed the inspection of his fingernails and said with glum fervour, 'I wish to God he were here with us now. We've got ourselves into a pretty pickle.'

It was characteristic of the kind of courage they

all had that the sharp knock on the door that followed this wish did not panic them. Not a man moved.

The Wolf said, '*Entrez!*'

The door opened. Colonel Roquebrun stood framed in the doorway, thickset, bull-necked, florid.

'*Renard!*' The word exploded from the blubbery lips of the fat Leopard. 'We were just wishing—'

Colonel Roquebrun came into the room, shutting the door carefully behind him. He eyed them coldly. 'You idiots,' he said, 'where are the pictures?'

The dark eyes of the Wolf glowed and his sardonic mouth permitted itself a smile. The old Fox was still the Fox. One did not have to draw diagrams for him. He said, 'In Jean's warehouse amongst the onions. Smelly, but safe.'

Contempt marked the scarred features of the Colonel. 'And what the devil do you think you are going to do with them? Give me a drink someone.' He sat down at the table while the Wolf reached behind to a cognac bottle and poured him a *fine*. They all sat and watched him like four guilty children while he knocked it back.

Roquebrun set down his empty glass and sat staring silently at the four, who eventually began to recover some of their lost aplomb. After all, they were grown men banded together in a dangerous adventure that was far from concluded.

The Colonel quickly felt the return of this truculence and challenged them. 'Well, my clever ones, and now that you have them stored amongst the onions what do you intend to do? Advertise for a South American millionaire? Take them on tour? Or transport them to Paris and set up a stand in the lobby of the *Folies Bergère*—GENUINE RENOIR! FOR SALE?'

The carnation-growing Tiger, the most mild-mannered of them all, chose to reply. 'There's no need for your sarcasm, Pierre, you know very well we didn't do it for gain. We were going to ransom the pictures for the poor.'

Colonel Roquebrun, who had been sitting tilted back in his chair in a somewhat superior attitude, was so startled by this that he returned his seat to the floor with a crash, repeating, 'Ransom for the poor!'

They were on him now like children pressing home an advantage.

'Two and a half million francs paid to an American so rich he cannot count his money!'

"And in France people are going hungry!'

'Imagine, one man owning paintings worth tens of millions!'

'And in the next house the husband of my neighbour, Madame Aubert, may die because they can't afford an operation and a hospital.'

'The Government steals from us in taxes and spends it on a rag with some paint daubed over it.'

'There aren't enough schools or hospitals.'

'The situation is rotten. This will call attention to it.'

Colonel Roquebrun said, 'What kind of talk is this? Have you all become Communists?' and he spat on the floor.

'On the contrary,' replied the Wolf, 'we merely propose to protect the rich from their own idiocies. It is they who create Communists with this madness of spending.'

'My father knew Renoir in Cagnes,' said the Elephant. 'They were neighbours. He said he was a modest little man, riddled with arthritis, who did not think himself a god or anything extraordinary because he put paint on canvas. He was content when he was young to receive 400 or 500 francs for a painting, or even leave a little sketch at a bistro in payment for his bill. What has happened to these same paintings of my father's friend to make them worth millions? Where has the money come from? Where does it go? Who is being robbed? Who is being enriched?'

The Colonel's self-possession was returning. 'No one, you donkey,' he said. 'No one is enriched; no one is impoverished. The wealthy trade these objects amongst themselves like children playing with picture cards found in packages of soap or cereals. If two youngsters set about exchanging postage stamps, who in the community is injured and in what manner has the economy suffered?'

The Wolf saw the point and grinned wickedly, but the others were making hard going of it. The Leopard shook his head and said, 'The rich always find a way to profit.'

The Colonel snorted. 'It seems to me, my innocents,' he said, 'that you have got hold of the

wrong end of the stick. You may be fighting a just
war, but against the wrong enemy. It isn't the very
rich who are a danger to any country but the
ignorant poor. It is the latter who are always trying to pull down the structure and entomb themselves with it, instead of endeavouring to learn
how wealth is acquired and following the example.
And for that matter, you half-wits,' the Colonel
continued, 'who is it that supports charities, en-
dows foundations, creates universities, aids hospitals and makes possible research intended to relieve every human ailment? It is the rich. The
world today would be unspeakably ghastly if the
philanthropies of the wealthy were to come to an
end. You can afford to leave them their toys.'

They sat blinking at the Colonel for a moment
taken aback. Then the Leopard heaved his huge
bulk in his chair, pursed his small mouth and said,
'What about the Government getting into your
innocent scheme and handing over millions of
our money for something which in our father's
day fetched no more than a few hundred francs?'

The Colonel said, 'Have you never encountered
the phrase "men cannot live by bread alone"?
The nation's pride reposes in the handiwork of
her gifted sons. It is something in which every
man, woman and child can share.'

The Elephant said, 'You weren't so damned
moral in the old days, Pierre, when we were under
your leadership. It was you who planned the robbery of the German Military funds from the
Crédit National at Aix from which we took 50

million francs; it was you who organized the capture of the gold transport convoy on its way to Marseille; it was you who evolved the technique of stripping the villas of the collaborators on the Riviera of food, wines and clothing.'

The memory of those times evoked a nod from the Colonel. 'Hah,' he said, 'I taught you the value of paper bullets in those days, did I not? We hit the Germans and the collaborators where it hurt them most—in the pocket book.' His glance strayed to the fingers which had no fingernails at their ends, and he grimaced involuntarily. 'And paid too,' he concluded.

The Wolf said stubbornly, 'I don't see the difference, Pierre. In the F.F.I. we fought collaborators. They were Frenchmen too, like ourselves, but they were enemies. France is menaced by as many enemies internally today as she was during the war. What is wrong with using a little of the same technique as we did in the past?'

'We thought we would put some real worth into those paintings, Pierre,' the Tiger said. 'As it stands now, you yourself are willing to admit that these values are false. We planned to ransom the Blue Renoir and the others for ten million francs and turn the money over to charity. Thus, the pictures would represent a hundred hospital beds, some thousands of tons of coal and hundreds of thousands of pounds of food and milk for the hungry. Then when one stood admiringly in front of the Blue Renoir one could say, "Ah yes, this is indeed a valuable picture. It has paid its way." Let the spirit be fed indeed, but bread must come first.'

The Colonel for a moment was so startled by this idea that he leaned forward in his chair. '*Mon Dieu!*' he said.

'That's it!' exclaimed the Elephant. 'We knew you would see it our way.'

The Colonel laughed and shook his head. 'Beautiful, poetic and immoral,' he said.

The Wolf snorted, 'Immoral!'

'Immoral,' repeated the Colonel. 'It will not do, my cloud-dwelling cuckoos. We all enjoyed playing Robin Hood in the world of 1943 when it was both necessary and effective. This is the world of 1967.'

'Eh? What's the difference?' the Elephant pouted. 'The old war was hot, the new one is cold. We're still combatants.'

'Why,' said the Colonel, 'just that the world of today is so infinitely more corrupt, wicked and immoral, that one more immorality piled on top of it only gets lost in the shuffle. Ransom is just another form of blackmail or bribery. The insurance companies would not hesitate to enter into a shady deal with you in order to cut their losses; the police would connive with you to split the reward and get back the stolen goods if they could; and the public would not ask any questions provided their treasure was restored. Whom are you educating? Instead of light you bring more darkness.'

They sat around silently, looking unhappy.

'Well now,' said Colonel Roquebrun, 'since you have practically admitted that you have committed the stupidity of the century, and that none of the reasons for your *coup* will for one moment bear the light of intelligent scrutiny, what other excuses have you to offer for abandoning the dignity of the good lives you have all achieved and turning yourselves into criminals?'

Once more the four exchanged guilty glances and in the end it was Antoine Petitpierre, the melancholy Tiger, who replied. 'Pierre, all of us suddenly found ourselves growing old: a toothless Tiger, a clawless Leopard, an Elephant with fading memories, a Wolf with failing appetite. We sat here one evening and talked of the old days when we made the Germans tremble. We longed for one final adventure.'

The Colonel threw back his head and let out a roar of laughter, and when it had subsided he cried, 'But now for the first time you have been talking sense. If you had only come to me when this feeling overwhelmed you we would not be in this pickle we're in today. There would have been some brains about the affair.'

The Wolf regarded the Colonel curiously. 'You say *we*, old friend? Do you really mean we?'

'Don't ask foolish questions,' the Colonel replied brusquely. 'Why do you think I'm here, with Captain Scoubide practically breathing down my neck? You, my dear Leopard, I'll wager left your signature all over the electrical work when you disconnected the alarm.' Here the Colonel's professional interest suddenly took over. 'By the way, how was that done? If there is any tampering with the alarm it registers immediately at the police station.'

'Oh,' replied the Leopard with superb innocence, 'I took the precaution of disconnecting it at the police station end.'

Again the Colonel shook with laughter. 'Worthy of the best Resistance group a man ever led. Bravo, friend Leopard!'

'What, then, do you suggest?' asked the Elephant.

'A little morality,' replied the Colonel. 'It might shine out like a light in the darkness. The pictures must be returned.'

"But how?' asked the practical Wolf.

'In such a manner as to cause the light to shine,' replied the Colonel, and for the first time they realized that he had the glimmer of a plan.

Colonel Roquebrun drove his Simca stationwagon up the twisting road into the hills behind Cannes until he came to an arched gateway with a small, modest sign at the side: Society Club— *Privé*—Members Only.

A hundred yards within there was a dark, sprawling villa and a parking lot. There appeared to be very little illumination. His neighbours in the car park were Rolls Royces, Bentleys, Cadillacs, Mercedes and several fast Italian sports cars. It was nine o'clock in the evening. He heard the rambling tinkling of a bar pianist. There seemed to be no one about.

Left to find his way, Colonel Roquebrun saw an outside iron staircase and climbed it to find himself on a balcony off which rooms opened. He came upon a young girl standing there in a night-dress, looking down into the shadowy garden. Even by starlight he saw that she was exquisite. 'Oh,' he said, 'I beg your pardon.'

The eyes she turned upon him were the misty, understanding, melancholy ones of the Hetaerae. She said ,'The entrance is below, just beyond that tree there,' and went back into the room from whence she had come. Colonel Roquebrun heard a man cough, and as he descended he reflected upon the nature of the Society from which the Club took its name.

He came to an entrance beneath a canopy. A doorman in uniform eyed him uncertainly and asked, 'Are you a member?'

'No,' said the Colonel, 'but—' and between his fingers there showed the yellow of a hundred franc note.

"Of course,' said the doorman, 'it can be ar-ranged.' The Colonel handed over his card and the note. The man took them and disappeared in-side.

This, the Colonel thought, was the fatality of the France of today. The words *Liberté, Egalité, Fraternité* rimming their coins might well be re-placed by the slogan 'It can be arranged.'

The doorman returned with a gold-embossed card between his fingers. 'Monsieur is welcome,' he said, and led him down a long, unlit corridor and through the bar which was also dark. The pi-

ano player was lightly fingering nostalgic, senti-
mental tunes. A dark-haired girl was leaning
against a doorway clad in a bikini and holding a
half-empty cocktail glass, a secret smile at the corners of her mouth. There were several men sitting
at the bar but no one was paying any attention to
her. The Colonel supposed there was nothing
wrong about a bikini at nine o'clock in the evening, but somehow the effect was extraordinarily
sinister. He was glad he had come.

Beyond the bar was the dining terrace. The
head-waiter in a white dinner jacket waved a
menu at the Colonel and led him to a table from
which he could look down upon the curve of
Cannes bedecked in her night jewellery spread
out below. On the terrace the only illumination
was the glow of tiny lamps on the tables. Roquebrun was aware that the place was already half-
filled. He ordered a Scotch. The piano tinkled
soothingly. The girl in the bikini stood for a moment looking out across the terrace with moist
eyes, then walked off down a path, her hips sway-
ing. From nearby came the gentle splashing of a
fountain, and off to the left the Colonel saw starlight reflected in a swimming pool. The setting
was superb. But Roquebrun was remembering
how it felt when he waited in ambush in the darkness surrounded by the Germans.

By ten o'clock every table but one upon the terrace had been occupied. The Colonel's eyes had
now adjusted themselves to the dim light to the
point where he could make out features, and he

felt as though transported into another world. Here was collected a kind of international scum— the froth that would come to the top if all the wicked of the world were boiled together in a cauldron. The men with their smooth, parchment-like faces and immaculate clothes sat behind their dark glasses, sleek, slick, oily, overbearing and arrogant; Americans, British, Spaniards, Italians, Frenchmen. Pretty girls decorated their tables and were paid no more attention by them than the furniture. These were no small dispensers of evil. These were the wholesalers. Somehow it was the dark glasses which oppressed the Colonel. Even in the murk of the Club these men could not bear so much as the gleam of a candle, and he thought of the sunless sewers where rats scurried. They were the smelly rich and their hangers-on who coined their money out of human weakness. Here were collected the vultures of the world pretending to be people. The Colonel felt as though he wanted a bath.

The head-waiter, with his menu card held high in front of him to show that important people were arriving, threaded a party through the narrow aisles of the crowded tables, and Roquebrun saw that it was Sarah Howard and her friends.

He noted that one of the girls was the dark-haired one now dressed, who had been in the bar in a bikini, and the second was of the same class. The third girl was obviously the English girl who was staying with Sarah. The man who accompanied her he recognized as Kip Trenchley from photo-

graphs of him he had seen in British newspapers,
and Roquebrun remembered now why the association had been unpleasant. Trenchley's speciality,
one gathered, was trafficking in feather-brained
debutantes. He lured them to the Continent, en-
tangled them, and then sold them back to their
fathers who paid to avoid scandal.

Count Paolo Andrea, the Italian, was easily recognizable. If there were remnants of nobility in
his features they were almost obliterated by weakness and dissipation. Roquebrun thought he could
guess his function in this unsavoury quartet.

But the man who raised the Colonel's hackles,
and for an instant turned him sick with apprehen-
sion for Sarah, was the tall one known as Harry.
He was wearing a lilac-coloured dinner-jacket and
his eyes were hidden behind the inevitable dark
glasses. The Colonel felt there was real reason for
this concealment for he was sure they would be
the cold, expressionless eyes of the killer. There
was no mistaking the cruel mouth. This was the
new type of American crook-of-all-trades that had
emerged from the army after the war, with Europe
as its field of operations. The fourth member was
Marcel Dufour. His sensitive face silhouetted
against the table lamp gave him the aspect of a
poet.

It was an ideal quartet, the Colonel thought: a
French gang leader, a British blackmailer, a shady
Italian and an American killer, and he thought
likewise what a jungle was this Riviera for all its
innocence and loveliness of the sea reflecting the
night sky, the beacons flashing from the moun-

tains outlined against that same sky, and the necklace of lights, like blue diamonds stringing the waterfront. How easily the two girls had become ensnared.

He had seen enough, and now the Colonel sighed with a kind of long ago remembered pleasure. Colonel Pierre Roquebrun, the respected antique dealer, was no more. *Le Renard* had returned, the old game was on again. He called for his bill, paid it and made his way out, passing their table on his way. Outside of the momentary dilation of her eyes, Sarah Howard gave no sign of recognition.

The abrupt departure of Colonel Roquebrun had left Sarah with a feeling of desolation. As long as he was there she had felt safe. Now that he had gone she became once more prey to all her fears and doubts. She wondered how long it would be before she would be able to contact him again and hear his judgment of the men with whom she had become involved. Then she remembered his instructions.

The swiftness with which this contact was realized was startling, for it took place, to be exact, when after waiting a precautionary twenty minutes she went to visit the ladies' powder room. The woman in attendance there, without saying a word, slipped a small piece of paper into her hand. There was no one else in there at the time. Sarah opened it and read: 'Not nice. Keep your nerve. There will be a ransom note. They will take over. Let them. They will suggest you go home. Do so. R.' For a moment Sarah felt the dizzy-

ing clutch of panic. Then the cool strength of the
hand that had been stretched out to her through
the note steadied her. She tore the paper into tiny
shreds, entered the *cabinet* and flushed them
away, and then returned to the table with the
sentences of the brief message darting through her
brain. There was no question as to the confirma-
tion of her fears. *Not nice* said it all.

Shortly after midnight, as they were debating
whether to go to the Casino or on to the nightclub
at Juan-les-Pins which was offering a new troupe
of transvestites direct from Paris, a waiter came
to the table and handed Sarah an envelope. Conversation died away and Sarah was conscious that
they were all staring at her.

Kip Trenchley tittered and cried, 'Oh, I say,
Sarah's got an admirer. Harry's going to be jellie!'

For an instant Sarah was again aware of the trap
into which she seemed to have fallen from the
manner in which the Englishman had coupled her
with Harry. She was already considered Harry's
property. She remembered Colonel Roquebrun's
admonition, *Keep your nerve*. She opened the envelope and read the printed note therein:

'We have your pictures. The identification
number 2XRYB5342 concealed on the Blue Renoir will prove this to your father. We are business
men and prepared to negotiate for their return.
When your father arrives in the morning bring
him in your white car to the cross-roads sign below Piol by *La Ferme Minoury* where you will be
met. We are in a position to see every road in the
valley leading to the rendezvous. If there is any

indication that your car is being followed or observed from the air by helicopter or aircraft, the pictures will be destroyed.'

A half-smile illuminated the gentle countenance of Marcel Dufour. He said, 'I hope it does not contain bad news, my dear?'

There will be a ransom note Colonel Roquebrun had written. *They will take over. Let them.* Sarah said, 'It's—it's about the pictures. A ransom note—they say—'

'The pictures!' It was almost like a conjurer's trick the way they had the note out of Sarah's fingers and were reading it avidly, passing it from one to the other. Harry rose quietly and left the table to reappear a few moments later. He said, 'Nix. Kid on a bicycle rode up, handed it to the doorman and blew.'

Sarah said, 'Ought we to notify the police?'

'No,' said Marcel Dufour, 'under no circumstances.'

Sarah was suddenly aware that she had been pushed completely out of the affair. The four had managed to switch seats with the other girls and were now gathered around two corners of the table, their heads together, re-reading and whispering. Harry had removed his dark glasses to see better, and as for an instant the light of the table lamp was reflected from his eyes, Sarah saw that they were filled with a curious kind of animal glare.

'I think the girls had better go home,' Harry said.

'Yes, yes,' Dufour added, 'we'll handle this for

you. We know how to deal with such matters. Leave everything to us.'

Count Andrea was already summoning the waiter for the bill.

Sarah suddenly felt as though she were acting in a play in which she was thoroughly grounded in her lines. She saw again the words from the Colonel's note: *They will suggest you go home. Do so.* How had he known?

Kip Trenchley said, 'I'll call a taxi for you and Diana.' When its arrival was announced and the Englishman rose to escort them to it, the other three did not even look up from their whispering conclave.

The Zoo Gang sat about uneasily on bags of onions at one end of the long warehouse, topping the hill above Piol behind Antibes. The windows were shaded with sacking to keep light from showing. Beneath the tumbled heap of sacks of onions gleamed one corner of a gold picture frame.

Colonel Roquebrun glanced at his watch. 'I must be going,' he said, 'I think your visitors ought to be along shortly.'

'I don't like it,' said the Elephant. 'Supposing they're satisfied to pick up the reward and go to the police—'

'They won't be,' said Colonel Roquebrun, 'and you'll have to like it.' He addressed them all now. 'You won't, I think, be hurt if you control your natural truculence, but that is a risk you must take. These are dangerous men. They have already killed once. You will most certainly have to swallow a certain amount of insults, and possibly put up with one or two indignities. Control yourselves and accept them.'

The Wolf grinned and said, 'If it comes off it will be cheap at the price.'

Colonel Roquebrun went to the door and said, 'They will probably come in a van from the Blue Grotto. Friend Elephant, you must be prepared to lose a few sacks of your onions as well as your pretty pictures. Well, good luck!' and he was gone.

It was indeed the van of the Blue Grotto restaurant which drew up before the warehouse shortly before four o'clock in the morning. The pick-up van of one of the best known restaurants on the Riviera paying an early morning visit to an onion wholesaler would not arouse police suspicion.

And furthermore, there were the insults and indignities which the Zoological Gang accepted with reasonable fortitude, particularly in view of the fact that of the trio that burst in upon them one was armed with a long-barrelled Luger.

They did not even bother to conceal their features, Dufour, Count Andrea and Harry. Thieves engaged in the profitable and invulnerable business of robbing other thieves had nothing to fear, particularly where those others were amateurs so stupid and untutored as to give away their hiding place in their ransom note. It had taken Marcel Dufour, who knew the district, only a few minutes with a survey map to figure out that the only spot from which all roads approaching the Minoury

Farm could be observed was the warehouse of the onion dealer, Jean Soleau.

They were rough too, needlessly so, and cruel, as indeed the Colonel had thought they might be, for the ease of the hijacking operation and the insoluble predicament of the four men they found collected in the warehouse with their stolen art treasures fed their arrogance to bursting point. Besides which there was jealousy. The Leopard suffered a cut cheek where he was hit with the pistol barrel; the Elephant had the wind knocked out of him; the Tiger was kicked in the groin.

When the pictures had been transferred to the van and buried beneath layers of sacks stuffed with fat, golden-brown onions, the gang leader's ego could not resist lecturing for a moment. 'This will teach you amateurs not to encroach upon the field of professionals. You should be grateful to me for taking these paintings off your hands and absolving you from the risks connected with disposing of them. For our part,' and the sensitive expression of Monsieur Dufour's thin lips and nostrils made it seem almost like a benediction, 'we shall always remember you as having saved us a great deal of trouble. We had planned to remove them ourselves from the villa next week after they had been returned from the exhibition.'

Then having cut the telephone wires and wrecked the carburettors on the engines of the cars in the garage, they departed.

The Tiger was still gasping from the brutality of his injury and trying to control moans of pain.

The Leopard, was weeping openly with tears of rage and frustration. '*Le Renard* owes me one for this,' he said. 'By God, I'll have it out of his hide!'

The darkly sardonic Wolf said to him, 'Keep quiet. You don't know how lucky you are—how lucky all of us are.'

For he was thinking of Colonel Roquebrun, where he would probably be at that moment and the telephone call he would be making, and the Wolf added, 'Thank God, the brains of the old Fox are still working.'

Colonel Roquebrun had not had much sleep that night yet this did not vary his morning routine of opening his shop the following day by so much as a minute. The Colonel had known times when he had gone fifty hours without closing an eye and yet remained alert and efficient. It was just twenty four hours since Sarah Howard had drawn up before his shop in her cream Jaguar. He wondered who his first visitor would be that morning.

A squeal of brakes and the crunch of tyres answered his question. It was Captain Scoubide.

The Captain appeared exactly as he had the morning before for he had not yet had time to change his clothes. The only difference was that the left sleeve of his shirt had been ripped from shoulder to hem, and through the gap there showed the red of a long scratch.

For the rest, the Captain was just as concerned that morning with maintaining 'correctness' as he had been the day before, and he fingered one or two of the more expensive items of the Colonel's stock to give him time to reflect before he turned and said, 'Thank you for the tip.'

'Not at all,' replied the Colonel.

'Concerning the matter of the reward,' here the Captain coughed, 'it may be necessary to split with me in order to avoid embarrassing questions.'

'I fully understand this,' agreed the Colonel.

'Still,' the Captain suggested, '250,000 francs is a tidy sum.'

The Colonel picked up a 14th century ivory crucifix. 'One always finds uses for unexpected sums of money.'

'Such as, for instance, the husband of Madame Aubert?'

The Colonel never batted an eye. 'Poor woman,' he said, 'she has indeed been passing through a difficult period.'

The Colonel's gaze was now so unmistakably upon the rent in his shirt that Captain Scoubide felt compelled to refer to it. 'Nothing,' he said, 'nothing at all—fellow at the door—he was momentarily argumentative.'

'The pictures?' suggested the Colonel.

'Oh yes,' muttered Captain Scoubide, '—quite. In the cellar. Not only the Renoirs but the others as well.'

'Ah,' said the Colonel, 'I thought perhaps they might—'

'A veritable *petit Louvre*,' the Captain said. 'The El Greco, the Van Dyke, the Moderns and two

Breughels which had not yet even been reported stolen. I believe they expected to transfer them to South America.'

'How embarrassing for Monsieur Dufour and his friends. I gather they were all there?'

'All except the Englishman.'

'The little blackmailer—'

Captain Scoubide permitted himself a grim smile. 'That pigeon will keep,' he said. 'Another time. He was not implicated in the actual robberies, he merely provided the wealthy contacts. Dufour was the brains, the Count the art expert who selected the paintings, and Harry was the gun. He killed the caretaker in the Cap Ferrat robbery.'

The Colonel nodded. 'He was also the charmer. He worked on the women so that they were reluctant to complain. Excellent! I trust everything went smoothly?'

'Well, actually—' the Captain began.

The Colonel sent an eyebrow towards the top of his polished skull.

'Harry,' explained Captain Scoubide. 'He was so imprudent as to produce his weapon. My bullet killed him after he had discharged it at me. I will receive a decoration for this, no doubt.'

'And deservedly, my friend, deservedly,' the Colonel congratulated wholeheartedly, and then added with satisfaction, 'That was a mouth that wanted stopping,' for he was thinking of Sarah and the alibi Harry would have claimed if he had come to trial.

'It was your warning that he would be armed

that enabled me to be prepared,' acknowledged
the Captain. The Colonel bowed. The liquidation
of Harry pleased him enormously. It was one of
those fortuitous bits of luck sometimes encountered. It had been a loose end which had worried
him, and in all his operations as Commander of the
F.F.I. in the Alpes-Maritimes the Colonel had
been a tidy man.

The Captain began to move towards the door,
but hesitatingly, and Roquebrun suspected there
might still be something on his mind. He was right
in his judgement.

Scoubide coughed once more deprecatingly and
said, 'By the way, some friends of yours who live
in the vicinity of the Minoury Farm have suffered
a little inconvenience. Their telephone has been
cut, their cars damaged; one of them has come by
an injury to his face, another a painful bruise.
Nothing serious though, I'm told.'

'How kind of you to let me know,' the Colonel
said. 'I must pay them a visit and extend them
my sympathy.'

The Captain remained yet another instant in
the doorway, an expression almost of tenderness
and affection on his features. He said, 'I'm very
pleased with you, my friend, pleased and proud.'
And then, since there was no way by which the
Colonel could receive a medal for his share in the
night's work, the Captain proceeded to decorate
him with one last little florid speech, which might
have proved embarrassing had it not been so utterly sincere. 'France survived her defeat in the

war and lives because of such as you.' Then he
turned and fled.

The next arrival was not unexpected either. It
was the Jaguar of Sarah Howard, only Sarah was
not in it. It was her father, Joel Howard, who was
alone in the driving seat.

The millionaire, a widower and a startlingly
handsome man bursting with American vitality,
wasted no time in getting to the point. He said, 'I
arrived several hours ago. Sarah was at the airport
and I have spoken to Captain Scoubide. I have
come to thank you.'

'Ah,' said Colonel Roquebrun, 'for the return of
the pictures—'

'No,' said Joel Howard, 'for the return of Sarah.'

There was a moment of silent understanding
between the two men before Howard spoke again.
He began at a tangent. 'The pictures were insured
—besides which they were only things. But Sarah
—' He hesitated and then said, 'Sarah has told me
everything. It's my fault that she has been running
a little wild since her mother died. I have ne-
glected her. I shan't again. That's when the Harrys
move in. She is a very lucky girl that you were
here.'

The Colonel managed to look suitably modest
and deprecating, hoping in the depths of his soul
that never, never, not ever would Mr Joel Howard
hear so much as a whisper of the renaissance of
the Zoological Gang.

Howard had fallen into a moment's musing at
the conclusion of which he said, 'My good friend

Pierre, I should like to do something in return, if
you would permit it. Something—anything—that
might lie close to your heart, for I know very well
what manner of person you are and the nature of
your charities. Would you permit it?'

Instantly the Colonel remembered his four former comrades in arms and the idea behind their
last romantic and abortive adventure. The reward money would help to alleviate local distress,
but theirs had been a grander idea. 'Yes,' he said,
'give us a hospital, Joel. Up to date, with every
modern appliance and always beds free to the
poor who cannot pay.'

'Done,' said the millionaire, 'you shall have it.'

'And I think,' Colonel Roquebrun was saying,
'—I think I should like it known as *L'Hôpital du
Renoir Bleu.*'

'Hospital of the Blue Renoir,' Howard repeated.
'What a strange idea.'

The Colonel's smile was a far away one for he
was thinking once more of his friends and how
pleased they would be. 'But a perfect one,' he said.

'I beg your pardon?' said Joel Howard. 'I don't
quite understand.'

But the Colonel did not explain.

How to Stick Up a Fifty-Million-Dollar Riviera Gala

THERE WAS a hot summer mistral blowing down the corridor of the Rhône valley, turning the corner when it reached the Mediterranean and whistling along the coast, making everyone on the French Riviera jumpy from St. Tropez to Menton and the Italian border.

This included such an old hand as Colonel Pierre Roquebrun, the antique dealer in his shop on the outskirts of a small village, back country between Vence and Grasse.

The Colonel jumped also because, engrossed in the admiration of his latest acquisition, he had not been aware of the entrance of Captain Scoubide until the Captain had been forced to produce a deprecatory cough to announce himself. The Colonel had neither heard the car of the Captain of detectives draw up outside nor, what was even more astonishing in one whose life had once hung upon that kind of sensitivity, had he even felt his presence in the shop.

The Colonel acknowledged the cough with a glance but continued in his contemplation of his prize, a great gilt, ornate clock with an exquisitely engraved face and beautifully rendered figures of the Four Seasons adorning the housing. It stood a foot higher than both of the men.

His visitor, Captain Claude Scoubide, chief of the detective forces of the Nice Branch of the *Service Régionale de Police Judicaire,* was as thin and dapper as the Colonel was broad and bulky. He was, as usual, clad in the perpetual disguise he affected; namely coloured slacks, sandals and short-sleeved, open-necked shirt and which made him practically invisible amongst the hundreds of thousands of tourists thronging the Riviera for the summer holidays.

While he was still gloating over his clock which he had brought into his shop the night before, the Colonel wondered what lay behind his early caller, since it was only shortly before nine and at least another hour before any visitors might be expected to appear. Roquebrun had read his *Nice-Matin* over his breakfast coffee and could recall no major crime which might lead to a visit from the Captain.

Since during the wartime days when he had been the underground leader of the Zoological Gang, the Colonel's eyes and ears had never closed. Now, even though he was retired from active service and was a knowledgeable and respected *Antiquaire,* news of the perpetrators of dark deeds had a way of reaching him, probably because that same mouth that refused to open for the interrogators of the *Geheime Staatspolizei,* remained as firmly closed throughout his after life.

The Captain now moved to Roquebrun's side and stood by him, his narrow head cocked slightly as he joined the antique dealer in admiration of the clock. He said, 'It is handsome.'

Colonel Roquebrun said, 'It is more than handsome. It is superb. A prize and unique. Come here and I'll show you something.'

He led Scoubide around to the back of the clock and pointed up to the metal back-plate on which was engraved a signature: *HENRI MARTINOT*.

The Colonel's clear eyes sparkled with pleasure and his bald head turned pink as the blood rose to it, but Scoubide's expression remained blank. He was not with it.

'Henri Martinot,' the Colonel explained, 'was clockmaker to Louis Quatorze. He had a workshop in the Palace at Versailles. This is one of the last he made for the Sun King before he died. It came into the hands of the family of the Duc de Rochetouquet. It has been in their *Château* ever since.'

'And now?' queried Scoubide.

'The *Duc* and I were friends,' Roquebrun replied, 'he left word that when he died, it was to be sold to me.'

They were now around the front of the object again, Scoubide regarding it with more deference and as the Colonel passed an affectionate hand over the polished side, the detective as always was compelled to notice that the gnarled fingers had no fingernails, the same having been left in the torture chambers and had never grown back. He asked, 'Is it valuable?'

'I shall ask 250,000 francs for it,' said Colonel Roquebrun.

'*Mon Dieu!*' Scoubide said under his breath, 'Fifty thousand dollars!' He had a habit from life on the Riviera, where so many American tourists foregathered, of translating francs in a big deal into dollars. 'Aren't you afraid of thieves?'

'No,' the Colonel replied.

Captain Scoubide glanced around the antique shop. There were no bars over the windows. The front door had an ordinary lock. 'You believe, then . . .' and here Scoubide sighed, 'as I suppose I do, too . . . that it is impossible to devise a security through which an intelligent and determined thief cannot break.'

Colonel Roquebrun nodded. 'Exactly! The burglar who took my clock would find his problems arising after and not before it was in his possession. There isn't a dealer in the world who would not recognize this rarity. One might hold it for ransom, but one could never sell it.'

Scoubide's mind flashed back to that episode a couple of years before when a number of priceless Renoirs *had* been stolen, and for the purposes of ransom, and wondered whether the Colonel was entertaining thoughts of the same affair. He nodded and said, 'That's true. Not like large pieces of jewellery which can be broken up, gold or platinum melted down, famous stones recut or reduced in size so that they could never be identified.'

It was not only the carelessness of the detective's voice that put Colonel Roquebrun suddenly on the alert. It was that the comparison, or rather the detailing of what happened to stolen jewellery, was just that much too long. 'Broken up' would have been sufficient. There had been then a subtle change and Captain Scoubide had managed to introduce the topic which was the reason for his visit. But why? There had been no news of a jewel job in the morning paper, nor had there been a really sensational one since a gang had cleaned out the entire contents of the jewellery shop of *Le Boutelier* in Cannes a few years ago and since when security in that area had been doubled.

'Are you going to the August Ball next week?' Captain Scoubide asked.

The question took the old Resistance leader completely by surprise. The annual August Ball and Gala, to be held this year at the Silver Sands Casino in aid of what was known as 'The Charity,' was the social event of the summer season. It was a strange question for Captain Scoubide to ask, even more so since the Colonel actually was going. 'Yes,' he replied, 'my wife and I and another couple are taking my niece and a young friend. She had just turned eighteen and will be going away to University. Her first big affair. Like all young things, she is mad about this American singer Tommy Rich.'

Tommy Rich was the new star who was making them forget Sinatra, The Beatles, Tom Jones . . .

Scoubide nodded and said, 'She will not be disappointed. He is a handsome fellow and sings excellently.'

Although the Colonel had spoken casually and seemed still to be admiring the proportions and ornamentation of the King's clock, his mind was now fully alerted—thieves, jewellery, August Ball and Gala, the Silver Sands Casino and an early morning visit from the shrewdest policeman on the Côte d'Azur. But he remarked still blandly, 'You've heard him?'

'He's rehearsing with the band at the Silver Sands. A true professional. I had a little chat with him and his bodyguards, four ex-policemen from the county of Los Angeles. Very tough. It would not be wise for anyone to try to play games with Monsieur Rich.'

The Colonel looked only mildly interested.

'In America this boy has come to the attention of the Mafia. He makes just too much money and they have a long arm.'

Roquebrun nodded and said, 'The old game. Extortion, eh?' But he was aware that this was not what Scoubide had come to discuss. So he merely added, 'Clever of the Committee to have engaged such a drawing card. There isn't a seat to be had.'

Captain Scoubide regarded his own polished fingernails and wondered what it would be like to have them pulled out one by one. Admiration for the chunky old man at his side surged through his own narrow chest, coupled with nervousness. He was always nervous in the presence of Roquebrun, not knowing absolutely for certain whether he might be on one side or another, yet the problem that had been dropped into his lap compelled him to ask the question:

'Have you heard anything?'

'Heard anything about what?'

'About a possible attempt to hold up the August Ball during the course of the evening?'

Colonel Roquebrun was genuinely shocked, not so much at Scoubide's reply as at the utter absurdity of the notion, and his expression showed it as he turned upon his old friend, 'Are you out of your mind, Claude? Who on earth would give anyone such an idea?'

'Marseille. Our people there are very good, you know. And some of our chaps in Nice.'

Roquebrun looked even more incredulous. 'You mean that they have actually heard . . . heard . . . that . . .'

'No, no,' put in Scoubide quickly, 'they have actually heard nothing. That is to say not exactly heard, but—well, perhaps it is a stupid word—felt. That's why they have asked me.'

'And you . . .' and both the incredulity and the friendliness had gone out of the Colonel's voice which had become impersonal and slightly chill, '. . . you come and ask me.'

Scoubide looked miserable for a moment and begged, 'Forgive me, *mon Colonel,* but I had to. You see, the stakes are too high.'

The point being that while no names were mentioned, there was no need to draw diagrams for

either of the men. During the war the Zoological
Gang, led by Colonel Roquebrun, had been nota-
bly successful in raising funds for the expensive
business of being beastly to the Germans. They
had opened the vaults of banks and post offices in
occupied territory as though they had been made
of tin instead of Vanadium reinforced steel, and
they had been equally successful in collecting con-
tributions from the homes of wealthy collaborators
on the three richest Capes of the Riviera—Antibes, Ferrat and Martin. Sometimes these do-
nations were in cash, at others in bonds and
jewellery. Sometimes the contributors were at
home when *Le Léopard*, *Le Tigre*, *L'Eléphant*, *Le
Loup* and *Le Renard* called, and sometimes not.
It really made no difference to them.

The inference was that when a job so enormous
and utterly insane as the sticking up of the new
Silver Sands Casino during the night of the biggest
Charity Gala in France was being bruited about,
he and his one-time companions in quasi Robin-
Hood style of crime could not be overlooked.

All these thoughts registered upon the battered
countenance of the Colonel, setting it into lines of
increasing severity.

'Forgive me,' cried the unhappy Scoubide again,
who had known that this moment must come
when he would be compelled to give probably unpardonable offence, 'but have you any conception
of the amount of money that such a *coup* might
realize—or at least the value of the loot?'

'No,' replied the Colonel, 'it isn't the kind of

merchandise in which I deal.' And he said it in such a way that the double meaning could not be ignored.

Scoubide chose to do so. 'Fifty million dollars,' he said. 'This is an estimate made by the writer of an article in the Paris *Herald Tribune*.'

Even Roquebrun was startled. 'Fifty million dollars!' he echoed, 'It would be the robbery of all time.'

The French detective reached into his hip pocket and produced a paper. He said, 'I have here a list of what is expected to be attending the Ball.' When it came to such an affair the detective thought only in terms of 'what' and not 'who'; namely the valuables that would be present and not their wearers. He opened a folded sheet and began to read from it, 'The emerald set: tiara, necklace, brooch, bracelets and rings of Mrs Cranston Marberry, widow of the oil king—value in the neighbourhood of two million. Flawless emeralds today are worth more than diamonds. The Natal solitaire, fifty-six carats, just purchased by Scott Regis the actor for his wife: a million and a half. The Winston diamond, only a few carats less, belonging to Lady Burdick. The *collier* of the Maharani of Saharanganj; the Van Gelder rubies; Mrs Hutchinson's sapphires, amongst some of the better known pieces. Here, read the rest for yourself. And, in addition,' Scoubide concluded, 'to these sets on which every burglar on the coast must have had his eye for years, every lesser woman guest down to the more ordinary tourist seated on the outer fringes of the room, will be wearing her best bits. You would be surprised how much such rubbish will bring when collected *en gros*. No problem in marketing the smaller stones, simply a matter of extraction. I would say fifty million was a conservative estimate. Were the insurance companies to begin totting it up . . .' He left the sentence unfinished.

Then, almost as an afterthought, he added, 'In addition to which the *Préfet* of the Alpes-Maritimes and his wife will be present, not to mention the fact that the Minister of the Interior from Paris and the British and American Ambassadors have signified their intention of attending.'

Colonel Roquebrun muttered to himself, 'It would be impossible, and yet for a strike like that . . .' Aloud he said, 'The Marseille police have actually heard . . .'

'No, no, no!' interrupted the Captain, 'I never said they had heard, nor did they. It is only that to be a good policeman you must be occasionally unusually sensitive. Sometimes you don't need to hear when something really big is brewing; it makes its own reverberations. There have been many past August Balls where great jewels have been on display and where no more than normal security precautions have been necessary, but this one . . .'

The Colonel knew exactly what the detective was talking about when he spoke of reverberations. He had encountered them often—atmospheric waves as though from some hidden evil broadcasting station, invisible tensions, crawly feelings at the nape of the neck, or just a discomfort in the region of the bowels having nothing to do with digestion. And all based on what? Nothing, but inevitably something; probably just the silent working of the law of action and interaction, which could be discerned by those sufficiently tuned in to pick it up.

Besides which, times were changing and one was very well aware in every branch of modern life that things which would have been either impossible or intolerable ten or fifteen years ago, were now both acceptable and ordinary.

Scoubide might have known more than he was letting on, but the Colonel doubted it. A rumour had reached the detective's ears and he was on a fishing expedition. And, if the truth were to be known, for all of his outward indignation the Colonel was just the least bit flattered that upon having picked up the merest faint whisper of a hint via the antenna that an efficient police organization keeps turning in all directions like a radar loop, Scoubide had come to him.

Nevertheless, he asked, 'And that is all you have to go on? Just a feeling?'

'Yes.'

Common sense took over in Roquebrun's mind. To hold up a Gala where nearly a thousand guests, several hundred waiters, not to mention cordons of police and plainclothes men were spread over the outdoor terraces of the Silver Sands Casino fronting onto the lagoon, was simply unthinkable.

'The whole thing is too utterly hair-brained. Why would any gang take such a chance when it would be much easier, say, to rob the villas where these jewels are kept?'

Captain Scoubide interrupted with one word, 'Egomania,' and brought the Colonel, his thoughts and his speech up short.

Neither said anything for a moment. Both men were thinking hard. It was Scoubide who resumed. 'There's always a second motive to great robberies: the sense of power that accompanies murder. To defy all the protective devices of modern security and make away with valuables going into figures that are astronomical must feed and revive a sick and retarded afflatus to the point where any risk must seem worth taking. The challenge is tremendous and in the case of some humans, as we know, irresistible. What mischief hasn't already been created by ambitions and limitless dreams in which holocausts are set off for the sake of one megalomaniac fling? Consult your history books, my friend.'

The Colonel said nothing.

'Even if there weren't the profit motive,' Scoubide continued, 'think of the satisfaction of knowing that you had engineered the greatest and most impossible robbery in the annals of modern crime!'

The Colonel was hardly listening any more. His thoughts had been turned back to the night when he and the Zoological Gang had penetrated the German Army, Secret Police and French Collaborationists' security forces as well to hijack the payroll of the entire German South Coast Command, and what the sight of the chests of bullion, D-marks and French francs had done to swell his ego, even to the point of sustaining him through the torture when later, like most of the Resistance leaders, he was betrayed to the Gestapo.

The insignificant little French detective broke in upon his thoughts, 'It would be a great scandal and shame upon us if such an attempt were even to be made, let alone succeed.'

The Colonel smiled. 'And you would be a great hero if you were to prevent it, or cause it to fail.'

Scoubide said, 'You and I know very well to whom I owe my decoration in that nasty case of the picture thieves.'

The Colonel, whose alarm had not yet been allayed, said, 'You are too modest, old friend.' But at the same time he wondered how much of the whole of that story Scoubide had known and he wished suddenly to be alone. He said, 'Well, if I should hear anything . . .'

The Captain said, 'One could ask no more. Let me wish you a splendid profit upon your beautiful clock and that no acquisitive eyes will be cast upon it, shall we say, after hours?'

The two men shook hands and through the window the Colonel watched the inconspicuous detective depart in his inconspicuous Peugeot. He went over and sat down on the bench by a heavy, gothic, 13th century monastery table and rested his head in his hands in deep and troubled

thought. What Captain Scoubide in effect had
said to him was, unless a hitherto unheard of, outside mob was contemplating this idiot caper, the
only ones capable of considering it and possibly
even of bringing it off would be his friends, the
aging members of the Zoological Gang.

The Zoological Gang was at its Sunday afternoon game of *Pétanque,* behind the greenhouses
of the Tiger's carnation plantation above Haut-de-
Cagnes, when Colonel Roquebrun drove up in his
black Mercedes and sat watching them quietly
through the open window, so as not to disturb a
breathless moment.

The Tiger was taking careful aim. His arm
swung. A steel ball the size of an orange flew
twenty paces through the air and there was a click
as it hit a rival sphere squarely, knocking it away
from where it had lain a few inches from the white
jack. The Tiger had always been a dead shot with
whatever weapon.

The Elephant said, '*Salaud!*' but the cry of ap-
probation from the Wolf was followed by the
shout from the four as they greeted their old
leader.

'*Holà* there, *Renard,* welcome! We hoped you
might come.'

'Take my place,' said the Leopard, 'it is becoming more and more difficult for me to bend over to
pick up the *boule.*'

The Wolf said, 'I hear you have acquired a wonderful old clock. Very valuable.'

Roquebrun remained sitting for yet another few moments, contemplating his former comrades, wondering how the Wolf had heard about his new acquisition but not at all surprised that he had.

The Colonel shed his coat, for it was hot, partnered the Elephant in two games which they won, even though his mind was less on the problems of the pitch, that is to say the terrain, changing with each game and more upon how he was going to manage to bring up the subject that had been gnawing at his mind ever since the visit of Captain Scoubide, two days before. It had given him no rest and he had known that eventually he would have to satisfy himself.

Before the third game could be started the Leopard said, 'Phew, isn't it too hot to play? Why don't we wait until it's cooler? Friend Tiger, what about something to moisten our throats?'

The Tiger clicked his two steel *boules* together and said, 'What's the matter with me? I'm a rotten host! Come into the garden, there's both beer and some bottles of 'Mistral' in the fridge.'

This suited the Colonel. Out of earshot of anyone, with a couple of cold bottles of wine he might be able to relieve his anxieties.

And so it was in the pretty little garden behind the house of the Tiger, who was a widower and lavished much affection upon flowers as well as dealing with them commercially, the five sat around an iron table on iron chairs. Wine and beer gurgled into glasses and good feeling prevailed. Sooner or later at these reunions the conversation would turn to reminiscences of the old days and one or another of their exploits against the Germans and when it did, Roquebrun felt that he would have his opening.

Sure enough, after the third bottle of Provençal wine had gone the rounds, the stout Leopard smiled smugly and said, 'I can never drink this without thinking of the night when we blew up the warehouse where the German Commandant had stored the entire supply of wine they had stolen from us for their officers. Believe me, this was the most painful blow we struck at the Boche during the whole campaign. The General came close to having a stroke of apoplexy. He was too fat—like me,' and he chuckled adding, 'and it was so simple!'

Colonel Roquebrun was ready. He said, 'It would not be quite so simple today any more. I wouldn't too much care to have to conduct operations of *grand sabotage* in these times.'

The Wolf, who had his chair tipped back and was examining his own reminiscent daydreams through the bottom of his glass, brought his chair back to level again and said, 'What? Nonsense! With the Arabs able to place bombs on aircraft at will, or blow up offices . . .'

'And invariably get caught,' said the Colonel. 'Besides which, that is small stuff. I am thinking of something of truly staggering effect, such as we used to perpetrate. You would find yourself up against quite a different proposition. Remember, any *coup,* to count, must be a hundred per cent successful. To lose a man shot, or one or two landed in jail afterwards and the rest scattered, is for idiots. Today, in France, you would be up against nine local and national police forces, all cooperating by wireless. Twenty-five years have opened up miracles of electronics and computerized dissemination of alarm. Their forensic laboratories pinpoint the criminals. They photograph or televise you on closed-circuit while you are at work; they pursue you with helicopters. No, no, old comrade, today we have quite a different bowl of *bouillabaisse*. I think if we tried any of our old tricks we might find ourselves behind bars very quickly, or trying to cough up a bullet from our lungs.'

The Wolf, who in those times had been the expert on penetration, did not appear to be convinced. He set his glass down upon the iron table with a clang, shrugged his shoulders and remarked, 'Well, there's the old saying, for every lock there is a key.'

And the mild-mannered Tiger queried, 'Isn't it just a matter of keeping up to date? Crime or outlawry is a good deal like a continuing war, isn't it, with attack and defence alternating in effectiveness?'

The Leopard added, 'One hears only statistically that crime is on the increase. And what about the Great Train Robbery in England?'

The Colonel said, 'The majority of them were caught, weren't they?'

The Wolf's white teeth gleamed as he said,

'*Renard* has something there. That English gang left its name and address all over that farm. At least they were caught by fingerprints and so most of them are looking out from behind bars. Bad organization; good police work. We would never have been so stupid. We wouldn't be today.'

Roquebrun thought to himself: *That key word 'today' has come up sufficiently; perhaps now is the time to proceed.* Aloud he said, 'Say, for the sake of argument, that the French police of the seventies were the Germans of yesterday, do you really believe you could pull off the kind of jobs we did then and get away with it?"

The Wolf threw back his dark head and laughed. He said, 'Even with the French police, who are ten times as smart as the Germans ever were, I know we could.'

Electricity was beginning to gather throughout the group and the Colonel was wondering whether, if he held a finger just above the iron table top, a spark would jump the gap. They must, he thought, be thinking of the episode of the twelve Renoirs they had stolen: an exquisite job of planning, timing and execution. But if they were, they must also be remembering that in the end it had been himself who had had to resolve the affair. He said, 'Since you consider yourselves all so clever— which, mind you, I am not denying—let me set you a hypothetical problem.'

'A problem, excellent!' said the mild-mannered Tiger, 'but first let me fill up our glasses so that we can sharpen our wits,' and he did so.

It was now the turn of Colonel Roquebrun to tilt back his chair, to simulate what he hoped would be a relaxed attitude. He said, 'Next Saturday evening the August Gala is taking place at the Silver Sands Casino for The Charity. The American star Tommy Rich will be singing; caviar will be served up by the bucketful; souvenirs for all the ladies; three bands; a super firework show to end it. At five hundred francs a ticket, the affair is a sell-out.'

The four men sat silently, fingering their glasses and listening, and the Colonel, whose range of vision was that of the most exquisite, wide-angle lens of an aviation camera, wondered whether he had caught the ghost of a glance passing between the Tiger and the Wolf.

He proceeded, 'It has been variously estimated in an article in the American journal, the *Herald Tribune,* by their society reporter, that not only will every *grande dame* on the coast be there, but that jewellery valued between forty and fifty million dollars will be on the premises during the evening.'

The fat Leopard let out what was a combination of an asthmatic wheeze and a whistle and said, '*Mon Dieu!* I had not imagined it would come to that much!'

It was the second tingle of alarm set up in the Colonel. The glance he had thought he had seen, or had he? And why would the proprietor of an electrical shop be estimating the value of jewels at a Gala? And then again, why might he not? It

was the writer of the article who had brought up
the subject which had been there for anyone to
read.

He continued, 'You all know in general the design of the Silver Sands.'

Their reaction to this could not be judged anything but normal, as their eyes went up into their
heads to aid them in visualizing.

The Silver Sands Casino, completed no more
than a year ago, had been constructed in the shape
of a huge 'T'. The stem of the 'T', and the only
approach to the Casino proper from the land end,
was a four-lane causeway leading to a huge rec-
tangular parking place. But the sides of the causeway were also a part of a marina with berths for
small yachts and motor cruisers. Beyond the parking space and comprising the head of the 'T', was
the Casino itself, a modern structure of glass, polished copper and concrete, with a wing at either
end; one containing an opera house, the other a
variety theatre and on the Mediterranean side, a
vast open terrace facing onto a Venetian lagoon.
Here was space and an outdoor set-up, including
a stage, for hundreds of tables for Galas. Beyond
the lagoon was the strip of beach that gave its
name to the Casino.

Its designers had been very well aware of the
fact that during the season millions of dollars
would be changing hands in the gaming rooms
nightly. The building was surrounded on three
sides by water; the only exit by land was the
causeway, which led to the coast road between

Cannes and Antibes with almost the nature of an autoroute, without any intersection for several miles. Emerging, one could turn either left into Cannes, or right towards Antibes and that was that.

'As you can well imagine,' the Colonel was continuing, his hands comfortably behind his head to aid his balance, 'the place will be swarming with flics inside and out. The approaches to the Casino will be closed to all those except ticket-holders. In addition to the local police the area will be stiff with the *Police Nationale Sécurité Public,* members of the famous C.R.S.—*Compagnie Républicaine Sécurité,* and the *Surveillance de Territoire.* The *Police Maritime* will be in evidence off the beach and the helicopters of the *Police de l'Air* won't be far away, and amongst the waiters and guests there will be enough plain-clothes men to alert the entire force at the first hint of anything out of the ordinary. Your *Gendarmerie Nationale* will have the roads cut off with their motorcycle men: a mouse would not be able to get through.'

The four were quite quiet now, none of them even bothering to drink. 'So much is just common sense under the circumstances,' the Colonel continued. 'Goodness knows what other modern protective devices, besides an arsenal that would equip a battalion, have been prepared to give maximum security to the guests at the Gala.'

The Colonel brought his chair back to level and set his glass down hard, so that the two crashes coincided deliberately as he rasped out, 'Well, you clever ones, how would you take them?'

Immediately the Colonel realized he had made a mistake in presenting the hypothesis as a bombshell in such a dramatic manner, as he observed the effect of his question upon the four.

Stunned silence, swift and perfectly perceptible exchange of glances not only between the Tiger and the Wolf, but all four. The Leopard wheezed a heavy sigh, reached over and poured wine again. The Elephant played with his glass, breaking the silence with tapping noises on the iron table top, and the Colonel kicked himself for being a fool. Were their eyes and looks shifty, questioning, guilty, or merely introspective? How would he himself have behaved under similar circumstances? What would be his reaction if he, a one-time criminal on the side of the angels, had suddenly been asked how he would plan the most sensational robbery of all time? Certainly he would have to think and the outward actions of men thinking differed. Some rolled up their eyes, others picked their noses, pulled on hair, tugged at a moustache, lit a cigarette and behaved in a manner which could be looked upon as wholly innocent or highly suspicious. By presenting the matter to them in this way he now realized that whatever came out of it he would never be certain.

Yet another thought assailed him. What if they suspected that he himself might be planning such a *coup* and was using this method to sound them out? The difficulty was that while they had all been comrades in danger and were still friends, they were close-mouthed and kept their emotions to themselves, and the passing years had not made them more communicative. There was also the little matter of that caper of the Renoirs they had stolen for the high-minded purpose of ransoming them to aid some of the poor and ailing in their neighbourhoods, and which they had done without letting him know so that he had been compelled to go to their rescue. Now, by his mode of attack, he realized he had got himself into a pickle.

Colonel Roquebrun mastered his emotions and changing the tone of his voice said, 'Come, we are all here together having a drink and the idea came to me from our discussion to hear how you think you would deal with a situation which, in my opinion, is impregnable.'

The Elephant said, half to himself, 'Nothing is impregnable.'

The Leopard murmured, 'Fifty-million-dollars of jewels! What a score! But then you would have to know that when you went to fence them, you would only realize half. Still, twenty-five millions . . .'

The Colonel had another uneasy qualm as he thought: *Heavens, friend Leopard already has them and is thinking of disposal!* And then he calmed himself. What was more natural? This was the problem of every theft. Those hyenas, the fences, yapping on the outskirts of organized crime, took half the loot without lifting so much as a finger.

The Wolf, who might also have been given the sobriquet of 'Love' from the manner in which he had laughed at locksmiths during the war, enquired, 'Have you given us correctly all the conditions surrounding the problem, *mon vieux?*'

The Colonel for an instant felt wholly relieved. Here was an absolutely normal reaction to a hypothetical problem, and then immediately doubt again rushed in. Was the Wolf fishing for more inside information?

'Those I have told you are the obvious ones,' the Colonel replied, 'that you yourselves might imagine. I don't doubt that the French police will have some surprises waiting.'

'I wouldn't give any police too much credit for imagination,' said the Tiger, 'though ours are pretty clever.'

'It really wouldn't matter, would it?' put in the Wolf. 'If one's organization is sound, the surprises would not work, whatever they were. No one goes into such an affair without allowing for the unexpected.'

The Tiger said, 'The problem, then, breaks down into three parts: immobilization of the police, removal of the jewellery from the persons of the wearers, and escape.'

The Leopard, who had been studiously examining the label on the wine bottle, murmured, 'Entrance.'

'Of course, entrance,' agreed the Tiger, 'but one should really not consider this a problem, since there are no steel doors, vaults or locks to penetrate. If I were to present myself driving a small van, on the outside of which was painted the name of a well-known confectioner, nobody would dream of stopping me or even looking within, where the three of you, or a half dozen, could be concealed beneath boxes of *petits-fours.*'

The Elephant shook his head and said, 'Of course it would work, but once you were inside you would be in trouble. The van, the cakes nobody ordered; waiters all counted, numbered and identified.'

'Well, as guests, then,' suggested the Leopard, 'One could rent a "smoking", though they would probably have difficulty to fit me.'

The Elephant snorted, '. . . and leave a trail behind you. No, the simplest and most effective would be as police.'

They all fell silent at this and Colonel Roquebrun was again aware of another swift exchange of looks between the four.

'One policeman,' explained the Elephant, 'who encountered a second policeman on his beat whom he did not know, would be suspicious. Amongst a hundred to a hundred-and-fifty policemen collected there as auxiliaries from, as you say, nine different departments, as well as on loan from different districts, there will be dozens who do not know one another and who will be able to enter and move freely throughout the area.'

The Wolf said, 'Jean is right. Nobody would suspect a policeman.'

'Agreed,' put in the Leopard, 'even a fat one,' and the Tiger nodded.

'Then,' said the Elephant, 'we are four police-

men, or *gendarmes*.' He turned to Roquebrun
and added, 'We are now inside. Do you agree?'

'It is the obvious method,' said the Colonel,
'since we spent a good deal of our time in the old
days in German uniform, but your difficulties are
just beginning.'

The Leopard had now produced an envelope
from his pocket and with a biro was beginning to
draw a sketch which very quickly turned into a
diagram of the outdoor auditorium of the Silver
Sands Casino, and when he had completed it he
pushed it towards the centre of the table, making
room amongst the empty bottles, and all four
heads bent over it. He said, 'Here, you see, on the
seaward side of the Casino, is a stage. It is built
upon elevators so that it can be raised or lowered.
Entrance can be effected from both wings and
also the centre. Then, here is where the tables are
grouped, some eight long ones to accommodate
large parties, outward from the stage and parallel,
seating up to eighteen or twenty, and here . . .'
and he filled in the remainder of the area with circles and squares, '. . . are the rest of the tables
which occupy the space to the very edge of the
lagoon.'

'The main kitchens,' he explained, 'are here,'
and he pointed to the area he had drawn, 'behind
and to the right of the stage. But there is a second
unit here, on the left, which takes care of the in-
door cabaret, and on the nights of outdoor Galas
both are in use and so the waiters can come in
both from here and from here.'

On the far side of the lagoon he had drawn a large, empty area and a few rectangles indicating buildings. 'This,' he said, 'is concrete between the lagoon and the beach and ordinarily is always filled with tables, where they serve the buffet lunch for the bathers. It is cleared on Gala nights for the fireworks men. And then, of course, these here are the changing rooms and then the actual beach with the deep-water jetty here, where the Rivas tie up for the water-skiers.' He suddenly seemed to remember something and made some marks jutting out from the inner edge of the lagoon and grinned, 'I forgot the gondolas,' he said.

Colonel Roquebrun examined the diagram with a sick feeling at the pit of his stomach. This simply could not have been drawn from the memory of one who might have spent a casual evening there, or even gone swimming by daylight. Besides which, as he very well knew, none of the members of the one-time Zoological Gang were likely to be frequenters of this luxury complex. He said, 'Business must be good, my dear Gaston,' addressing the Leopard, 'if you can afford outings for yourself and your family at the Silver Sands.'

The Leopard's moon face dissolved into a fat chuckle. 'Not me,' he said, 'but I worked on the electrical job. It was too big for the builder; they were in a hurry, so they sub-contracted to a lot of us little fellows. I put in eight weeks.'

This explanation relieved the Colonel momentarily; the sick feeling returned immediately as he

thought: *And therefore you know the location of
every wire outlet, input, switch box and emergency systems.*

The Wolf, his eyes sparkling, was leaning forward examining the sketch, 'Splendid, Gaston!'
he said, 'Now we are not only inside, but know
exactly where we are, where we have to go and
what we have to do.'

The Colonel, too, looked at the drawing as
though hypnotized, for in his mind he was seeing
these four ruthless, capable, one-time unscrupu-
lous men on the loose within the Casino area and
suddenly the foundations of all the security
seemed a great deal less solid.

The Elephant now said, 'The first problem,
then—immobilization of the police.'

'The most difficult,' said the Leopard, 'a hundred and fifty armed men. . . .'

'The simplest,' put in the Tiger. They all stared
at him. 'Hostages,' he said.

'Oh, my goodness,' put in the Wolf admiringly, 'but where do we keep them?'

'In the lagoon of course, in one of the gondolas.
Out there in the centre of the water, safe as in
your own home.' They all bent over the Leopard's
map again.

The Tiger had a fingernail on one of the black
marks by the lagoon. 'We embark them here.
There will be no interference. They will be
afloat before anyone knows what's happened.'

The Elephant gave a grunt of satisfaction, 'Excellent! The newspapers have indicated that the

Préfet, the Minister of the Interior and the British and American Ambassadors will be present. We collect them one by one. A gun in the back, a whisper in the ear.'

'What? With all those lights glowing?' asked the Leopard, 'And plain-clothes' detectives?'

The Wolf said, 'You know where the master switch is located.'

'*Crétins!*' said the Tiger, 'what has become of your brains? We do it under cover of the fireworks. Lights are out and there's the noise of the explosions to cover pistol shots. I recommend we pick up a couple of young girls as well; the prettiest.'

'What for?' asked the Elephant.

'To kill if necessary,' replied the Tiger. 'At the first false move from either a patron or the police —and you may be sure there will be such—we shoot one.'

Roquebrun felt a wave of horror such as he had not even known during wartime pass over him. 'Antoine!' he cried at the Tiger, in genuine outrage, 'what the devil are you saying?' It had been so long since such utter callous cruelty had been almost a daily necessity amongst them.

Antoine Petitpierre, the Tiger, the thin, gentle-looking carnation-grower, now turned to the Colonel and asked, 'What are you so exercised about? You have set us a hypothetical problem; I have just shot a hypothetical girl. We want this caper to succeed, don't we? For a great robbery it is necessary to freeze the victims with horror.

They will then believe that you will carry out any further threats.'

There was no denying the calm, sane logic. They were playing a game, as the Tiger had taken the trouble to remind Roquebrun-*Renard,* amusing themselves with finding a solution to an impossible problem. Yet was it a trick of the light, for the sun had begun to dip into the west, or had the Colonel—as the Tiger had turned his head towards him to speak—seen for a moment the mild eyes of the horticulturist change to that slate-grey opaqueness that the Colonel remembered when the Tiger had had a murder to perform?

Then, the blood once more freezing in his veins and as though transported in the palm of some monstrous, evil genii, Colonel Roquebrun saw himself there the night of the Gala, with his young niece Madeleine Renault in the darkness, the exquisite, delicate face and shining eyes uplifted in enthralled excitement to the green and gold, the red and silver bursts of fire in the sky, the bouquets of burning flowers showering the night, to the thunder of the air bombs. She would be dressed in white, her first long ball gown. He had seen it, the 'V' crossed modestly high over the young breasts, chiffon floating; the moment in a young girl's life when down through the centuries she could serve as the model for the angels.

He imagined an interval of darkness between the ascending, tumbling shells of the fireworks, the child torn from his side before he was even aware of what was happening. In the sky a glorious fall of jewelled rain; a scream, a faint pop. In the light of the fireworks Madeleine slumped over the arm of a policeman, the white chiffon already stained dark red. The man was gone. She lay in a small heap on the ground between the aisles of the tables, a slain white bird.

'Collection,' the Wolf was saying, and Colonel Roquebrun was once more back in the garden by the iron tables, with his glass of wine in front of him, but much shaken. Whatever had made him initiate this horrid game? Then he remembered Captain Scoubide.

The Elephant said, 'Three of us with sacks could handle it pretty efficiently, I would imagine. Wire cutters, of course, for necklaces and bracelets—one snip and they're off.'

The Leopard asked, 'What about rings?'

The Tiger said, 'I should think there would be not too great a problem. The patrons would be asked to remove them and have them ready. Should there be hesitation, the holding up of one or two severed fingers would, I am sure, expedite the rest.'

Colonel Roquebrun shuddered again but said, 'The police inside the area ...'

'Will do nothing,' concluded the Tiger. 'The police outside will be equally helpless. I am sitting in the middle of the lagoon, holding a Sten gun on four men, the killing of whom would have most serious international consequences, plus a young girl from a prominent family. Remember, we have already shot one.'

'Twenty minutes, if the rest of us work fast,' put in the Elephant. 'The fireworks are scheduled to last half an hour.'

'Bringing us to the third problem,' added the stout Leopard, 'escape.'

'By helicopter, I suppose,' said Colonel Roquebrun and wondered whether the bitterness in his voice would be apparent to them all.

It was the turn of the Wolf to let out a great snort, 'Hah! Now it is you, comrade *Renard,* who are being old fashioned and not up with the times. A helicopter? We would be shot down in two minutes. Remember, that while the police within are immobilized, those on the outside are not. They will be hearing what is taking place, even though they cannot interfere. With all roads blocked and the marine police alerted, they will know the only escape route is by air. The military airfield at Toulon will have been alerted—Helicopter, indeed!'

The Colonel found himself fascinated again 'Then what do you propose?'

The Wolf leaned back, his hands behind his head and said, 'Some of that modernity you said would make it impossible for us to operate today —VTLA.'

'What?' the Colonel asked sharply.

'Jump jet,' replied the Wolf, 'Vertical Take-off and Landing Aircraft.'

The Colonel recalled, now, that the Wolf also had been their aviation expert. When any type of flying had to be done, he had been at the controls.

'The timing will have to be right,' the Wolf continued, 'The jet descends onto this concrete area here,' pointing to the sketch, 'We embark and take off. Even if there are military planes in the area, they won't be looking for a VTLA and by the time they twig, it will be too late to catch us. The latest models fly at 1200 miles per hour. In twenty minutes we will be over Algeria. Then let anyone try to find us.'

'*Quod erat demonstrandum!*' said the Elephant.

'Wait!' cried the Colonel, 'Not so fast. Who is flying this affair? One of you is still on the lagoon with the hostages and three of you have been collecting the swag—Well?'

The Tiger said calmly, 'Oh, outside assistance of course, arranged beforehand. You never said the affair was to be strictly limited to us four. You only asked us to work out a means by which a robbery on so vast a scale could be effected. I think we have done so. Are you satisfied?'

The Colonel now found himself wholly caught up in the game. He said, 'One more inside man is needed. Someone to direct the affair, give the instructions to the patrons and the police. How do you propose to accomplish that, and with whom?'

The Leopard, the electrical expert, said, 'There would be no difficulty since the performer having just completed his act, there would still be a microphone on stage. There isn't a modern singer today who can be heard above a squeak without the aid of amplification, including the great

Tommy Rich. The fifth member will take over
the microphone as a kind of master of ceremonies, announce that a hold-up is taking place, that
anyone resisting will be shot, point out the in-
vidious and helpless position of the police, indicate the presence of the hostages in the centre of
the lagoon and advise the ladies to be prepared to
relinquish their valuables with the least possible
fuss.'

All four members of the one-time Zoological
Gang were now grinning broadly and the Wolf
said, 'We, of course, have reserved this important
and dramatic role for you, my dear *Renard,* one
that would fit your presence and attainments. You
hold fifty million dollars in the hollow of your
hand—Do you accept?'

Colonel Roquebrun forced a laugh which did
not at all come from his heart or sense of humour.
'No, thank you,' he replied, 'I have never been
much use at public speaking and I am not sure
that my nerves are any longer what they were. Besides which, I don't like killing.' And then he
added, dropping the artificial jocularity and now
sincere, 'The horrible thing is,' he said, 'that I
think it might work. The jump jet had not occurred to me. The right man approached at a military air base, promised one fifth of the swag, the
fireworks would guide him and he would be able
to land by their light. It fits. That's clever, friend
Wolf.'

Alphonse Cousin acknowledged with a slight
bow, and they all fell into silence once more. The

Colonel went into some frantic soul-searching.

The minds of the four had most certainly been turned to crime by this little game, if they had not been before. Had he put ideas into their heads? Fifty million dollars! True, the only caper in which they had indulged since the war had been for benevolence, but for fifty million dollars charity might, for once, strike them as beginning at home. Or they might have latched onto some quixotic idea that as the August Ball was itself for charity, they would make a good job of it, since it was well-known that only a small percentage of the proceeds of such affairs ever really reached the needy.

For one impulsive, almost insane moment, it was on the tip of his tongue to say, 'Are you four lunatics actually contemplating a crime so vast and willing to take innocent lives to accomplish it?' when in the nick of time the enormity of the impossibility of saying such a thing, of imputing something so monstrous to these men who were living as good, simple citizens, carrying on their daily lives, came home to him. He realized that he could never do this. He needed to get away alone and think and did so by examining his wrist watch and saying, '*Dieu!* Look at the hour! This is when the tourists begin to arrive and I don't like leaving my wife alone in the shop.'

He took his leave with a handshake all around, climbed into his Mercedes, waved to them from the window and was off. The Four watched his departure silently and when the noise of his car had died away, the Elephant murmured, 'Welll'

The Wolf said, 'I'll wager he's going to have a word with Captain Scoubide.'

The Leopard said indignantly, 'He wouldn't!'

The Elephant addressed the Tiger saying, 'It was your killing that upset him. Wouldn't it work without that?'

'No,' replied the Tiger, 'you know it wouldn't.'

All four men were thinking hard, for they were no fools. 'And if he were to warn Scoubide?' said the Wolf.

'It would be unpardonable,' the Tiger stated flatly.

They continued to sit a while longer in uneasy silence.

The next twenty-four hours the Colonel went through such hell that he wished every curse and malediction possible upon the head of the wily little Riviera detective, Captain Scoubide. 'Have you heard anything?' he had asked in seeming innocence and good faith. The Colonel now had heard plenty, and he only had himself and his curiosity to blame for his dilemma. He could have replied originally, 'I have heard nothing,' and there the matter would have ended.

He sat in the shop late at night with his own sketch of the Silver Sands lay-out before him, studying, scheming, racking his brains to try to think of some other way to pull off a job like that. If he succeeded, then the plans of his four friends could be considered truly hypothetical. But he could not. Unless one were to descend upon the area with an army of several thousand men, cordon it off and eliminate the police, it was impossible. Theoretically the Zoo Gang's analysis was practically foolproof, provided its viciousness was adhered to and he shuddered as he remembered the utterly calm and cold-blooded proposals of the Tiger.

Again in his mind arose the picture of his niece, Madeleine Renault, her white garment stained scarlet and with equal horror, the thought of a jewelled finger clipped off by the wire cutters, held up as an example. He thought that only in the world of today could such monstrous violence, even in the imagination, be devised against innocent persons.

What to do? Warn his friends off? Inform Captain Scoubide? He could not bring himself to impute such a murderous scheme to the four without an iota of proof beyond the fact that the police 'felt' that something was in the wind and they had come up with the way it could be done.

But what if these brave, once dangerous and reckless men had actually come together for one last throw of the dice? And as soon as he thought of this it coloured all his suspicions that had been aroused by the glances he thought he had seen pass between them. Yet, as one who himself had been betrayed, it was against every fibre of his nature to betray. But the picture of the hypothetical, dead girl would not go out of his mind.

It came as a shock to him that the lights of his

shop, beneath which he had been working through the night, were no longer needed. He looked out of the window. It was daylight—Monday morning. He reached for the telephone.

A great Riviera Charity Gala is an unforgettable event to anyone who has ever attended one of these extravaganzas where beauty, show, chic, vulgarity and gluttony are all combined beneath a canopy of stars. Music, chatter, clatter of dishes and the glow of the table lamps reflect from flushed faces, shirtfronts, bare shoulders and the contained fire of jewels, jewels, jewels.

Caviar is ladled out from kilo-size tins; chunks of equally expensive *foie gras* plugged with equally expensive truffles appear as though by magic over one's shoulder; only the flask-shaped bottles of Dom Perignon or Cristal, the most expensive champagnes, gush their foam.

The women are either exquisite beauties of every class from aristocrat to *poule,* or rich old bags, the lines of whose face-lifts do not show in the lamplight. But young or old, their gowns are the latest exclusives from the Paris houses and their equally exclusive perfumes lace the soft night summer air. The decor surrounding the enclosure has been devised with lights and paint and canvas into some kind of modern fairyland by a Parisian designer.

Enjoyment consists of the knowledge of being there amongst the people who are acknowledged —by themselves at least—of being the best, in surroundings of the best, with food of the best and everything in the greatest luxury which a luxurious era is capable of presenting.

For a table for six the Colonel had splurged six hundred dollars, with wine costing him another hundred or so, plus the hundred-franc notes he handed out and which were fluttering at every table as pretty girls came around throughout the dinner selling lottery tickets for the car, mink coat, the diamond brooch, the various vacations by air, and merchandise donated, and which would be drawn at the end of the evening.

His was one of the first, close to the stage after the long tables drawn up in parallel lines where sat the celebrities. The Colonel thought that if robbers were only to limit their attention to those big parties, they would garner gems enough to make the job worth while. From where he sat uncomfortably, he could see the glow of the Van Gelder rubies, the brooding reflection from the Marberry emeralds and the diamonds of the Maharani splintered by the lamplight into every colour of the rainbow.

The reason why the Colonel was sitting uncomfortably was that his wallet, stuffed with hundred-franc notes, had been transferred to the inside of his dinner jacket, while in the hip pockets of the trousers rested two loaded .38-calibre automatic pistols. Nor was there any more comfort in his mind. His wife was delighted with the treat, so were his friends and the young people were ecstatic, but the Colonel, as he kept trying not to be caught looking about constantly to see if he could locate any members of the Zoological Gang, was miserable.

He kept searching for them disguised as policemen, but there were no uniformed men visible in the area around the tables, though he thought he saw a dash of blue and a glimpse of a pistol belt at some of the distant entrances to the outdoor enclosure. And then he was assailed by doubts. 'Gain entrance dressed as police,' the Zoo Gang had said was the simplest, but there were other possible masquerades. The delivery van idea was perfectly feasible, so were extra waiters, not to mention the crew connected with the stage show—scene shifters, mechanics and electricians.

The area of the Gala was one gigantic pool of light through which bustled white coated waiters, black-coated Maître D's, lottery ticket sellers, guests stuffing themselves at their tables. Beyond lay the darkened lagoon and across it the Colonel could see the torches of the fireworks men as they went about setting up and checking their production.

The Colonel felt more and more uneasy; the short hairs at the nape of his neck told him that *something* was going to happen. He wondered whether he ought to excuse himself and hustle down to examine the gondolas, to see if there was one with weapons concealed in it, and then thought he would only be making a fool of himself.

Five tables away Roquebrun saw an enormously fat waiter bending over, offering *Filet de Charolais en Croute Parisienne* and he was so certain it was the Leopard that he felt himself close to panic and half rose from his seat. The waiter turned around for a moment. He was not the Leopard and the Colonel realized that if he were anywhere on the premises, he would be backstage with the electricians, where he could get his hands on the main switch. His mind turned to how the gang would divide their labours if they were there. If there was to be killing, the Tiger would do it. No question.

The Colonel jumped as a waiter brushed over his shoulder to present him the beefsteak in its crust of dough, stuffed with *foie gras*. His nerves were getting out of hand. He had no appetite but took his portion and even toyed with it, as he forced himself to remember that for the robbery to have any chance whatsoever of success, nothing would happen until the lights went out and the bangs of the fireworks began. When that moment came it would be time enough for him to decide what to do and how to do it. The guns on which he sat no longer felt uncomfortable. He was very glad they were there.

The dinner came to an end; the atmosphere thick and heavy with the smell of food now mingling with the perfumes and the fumes of alcohol. Voices were crescendoing and laughter louder as the endless glasses of champagne took effect. The tables were cleared, the lights dimmed, the stage illuminated and the show began.

Afterwards the Colonel could remember nothing but whirls of colour and fluttering fabric as girls and boys went through formation dances. There was an inept magician, and it was not until later the Colonel realized he had been a comic and was missing his tricks on purpose. And then, at last, the star's turn; the American singer Tommy Rich.

The Colonel was alert to him because, his nerves brought under control, he was now alert to everything since the fireworks would follow the singer. When the young man, to a polite patter of applause (it was not considered chic to be enthusiastic about anything on the Riviera, even a great star), placed his microphone to his lips, he was aware of the boy's bodyguards, their bulky chests almost bursting from their dinner jackets, below the stage which had now been raised upwards three feet from floor level, standing on either side. They were toughies. If any attempt were made to seize Tommy Rich as a hostage, all hell would break loose there. When the possibility of staging a robbery had been discussed with the Zoo Gang, no one had thought to mention or consider the presence of this armed group of Americans prepared to defend their charge. How would they react? How many innocent guests would die in the cross fire of bullets?

In spite of themselves, the smart crowd was falling under the spell of the singer.

He was young, twenty-four, a dark, sleek, handsome boy with moist, glowing brown eyes which, when a song was plaintive, seemed to be glazed with tears. They were a feature of his face and yet in one sense disturbing, for they were placed just that much too close together on either side of a dominant nose.

He differed from the modern singer of the day in that he could sing. He had been trained; his voice was a beautifully timbred baritone, his phrasing and musicianship were exceptional. He gave delight.

Roquebrun looked across the table at his niece and his heart warmed at the expression on her face. Her cheek resting against her clenched hands, she was transported. The magic of the singer was that he could make one remember and think of all the sad, the joyous, the painful and the wonderful things that one had ever experienced.

And therefore when it happened, the Colonel was unprepared for it.

One can think about, talk about, imagine an event but it is never like the actuality itself which has its own particular rhythm of going forth at a pace quite different from what one has anticipated, far more swift, unobtrusive and inexorable.

The last encore had been sung; the boy had taken his final bow in response to the ovation and skipped into the wings; the audience had settled into a hum of conversation when every light in the outdoor theatre, with the exception of the distant 'Exits', went out, plunging the area into darkness except for the high glow of the Milky Way. A spark climbed into the sky, tumbling over and over and there was a shattering explosion as the first of two thunderclap shells announced the beginning of the fireworks.

Simultaneously the blood seemed to freeze in the veins of Colonel Roquebrun, for he was remembering what he had forgotten. There was enough starlight for him to see a shadowy figure emerge from the wings and seize the microphone and a voice, a familiar one, rang out over the audience, 'Ladies and Gentlemen! All of you remain in your seats and do not move. This is a . . .' and here the voice was suddenly cut off. Nobody seemed to have heard.

A second explosion followed to herald the first firework and then from across the lagoon came the 'thup, thup, thup, thup, thup,' of the shells fired heavenwards from their mortar tubes. The Colonel leaped to his feet, dragging his two pistols from his pockets and rushing around, leaned over his niece, covering her with his body.

Dwarfed by the violence of the blast in the sky, Roquebrun heard a snap from the direction of the stage, rather like the sound made when pulling a *bon-bon* or Christmas cracker, and a cry. Every nerve on edge, the Colonel thought: *My God, have they already shot a girl?* He had a momentary glimpse of figures writhing on the platforms and sounds of a scuffle below, and then from overhead the display flung skyward burst with an earsplitting cannonade into a canopy of gold and silver, rubies and diamonds, showers of colour; one burst emanating from another bathing the upturned faces below in brilliant light. From the throats of the audience came the first appreciative 'Ahhhhh!' which always seemed to go with the climactic flowering of rockets, as well as applause.

Colonel Roquebrun's face was not upturned. Still covering his niece and with a gun in each hand, the safety catches removed, he had turned towards the stage. But there was no one there any longer. The figures he had thought he had seen had disappeared but he noticed that the microphone had been knocked over and was lying on its side. Nor were the burly forms of the bodyguards visible either.

'Thup, thup, thup, thup,' went the next series of shells to light the heavens in a symphony of blue and white stars.

Madeleine Renault cried, 'Uncle, uncle! What are you doing? What's the matter? Oh, do be careful! My hair!'

The Colonel's nerves were still tingling violently but he had the feeling as of something that had passed, a danger that was no longer. He said, 'Forgive an old fool, my dear, for an attack of war nerves combined with, I suspect, too much champagne. When those cannoning blasts went off I thought I was back in combat once more,' and with this he quickly pocketed his pistols, thanking goodness that with everyone looking upwards, no one had seen him waving two automatics about.

The young girl looked up into the countenance of the veteran and, because she was a woman and sensitive, she understood or at least she believed the gesture of protection and reached up and kissed the scarred face. The Colonel moved back to his seat.

The rest of the show was superb. There are producers of such performances who can write coloured poetry in the sky and this was one of those occasions, but it also offered a most unexpected climax. For just before the finale, when the fireworks men were about to let everything go in one magnificent culmination, there came a buzzing sound from overhead and there, picked out by the illuminations, was an aircraft; no helicopter but an airplane hovering, looking like a gigantic black beetle and descending slowly, vertically into the spurting silver fountains.

Here was the surprise supreme, or so it was accepted by the audience, and a great wave of applause greeted this phenomenon as the jump jet slowly settled down on the concrete surface beyond the lagoon.

The Colonel mopped his sweating brow, face and neck with his napkin. 'My God!' he murmured to himself. 'So it was true after all!'

Opposite the lagoon, which was momentarily dark except for the torches of the fireworks men, what happened to the aircraft after it landed or who had been in it no one could see, for the next moment one and all were transported by the violence, the beauty and the glory of that last number known as The Battle in the Sky, when fifty shells all discharge their contents at once and set the firmament afire. The patrons were getting their money's worth.

The last coloured stars faded and vanished, the table and side lights of the Gala came on. Overhead, the curtain of grey smoke drifted out to sea and the audience resumed its excited hum about the show they had seen. Madeleine, her face flushed and her eyes themselves like unexpired fireworks cried, 'Oh, Uncle! This has been the most happy night of my life!'

Roquebrun's wife said, 'Pierre, I am simply exhausted! What a wonderful treat you have given us!'

The Colonel made a desperate attempt to wrench himself away from all the unanswered questions and smile acquiescence, but he was far from feeling at ease. That some kind of an attempt had been made, that he had not imagined the whole affair, he was certain but he was not sure that the Zoo Gang had not been involved. Yet was it possible for two independent parties coincidentally to hit upon exactly the same idea? And he worried the thought like a dog with a bone until, as he remembered his all-night-long wrestle with trying to find a different way of doing it, he realized that the word 'coincidentally' was what was leading him astray. There was only one way to solve that particular problem, just as there was only one key to every lock. It might vary slightly in detail, but the main elements would have to be basic.

The stage had lowered again until it was level with the tables, the band was back in place at the back, the musicians' racks illuminated. The conductor posed his baton, the burst of music smoth-

ered the overall hum of talk. Roquebrun's niece
and her boy friend arose to dance before the floor
should become too crowded. The Colonel's friend
at the table invited Madame Roquebrun to the
floor and an acquaintance from across the aisle
asked the other wife to dance. The Colonel found
himself alone, that is until he was aware that
someone had slipped into the chair next to him
and was saying, 'Thank you, _mon Colonel,_ I will
never forget what you have done for us as long as
I live.'

It was Captain Scoubide disguised in a dinner
jacket, except that in this instance it was less effective for its cut was slightly old-fashioned and
with his narrow face and small moustache he managed to look more like a head waiter than a dinner guest. But his eyes were glowing with gratitude and he had placed his hand upon the Colonel's arm in a gesture of affection that was almost
tender.

The Colonel was still shaken and uneasy. He
tried to steady his voice as he asked, 'You have
them all?' Even though he had not been able to
spot any of them, he was still terrified that somehow his friends had been implicated in the affair.

'All,' replied Scoubide, 'all five of them, plus the
fellow in the aircraft.'

'Five!' exclaimed the Colonel and for a moment
his heart leaped, until he remembered that in their
planning of the robbery the Zoological four had
admitted the necessity for a fifth and, of course,
also the pilot of the jump jet.

Scoubide said modestly, 'I had to shoot one. He

had his weapon all ready to fire.'

'Was he seriously injured?' the Colonel asked.

'Fatally, I'm afraid. There was no time to choose a disabling spot and besides which, we didn't want the fellow thrashing about and creating panic amongst the guests.'

'I heard the shot,' the Colonel said.

Scoubide nodded and said, 'Of course, you would have been waiting for it. But for the rest it was covered by the fireworks.' He added, 'Your analysis was brilliantly conceived! Absolutely brilliant!'

The Colonel had a moment of deep sadness and he wondered whether the little detective was giving him the needle in any way.

'Particularly,' Scoubide continued, 'the clue of the four policemen.'

'The four policemen?' queried Roquebrun, and for the first time his heart lifted with hope. He had seen no policemen.

'Yes, it gave us the break,' Scoubide replied. 'Once we knew of that proposed method of gaining entrance to the area, we checked and double checked every one of our own men assigned to this evening. There was not a chance. Therefore that left . . .'

'Yes?' put in the Colonel. He had picked up a spoon and did not realize that he was bending it almost double between his fingers.

'The other four policemen—the ones from Los Angeles.'

The Colonel looked at the ridiculous article he had made of the spoon and straightened it back to its original shape. It did not escape the dark, intelligent eyes of the detective who increased the pressure of his hand upon the Colonel's arm and said, 'My friend! My very dear and noble friend, I should have told you before, but we were certain only at the very last moment, and locating the fellow in the Air Force who would steal and fly a jump jet took some doing. And that, too, was a magnificent analysis and one that had not occurred to us. Our minds were on helicopters. The jet would have made a clean get-away.'

'Those four policemen?' said the Colonel, for now that he was reassured he wanted still more.

'The bodyguards of the American singer,' Scoubide said. 'They were the only ones left. We contacted Los Angeles. There was no record of them. We had them secretly photographed and the prints sent by wire. They were identified as four ex-convicts.'

The Colonel said with sudden asperity, 'Then why didn't you move immediately and pick them up? Why wait until the last second?'

Scoubide nodded and said, 'Of course, except that there were no charges pending against them and there is nothing to say that a singer who had been ostensibly threatened by the Mafia may not engage four ex-convicts to perform as his bodyguards. The four lied about their former connection with the Los Angeles police, but that's no crime. In fact it wasn't even a total lie. Our friends certainly had been connected with the police, but not in the way they would have had us believe. And remember, we had no evidence of any intent to commit a robbery, only—thanks to you—a preview about how such a crime might be committed. Our laboratories are not yet able to pierce the front of the skull and read the messages on the lobes that lie behind. And so we did the next best thing, acting upon . . .' he hesitated, '. . . what seemed to be the only possible way of committing the deed, we made every preparation and took every precaution.'

The Colonel drew a deep breath and said, 'Ah, but the fifth member—the fellow who made the announcement from the stage, or rather started to make it. I recognized his voice.'

The beat of the band changed to a samba and for a moment the dark eyes of Captain Scoubide rested upon where the stage had been and it was now crowded with men and women in evening dress, leaping up and down like Red Indians in a war dance. When he looked away again he was smiling. He said, 'To be sure. You mean Tommy Rich—or rather, Tomaso Torrino, a Mafia boy himself and in with the plot for the big score. It was the final proof we needed.' He laughed suddenly, 'Do you know who identified him for us? Do you remember old Marcello Rufino, the wood merchant who has a place behind Villeneuve-Loubet?'

'What?' cried the Colonel in astonishment, 'Our own homegrown Mafioso? I thought he had been disposed of long ago.'

'Well, he hadn't,' said Scoubide. 'He recognized Torrino, the right name of the singer, or knew about him, probably through a family resemblance or connection, and his nose was put out of joint because he had not been invited to join the party. And now we knew exactly who we had to watch. There were eight of us at each of two tables at either end of the stage, including four of our younger members who accepted the humiliation of appearing in what the Americans call "drag". I assure you their jewels from the Monoprix sparkled as seductively as any at the adjoining tables. It was just a question of timing. One of the bodyguards produced a Sten gun and went for the head table. When they moved, so did we. Except for the one shot, they were overpowered so quickly that no one noticed. Everyone was looking upwards. Our squad in the wings swept up Mr Torrino and when that pretty bird came down out of the sky, the reception committee was waiting for him. *Quod erat demonstrandum.*'

With a shudder as well as a blessed wave of relief the Colonel remembered that the Latin quotation was the exact same one that had been used by the Elephant at the conclusion of his friends' diagram for robbery.

The band crescendoed to a stop. The wild stomping, whirling and leaping came to an end and flushed, laughing and happy couples came off the dance floor, not one aware of the drama that had been played out under their craning necks so to speak, and the tragedy that had been averted.

Captain Scoubide arose, his hand still upon the Colonel's arm. He said, 'Your friends will be returning. *Mademoiselle,* your niece, she has the face of an angel. I'll say thank you again and I suspect that you will be receiving further official thanks—of course, as I know you would wish it, very much beneath the rose bush.'

The Colonel's party converged upon the table and Captain Scoubide turned away, but not before he had managed quickly to lean towards the Colonel's ear and whisper, 'Will you make my sincere and abject apologies in—the proper quarters,' and he was gone.

'Oh Uncle!' cried Madeleine, 'what wonderful music! I didn't know life could be so heavenly!'

It was four in the morning when the party broke up, and the first lightening of the eastern sky that presages dawn when the Colonel drove his wife and niece to his house, put the car away and then headed down the path in the direction of his shop.

Madame Roquebrun, who had been waiting in the doorway, said, 'Aren't you coming in, Pierre? I haven't been up this late since I was a girl!'

The Colonel replied, 'In a moment. I would just like to check that all is well with the shop.'

He crossed the road and approached the building. The stars overhead had begun to dim. Through the window he saw the light that he always left burning so that passing patrol cars could look inside. Automatically he tried the door. It was locked. Everything was as it should be. And yet, even as he drew a bunch of keys from his pocket and inserted one, he knew—as he had often known things beforehand—that all was not as it should be. He turned the key, went inside, pressed the switch that flooded the showroom with light and then saw.

The clock was gone. The prize of his career as an *antiquaire,* the great gilt timepiece built for the Sun King by Henri Martinot and signed by him, this exquisite museum specimen in mint condition was no longer there.

And the Colonel also guessed, or pre-experienced the next move even before his eyes turned to the floor where, in the space that the clock had occupied, was a white envelope addressed to simply *'LE RENARD'*. He picked it up. It had not even been sealed and extracting the sheet of notepaper he read the letter:

'My dear *Renard,*

'We are afraid that you have been very naughty. We accepted in good faith that you put up to us a hypothetical question of how it might be possible to perpetrate the crime of the century and hold up the August Gala for fifty million dollars-worth of jewellery. And a very interesting game it was to lay before us your friends, four old experts who joined in and did their best on the spur of the moment. Given more time, we could have made it absolutely fool-proof.

'But when your very obvious expressions and writhings suddenly indicated to us that you actually suspected we might really be planning this, including the slaughter of the innocents, the affair lost its amusing elements and became somewhat more serious, to the point where we even suspected *you* of wishing to become involved in such an affair. Not until the end did it become clear that you were pumping us, had convinced yourself of our guilt and in some manner or other were going to give us away.

'It was not long before it was apparent that you had sung to Captain Scoubide, since for three days after our little Sunday pastime the four of us were shadowed until it must have been obvious to even the most idiotic of policemen that we were minding our own business and as innocent as the snowiest newborn lambs.

'Thirty years ago, dear *Renard*, we would have executed you out of hand for such a betrayal. However, after a meeting we came to the conclusion that none of us is getting any younger and that an ageing brain is no longer wholly responsible for the directives emanating therefrom. Hence, allowances must be made for what we choose to believe was a temporary aberration. Also, we are all extraordinarily fond of you and, I am sure, would afterwards greatly regret anything so drastic.

'Still, a punishment is indicated. You cannot play with feelings of old friends in this manner without some kind of forfeit and so, as you will note, we have removed your clock.

'You have spent an evening in aid of charity. Continue then, this charitable impulse. As always, we have intimates, acquaintances and favourite fellow labourers in the vineyard in dire straits; an operation needed, a mortgage due, the loss of a job—you know the kind of everyday disasters that befall one's friends. Shall we say that a matter of

250,000 new francs will be sufficient to liquidate current distress in our neighbourhoods? A cheque for this amount made out to 'Bearer', and mailed to any one of us will see your clock magically restored to you in the same manner that it was removed, and your image, as well, refurbished in the eyes of your four devoted colleagues,

'The Tiger, The Elephant, The Wolf and The Leopard.'

The Colonel read the letter over twice, first with his eyes half blinded by tears and then followed by such gusts of laughter that he thought he would never catch his breath.

But finally he did and wondered what the Zoo Gang would think and say when in that morning's paper they read about the abortive attempt at the Silver Sands Gala.

But the fact of its having taken place, he reflected, did not alter the circumstance that they were right and that as they had written, he had been 'very naughty', and a punishment was in order.

Refusing even to wait until the morning was official, he went to his desk, sat down, wrote out the cheque and inserted it into an envelope, addressing it to, '*Monsieur Alphonse Cousin, Le Bar Perroquet Rouge, Antibes.*' Then, slipping it into the pocket of his dinner jacket, he put out all the lights, since the east was now rosy with a promise of day, locked the shop and marched slowly up to his home.

Snow Over the Côte d' Azur

Wednesday, August 5, 1970

THE SUMMER of 1970 over the French Riviera was unusually hot, sultry and restless with the reverberations of crisis from distant countries as well as troubled neighbours.

For the first time one was aware of the extent of the pollution of the beaches where disgusting, unnameable things floated amidst scraps of paper, orange peel and other garbage setting the tone for a different kind of pollution, that of Juan-les-Pins by another kind of wastage—the dregs of the lost generation of the young.

There used to be an innocence about Juan-les-Pins with its nightclubs which were nothing but discotheques masquerading under such names as 'Whisky à Gogo' and 'Voom-Voom', an occasional striptease and the Casino itself; its rows of 'with-it' shops one jammed next to another selling costume jewellery, postage-stamp-sized bikinis and the latest models of clothes two years behind Carnaby Street; *crêperies* cooking up pancakes laced with watered Grand Marnier, dodgem cars, ski-ball games, sidewalk cafés; beaches and the bicycle man, the ex-circus clown who came every night and performed tricks in the square and then passed his hat.

Juan-les-Pins was for youth and in the days of its guilelessness during the warm, summer, vacation months you never saw a drunk on the streets or heard of anyone being rolled or mugged. It was a place of light, fun and gaiety—until the hippies came and soiled it.

And with the lowest of these new type parasites came filth, beggary, stench, arrogance, petty thievery, ugliness, obscenity, public concupiscence and copulation on the beaches and inevitably drugs.

Up to that time France, and in particular the Riviera, had been reasonably free of this new curse visited upon mankind for its idiocies but the hippies brought their addiction and cravings. The pushers followed and suddenly France appeared to the Syndicate as virgin territory to be exploited. When the stuff began to show up on the steps of the school house the French woke up to the fact that they had become a way station along the international narcotics underground.

One August evening when the moon was full and hung so ridiculously poised like a glowing orange over the flat calm Mediterranean that jokes were made—'How do you like our prop moon we had hung up there for you?'—and the leisurely crowds were shuffling through the neon streets of

Juan-les-Pins window shopping or just sitting in
sidewalk cafés, people-watching, the hippies were
gathered at the end of the street by the beach
promenade, sprawled on the promenade or
benches. They were dirty, unlovely, hostile, gig-
gling and sniggering amongst themselves, lying in
obscene and unlovely postures, occasionally strum-
ming a guitar or just sitting, hugging their knees
and staring stonily ahead of themselves for the reason that this was what they were—stoned. Not
even the golden electrical glow from the property
moon could soften the squalor. It was as though
the daytime litter of the sea had been washed up
there at night and remained. They were revelling
in the attention they were attracting from the
tourists and passersby, in particular the staid members of the French *bourgeoisie*, families who
looked upon them with utter astonishment since
they were so recent a phenomenon in that country. Some of them acted up showing off; others just
stared with the peculiar insolence and self-satisfaction of this new breed of hobo. Several rolled
up in filthy blankets were stretched out asleep.

One of these groups contained three boys in
jeans and leather jackets stiff with dirt, hairy as
orang-outans, two girls equally bedraggled in long,
gypsy dresses, felt hats pushed on the back of
heads that had not seen soap and water for weeks.
One of the boys was plucking at the strings of his
guitar and producing nothing worth listening to
out of it. A third girl in a long, white chiffon
gown that was now no longer white, lay stretched

out on her back on the pavement ostensibly asleep. Every so often one of this group would throw her an uneasy glance and then they would murmur to one another, and to cover the murmuring the boy with the guitar would bang discordant chords from his instrument.

Between the shops, the moon and the mercury globes of the promenade it was light enough to see the grime under the fingernails of the boy with the instrument, the curious glaze of their eyes and their bare, dust-coated feet.

It was also light enough to see that the ostensibly sleeping girl was not well. Her breathing was that of one who even though unconscious is fighting desperately for the air needed to live. Her colour was that of what her frock had once been six months before, when she had run away from a well-to-do French middle-class home.

An elderly woman, a British tourist momentarily separated from the friends with whom she was visiting the Côte d'Azur, passed by the group, her lips curling in disgust and then, having passed them, stopped as though something had struck her and went back.

The extraordinary thing is that no one ever knew who she was, or her name, except that apparently during the war she had been a nurse, for this she told to the police when she summoned one. But having played her part in the tragedy and just too late, she thereafter vanished from the story.

Having turned back she went and stood over

the girl who was no more than eighteen or nineteen with the pale, pinched face of a sick child, and said, 'This girl is very ill. What's the matter with her? Oughtn't she to be looked after?'

She had spoken automatically in English and was answered in the same language by one of the boys who said, 'She's all right. She's sleeping. Buzz off!' The insolence aroused her to anger.

She knelt by the side of the girl, felt her pulse, put her hand on the heaving breast, lifted her eyelids, noted also the clammy skin, and rising said, 'Can't you see that this person is desperately sick and you're simply standing around, doing nothing?'

One of the girls said, 'We don't know who she is. She was just there when we came.'

And the other boy sniggered and said, 'Why don't you mind your own bloody business, Mom?'

The lips of the elderly lady tightened and she said, 'I will. This girl ought to be taken to a hospital at once. I am going to fetch a policeman and ask him to call an ambulance.' She turned back on them and marched away.

Twenty minutes later when two *gendarmes* arrived simultaneously with an ambulance and the ex-nurse, the group had vanished but the sick girl was still on the pavement unattended.

The young doctor confirmed the seriousness of her condition. She was taken into the ambulance and driven away. The *gendarmes* took a few notes from witnesses in the crowd, including the names of another group of hippies. The British Samari-

tan having done everything she felt that she could,
and having no wish to have her holiday disturbed
by involvement with the police, moved off quietly
and was lost in the crowd. And because she neither spoke nor read French, she never later either
knew the identity of the girl or the consequences
of her actions.

The doctor in charge of emergencies in the
Hôpital Mixte at La Fontonne who made a pre-
liminary examination did not like what he saw.
First of all, the nature of the illness from which
she would not recover and, secondly, because beneath the grime, he was aware that this was a
French girl of gentle breeding. He therefore had
summoned Captain Claude Scoubide, Head of the
plain-clothes detective bureau of the *Service Régionale de Police Judiciaire*. Appalled, the Captain recognized her and telephoned not to her
parents but to her uncle, Colonel Pierre Roquebrun, the antique dealer.

The Colonel was there in a scant half hour,
identified his niece, his eyes closed nearly shut to
hold back the tears of rage, his bald skull and once
tanned face now so white with anger that every
ancient cicatrice left upon them by the Gestapo
in days bygone showed up as red weals.

The Colonel said to Scoubide, 'Notify her parents.' He went and stood by the window, looking
out over the garden of palm trees and tropical
shrubbery in which the hospital was set. He was so
old a hand at the approach of death in every aspect
that he knew the child would not live. Here then,

in this bare, horrid room with its plastered walls
and antiseptic stink, the murder of Madeleine
Renault would come to an end and this once
bright, gay, happy being who, since he was childless himself, had been like a daughter to him and
his wife, would be snuffed out.

He himself had taught her to swim and sail, had
watched her progress on water skis and he remembered how she was happiest in, on and about
boats: the fast Rivas or cabin cruisers where she
would perch on the foredeck between sun and
sea, her loose hair one with the wind, her heart
soaring. She had always been a free spirit and one
that had found itself at home more with him than
with her own family. He had understood her; her
father, Roquebrun's brother-in-law André Renault, a member of the City Council of Nice, was
something of a stick.

Perhaps it had been a mistake to send Madeleine
to a University away from home, where her un-
tamed nature would be captivated by the youthful
revolutionary movement. But on the other hand,
it had been on the Riviera that she had died of
drugs; the Riviera where, for all of its so-called
sophistication, a child could be brought up in innocence untouched even by the naïveté of some
of its wickedness. This was something different, a
world apart and of no danger to a girl with a
healthy mind and a decent upbringing. So much
of the Coast's naughtiness was so ludicrously plain
and absurd that it was laughable to a young person brought up in its proximity. That is, it was,

until the drug pushers came, dedicated to the destruction of youth, body and soul.

There was a stir at the door. Colonel Roquebrun turned; it was the parents of the girl. They came in and were present in the early morning when the laboured breathing of nineteen-year-old Madeleine Renault ceased for all time.

The autopsy revealed galloping hepatitis as the result of infection from a dirty hypodermic needle, used for the injection of heroin. If the hepatitis had not killed her, the girl was already on so high a dosage of the drug that this also must have destroyed her eventually.

The *Nice-Matin* covered the story under the headline '*TRAGÉDIE DE LA DROGUE ET LES HIPPIES SUR LA CÔTE D'AZUR'*, and the story dealt with the tragic circumstances of the death of Mademoiselle Madeleine Renault, aged 19, daughter of the respected lawyer and member of the City Council of Nice, André Renault, who had succumbed at the *Hôpital Mixte* at La Fontonne from an overdose of drugs, combined with acute hepatitis, as a result of the self injection of heroin with an infected needle.

Because of the prominence of the father, the story skated carefully and tactfully around the fact that she had become a member of the activist, leftist movement of the University of Grenoble and involved in the May revolution. Apparently, she had then given up her studies to join with a so-called youth-movement. The father, Councillor Renault, refused to discuss his daughter's actions, saying only 'We always tried to give her the best of everything in our home. Please leave us to our grief.' But one gathered that the girl had managed to become mixed up with a bad crowd and had left home.

The newspaper was compelled to report that the girl had been found in dying condition on the Promenade in Juan-les-Pins and quoted one of the group, to whom, it appeared the girl apparently had attached herself recently. John Fraser, aged 23, British, of no fixed address, said, 'We picked her up in St Tropez two weeks ago. We didn't know how far gone she was already on the heavy stuff. She seemed to have plenty of money and was a good kid. We just worked our way up the coast and when she got sick, we got scared on account of, see, she was on the heavy stuff with the needle, and we don't want any trouble like this. She said she had been on it for four months and it was easy to get it down here. Anyway, this kid was getting all she wanted, and I guess she wanted plenty, but that was not our business. She started out with another bunch, some English and Americans, last winter, she said, and I guess that's where she got going on trips. That's all we know.' The newspaper, then, did some viewing-with-alarm on the apparent increase in the appearance of the heavier and more dangerous drugs on the *Côte* and remarked that the police did not seem to be able to cope with the increasing traffic.

The story concluded with the date and hour of the interment. There was no mention in any way

of the uncle of the girl, Colonel Pierre Roquebrun, *antiquaire* and former Resistance leader,
whose sister Antoinette was married to Councillor
Renault.

The Colonel, along with his wife, Marianne, did
their grieving for the niece who had been so close
to them, in an orderly manner, with the minimum
of public show to their neighbours. When the official period of mourning could be said to have ex-
pired, the Colonel advised his wife that he would
be going away on a trip for what might be a long
time and perhaps that since this was the height of
the summer season, she ought to have her sister
come and stay with her to help look after the
shop. He then packed a bag, and leaving both his
cars in the garage—his black Mercedes as well
as his Peugeot station wagon which he frequently
filled with acquired merchandise—he took a taxi
to Nice and boarded one of the Paris trains. The
ticket he purchased would have taken him as far
as Valence which he never reached, and where it
was he got off, no one ever knew or ever found
out. But it became increasingly obvious in certain
quarters as time went by that the old fox, or
Renard, as he was known in the Resistance, had
gone to ground.

Friday, April 9, 1971

Claude Scoubide sat at his desk in the ancient
building housing the *Service Régionale de Police
Judiciaire,* overlooking the old market in Nice

and on to the end of the Quai des Etats Unis, the
sea front of Nice where the first of the Easter in-
flux of tourists were raising white faces to the wel-
coming rays of the Riviera sun. With his pointed
chin sunk into his hands, he brooded over the
strangest problem ever to face an intelligent and
imaginative detective; the non-commission of a
vast crime, the non-existence of a group of criminals who should have committed it. To Scoubide
it was like staring into a great dark void, a bottom-
less hole where there should have been something
but there was not. This was one of the two worries
which were making him feel like a fool.

The second was that long absence or put it, if
you like, 'disappearance' of Colonel Pierre Roquebrun after the unfortunate death of his niece Madeleine Renault, an absence too readily explicable
since the Colonel was always going off on trips in
search of antiques for his shop. This was what
made Scoubide's worry absurd because the Colonel had eventually returned some seven weeks
after and eventually exposed a treasure trove of a
set of the most exquisite 16th Century pewter
dishes, candlesticks, jugs, bowls and chamber pots
purchased from goodness knows what convent,
since dealers never revealed their sources.

He had surfaced late in October and had been
visible ever since conducting his business and fre-
quenting his usual haunts. But barring the purchase of the pewter, which if Scoubide had
wished to he could have run down, where had he
been during that interval? What had he been up

to? For there had not been a single, solitary trace of him.

And the non-crime—why hadn't it taken place? The non-criminals—where were they? For the fact was that in the past six months the import, distribution and sale of *stupéfiants,* as the French call narcotics, had practically dried up in his whole area of the Alpes-Maritimes, an area which in American terminology would be considered a large county but in the case of Captain Scoubide covered one of the most romantic and dramatic areas of France, that part of the Riviera stretching from Fréjus to Menton, and including Cannes, Antibes, Nice and the Capes. As Captain of Detectives in the *Service Régionale de Police Judiciaire,* Scoubide was responsible for the suppression of crime in a region made difficult by the fact that it contained the highest proportion of mixed foreign population anywhere in France: Italians, Spaniards, Algerians, Moroccans as well as the *Pied Noirs*—Algerian-born French exiled from there, residents, tourists of almost every nationality, as well as a floating group of vagrants and shiftless persons of no fixed address, attracted by the climate, the sun and the pickings.

The sudden shutting off of the supply of narcotics which previously had begun to flood the Côte d'Azur would have been a tremendous feather in his cap if he had been able to claim credit for it. Even more so would have been the smashing of the organization needed to conduct such traffic, had he done so.

Or, to make matters even more abstruse, was the fact that where this hole of the non-present, non-existent criminals was, there had not been even really officially a non-hole or identifiable criminals.

For at the meeting of the Congress of International Narcotic Agents in Marseille, which had taken place in the winter and which he had attended as an observer, the brains of the international forces arrayed against this horror traffic had been able to do no more than advise the police that a gigantic new syndicate had come into being and that the largest shipment ever of hashish, cocaine and opium was due to be introduced into the French Riviera. And thereafter the buck had been passed to the police. The consensus had been, 'As yet we don't know who they are, or how many, or where, or of what nationality. Just go out and find the biggest load of drugs ever scheduled to come into France and the men behind it.'

And the results thereafter of hard and determined investigation on the part of every department were nil; no gigantic shipment; no super syndicate. But also, suddenly no drugs, only the hole where there ought to have been evidence of something having happened.

Captain Scoubide stared across the slanting roof of the bustling market place and over the low buildings fronting the sea to the strollers, lost in thought as though somehow he could wrest secrets from those distant, wandering strangers. People, people, people! In the end everything—all good-

ness, all feeling, all charity, all crime stemmed
from those two-legged animals marching by. And
who was to say who was all good and who was all
bad? For he knew himself to be no angel. No angel could hold down the job of chief of detectives
on the Côte d'Azur. True, he was on their side but
from time to time he was compelled to hope that
they were not watching. No policeman could be
wholly honest and carry out his duties of protect-
ing the public. Stoolies had to be used; nasty traps
laid; even deals made to keep the balance between
crime and law and order at a tolerable level.

In sudden irritation he bit his lip and pounded
his desk with his fist: 'Scoubide, you fool! You're
being paid to uncover crime and not non-crime!
Forget it and perhaps since Colonel Roquebrun
seems to be minding his own business, it might be
healthier for you to mind yours.'

And then, having decided to put it out of his
mind like all nagging questions, it refused to stay
out. If the drug supply on the Coast had indeed
dried up as it had appeared to, he would have to
find the explanation someday as to why, and what
was more, keep it out. He turned once again to the
dossier of the felonies and oddities for the past
year; the volumes adding up to the thickness of
his fist, not only those in his own *Département*,
but in the neighbouring one of the Var, which extended on down the Coast to embrace as far west
as St Tropez and Toulon.

There were the usual unsolved things; missing
persons, an important robbery or two, the burn-

ing of the chocolate factory in Toulon—a fire suspected of incendiary origin—lorry hijackings;
stick-ups and murders, of course. Murders solved,
and very proud he was of this, that in his area
every killer had been brought to book; no detective story mysteries. And of the breakings and en-
terings, the major part of the loot recovered.

There was still the ridiculous and slightly hu-
miliating mystery of the missing Carnival Float
No 19, lost, strayed or stolen from the recent
Mardi Gras Nice Carnival parade, which had oc-
casioned more laughter than concern, since it was
an enormous affair and its vanishing probably the
prank of students from the University who usually managed some rag or other during Carnival
time.

He went over the disappearances again, not that
this was part of his department until such disappearances could be connected with actual crime,
for here seemed to be the only coincidence in
that there were seven and all of them appeared to
have been registered within a space of ten days,
but from such varying areas as Grasse back in the
hills, Cap Martin, Nice, Théoule, St Tropez, Draguignan inland from St Raphaël, and Le Lavandou. But on rereading the reports there had not
seemed to be the slightest reason for connecting
any of them. Three of them had been reported by
wives whose attractions when interviewed had
been such as to make the theory of the decamped
husband almost mandatory. Two had been tourists in widely separated areas; one in Théoule, the

other in Cap Martin, who had failed to return to
their hotels to claim their luggage which had
been seized in payment of their bills. One was
supposed to be missing in a sailboat after a blow
off Le Lavandou, and the seventh was the owner
of an expensive Mercedes with German licence
plates found abandoned in a side street in Nice.
When, after it had been there for days and the
police finally looked into it, checking its registration, the name and address of the owner, the people at the address claimed that they had never
heard of such a person or ever seen the car. Captain Scoubide did not like this. A false registration
smelled of skulduggery but there was no one to ap-
prehend and the car having committed no crime
except obstructing the public highway had been
impounded.

He kept thumbing through the dossier; bank
thefts, vengeance killings, Mafia, *crimes passion-
els,* and the photographs—corpses here, corpses
there, from newspaper cuttings as well as official
police photographers—those *paparazzi* of the dead.

And then why hadn't the Colonel taken his car
—either the fast, black Mercedes or the roomy
station wagon—if he were going off, as he had told
his wife, on a purchasing expedition?

Madame Roquebrun had had a perfectly legitimate explanation of this, when he had dropped
in upon her, ostensibly to pay a social call after the
news of the Colonel's departure had reached him.

That is to say, as Scoubide knew, all explana-
tions were legitimate as long as they remained so.

Madame Roquebrun who, with her sister Antoinette, was tending shop—this had been early
September of the year before—had told him that
recently the Colonel had complained that he was
getting too old for those long car trips; the strug-
gle on the roads with summer traffic, inhaling the
fumes of buses and double-trailer trucks obstructing the roads for miles. Unless it was a short jour-
ney he was inclined now to take a train to a size-
able town in the area he wished to explore and
then make use of a hire car if necessary. Goods
he purchased would arrive later by express.

Scoubide had nodded and said, 'Intelligent. The
summer traffic is becoming impossible.' And then
making a gesture of impatience he added, 'Tsk!
tsk! There was something I wanted to ask him.
Have you heard from him?'

'Oh yes' Madame Roquebrun had said, 'we've
had several postcards. I'll show them to you.' And
going to the back of the shop she produced three
pretty views from Le Puy, Le Mont-Dore, and as
far off as Périgueux, all indubitably in the hand-
writing of the Colonel with the messages of a faith-
ful and loving husband.

'Ah, well then,' Captain Scoubide had said,
'probably he will not be away much longer. Will
you say that I called when he returns?'

He naturally did not reveal to Madame Roquebrun that he had already read the postcards in the
central post office at Vence, where they had been
held for his perusal before delivery. And also that
when he had talked to colleagues at Le Puy, Le

Mont-Dore and Périgueux there was quite naturally no trace of the Colonel ever having been there. This did not surprise him, since he knew that the old Resistance leader had friends all over France and only had to send a postcard already collected on some other trip, written and stamped in an envelope, to an old pal in that town with instructions to mail it.

This could be coupled with the fact that it was the end of August, an important time for selling and the worst possible month for a buying trip with everyone away. Also there was the slight indecency of a business trip so hard on the heels of a personal tragedy which made the explanation slightly less legitimate.

Upon the Colonel's return Scoubide naturally had not been able to query him as to where he had been, since it was none of his business, and if the Colonel had known—as he probably did—that France's most efficiently administered, up-to-date and interlocking police organization had been making discreet enquiries about him, he gave no indication.

In his sixties and a well-known figure the length and breadth of the Riviera, and almost equally well-known in other parts of France, actually nothing would wholly disguise his chunky, bulldog figure, the extraordinary blue of his eyes, their intelligence, or the aura of power of his personality. Anyway the Colonel had never been one, during his active days in the Resistance, for dressing up or masquerading. He simply could not hide if he were going about his normal business.

But hiding he unquestionably had been during that period immediately after the death of his niece, and therefore he must have been concerned with possible police enquiries as to his whereabouts. As he had in the days of the German occupation, he had gone underground and, as the Nazis had learned to their sorrow, he was nowhere and he was everywhere with his four associates, the Zoological Gang; five men engaged in intelligence and sabotage and yet remaining unseen.

And this was what really had upset Captain Scoubide. Whatever he had been up to, he had been playing a lone hand. His old Resistance companions, the Zoo Gang, had been able to convince the Captain that they had not the faintest notion of what had become of their former leader.

If the Captain of detectives had not known where Colonel Roquebrun was, he thought he had known very well why, so to speak. The old *Renard,* for this had been his own pseudonym, could have been on the hunt for the murderers of Madeleine Renault.

Scoubide's worry at that time had been that Roquebrun would find these merchants of destruction, who pushing heroin had brought about the death of an innocent girl, before he or others did in cooperation with the *Brigade des Stupéfiants* from Paris and the International Narcotics agents.

When a man has several times anonymously been the instrument of one's advancement as the Colonel had been to the detective there are bound to be emotions of gratitude and admiration in-

volved. And so yet another cause of his worry had
been that Captain Scoubide loved the Colonel and
did not wish him ever to become the quarry with
himself of necessity the hunter.

The Captain was no longer seeing with his eyes
what was passing before them but was now looking moodily within himself.

The area known as the French Riviera may be
said to stretch along the shores of the Mediterranean from Marseille to the French border town of
Menton, taking in as well the Principality of Mona-
co. Beginning with St Tropez and Ste Maxime,
the names of towns as one proceeds eastwards
sound like chimes in a symphony dedicated to the
playground of the rich: St Raphaël, Théoule,
Cannes, Juan-les-Pins, Antibes, Nice, St Jean-Cap-
Ferrat, Beaulieu, Monte-Carlo and Menton and
thereafter with Ventimiglia came Italy.

Some of these are separated by woods or cliffs
of red rocks that spill down into the sea and others, like Cannes, Juan-les-Pins, Antibes and Nice
are so contiguous—one running into the other
along both the coast road and the 'N.7', that they
might be one sprawling community except that
each one could not be more different from the
other; Cannes the playboy, Juan-les-Pins with vine
leaves woven in her hair and Antibes affecting
the working man's cap, particularly during the
massive project of the construction of the new, all
concrete Port Vauban there. This was an enlarge-
ment and modernization of the one which had
done very well for the Phoenicians, the Greeks,

the Romans not to mention the Sun King whose
military engineer Vauban had strengthened it
with his ramparts and Fort Carré jutting out into
the Baie des Anges. And Nice? Nice, well, perhaps
with a motherly shawl tucked about her shoulders
even though it was the fourth largest city in
France. It saw mostly elderly people sunning
themselves there. Or, if you cared to look behind
the golden front of the Promenade des Anglais,
you could also characterize Nice by a mask and
cosh, for like Marseille at the other end of the line,
it was a hotbed of crime.

What made this particular stretch of coast so re-
markable, so attractive, exciting and newswor-
thy as well as a magnet for the unholy, was that
the concentration of wealth there must be reckoned in billions in the fortunes of the owners of
the villas, the villas themselves with their contents
of paintings and jewellery, the yachts, the price
of the land, cars and pure liquid cash passing usually one way through the casinos of which between Fréjus and Menton there are nine, where
the wheels spin constantly.

Such wealth invariably spells romance and excitement, attracts beautiful women and un-
scrupulous men. And it was along this stretch and
perhaps as far as such cities as Aix-en-Provence,
Draguignan and Grasse, that the Zoo Gang and
others of the French Resistance known as the
F.F.I. had operated during the German occupation under the leadership of Pierre Roquebrun.

This organization had put Roquebrun in a kind

of temporary alliance with various branches of the
underworld who preyed upon the rich. These out-
laws were callous, often brutal and not too concerned with the value of human life. But they
were also clever, brave and in the face of the
super-brutality of the Hun many of them had
turned patriot and at the risk of their lives worked
for the underground. The good and the bad
united in harassing the enemy, destroying his supplies and making life a misery. During those days
some strange friendships had been formed.

But all that was thirty years ago and since that
time the Riviera had changed physically, and not
for the better with hundreds of hideous square
blocks of flats going up as well as towering hotels
and apartment buildings connected with Ma-
rinas and whole new communities such as Port
Grimaud and La Galère. Even the oldest harbour
on the coast, Antibes, which had known the
triremes and galleys of the ancient Phoenicians,
Greeks and Romans was in the throes of suc-
cumbing to modernity.

Yet none of this had altered the basic nature of
this fabulous stretch, the famous villas on the famous capes were still there and so was the way of
life. And so, too, as in the case of Colonel Roquebrun, some old friendships had been maintained
down through the years, friendships not exactly
edifying but when one's life has been saved by certain parties not once but perhaps even twice or
three times, one from then on would find oneself
able to overlook the morals of the saver. These

men had once been true patriots and if ever France again were similarly endangered, they or their kind would be again.

It was for this reason that Colonel Roquebrun, when he had wished to do so, was able so thoroughly to vanish that even Captain Scoubide eventually had recognized the futility of trying to turn him up. Nevertheless, this was unfinished business; the business of knowing everything that went on about everyone in his area, and the Captain considered himself a paid, professional enemy of mysteries.

All thoughts of that particular one were driven from the Captain's head by what followed the knock on his door and the entrance of Sergeant Marcel Pelissier, and what he had to tell.

Saturday, October 10, 1970

Saturday night and Sunday afternoon were the weekend foregatherings of the Zoo Gang, rain or shine and in particular since the absence of Colonel Roquebrun they had been careful not to vary their habits by one iota. They knew very well that they had been under surveillance and that only strict adherence to routine would convince the surveyors that whatever was going on they were, at least at the moment, in no way involved.

The Saturday night meetings took place in a back room of the bar, the *Perroquet Rouge*, owned by Alphonse Cousin the Wolf, where they sipped *pastis*, gossiped and occasionally played

cards. The fact that there was not and could not
have been any kind of bugging in the place was
the guarantee of Gaston Rives, the Leopard, since
during the days of the Resistance he had been the
electronics expert of the Gang for radio transmis-
sion and listening devices, and there was nothing
ancient or modern that he did not know about this
type of eavesdropping.

The Sunday afternoon sessions were devoted to
the outdoor game of *boule* and wine at the carnation farm of Antoine Petitpierre, the Tiger. For
the rest of the week they went about their daily
business which included Jean Soleau, the Elephant's dealings in the wholesale purchase and
dispensing of onions and garlic that took him from
his warehouses back-country to the cellars in Antibes which were his stockrooms, and the market
there, behind the ramparts. And in the process of
pursuing these simple duties the four were likely
to hear anything that was going on in the neighbourhood and, since they also were who they were
and what they had once been, a good deal more.

Through this addiction to routines and other
circumspections they had, thus, over a period
been able to convince Captain Scoubide that they
had not the faintest idea where Colonel Pierre
Roquebrun, *ex-Le Renard,* their one-time Resistance leader, might be. Which, indeed, they had
not. It was at one of the Saturday night musters
in the back room of the bar that the Elephant
asked the question, 'How long has he been gone
now?'

The Tiger counted on his fingers, 'Seven and a half weeks.'

The Leopard said, 'And no news of any kind? Madame Roquebrun . . . ?' He left the question hanging in the air.

The Tiger, who lived closest to where the Colonel had his shop and home near Vence, shrugged and said, 'Oh, there have been postcards.'

The Wolf merely grunted. He knew as well as did the others the old postcard trick.

'And no unidentified *cadavres*,' remarked the Elephant, 'I have combed the *Nice-Matin* carefully and they are usually pretty thorough.'

The Tiger sniggered, took a sip of his milky *pastis* and set the glass on to the table with considerable severity. He said, 'You know we never left any corpses about. That was *Le Renard's* speciality. That was why the Gestapo half killed him, trying to find out. No evidence. You can bet that if Pierre has found the one, or ones he is looking for, there will be no *corpus delicti*.'

Roquebrun had been one of the masters at this most difficult game. There is nothing more complicated than to get rid of a body.

The Leopard now said with a sudden anxious note in his voice, 'They wouldn't have got him . . . ?'

The Wolf shook his head decisively and said, 'I would have heard.'

They accepted his statement without question. Next to the Colonel himself, and naturally through the grapevine closely in touch with the old pals

of the Underground and who would be most likely to hear if anything untoward had happened to
Roquebrun.

'Well,' queried the Elephant, 'what have you
heard?'

The Wolf shrugged, 'Rumours of a big deal in
narcotics. A new outfit. Nobody knows who they
are. My friends, the little thieves of the *Côte,* don't
like it, since first of all most of them are respectable, family men who understand how vile the
traffic is and secondly, it interferes with their
work—nice, clean, neatly executed robberies. Nobody hurt, nothing disturbed but what they are
looking for, no mess, no damage. The addict, on
the other hand who must have money is addled,
stupid, messy and frequently murderous. He will
beat an old woman to death for a few francs, or
rampage through an entire villa not knowing what
to look for. He is far too handy with the knife or
gun, kills policemen as well as civilians thereby
arousing them too, and spoiling the game for
everyone. Yes, I think one could count upon help
from honest burglars, if it were ever needed, or at
least a word let fall where it would do the most
good.'

The Leopard asked, 'Why do you suppose Pierre
hasn't called us in on this? What's he doing? This
isn't like him. He should have contacted us long
ago.'

It was the gentle Tiger who replied. He said, in
his quiet, sometimes hardly audible voice, 'Because, my dear *copains,* he is very angry and it is

only I, who myself was once so angry that I lost all humanity, who can judge of his. And when one is that cold and hard and unforgiving, one wishes at first to be and to work alone.' Sitting there for a moment and looking into the remaining *pastis* gathered in the bottom of his glass, it was as though he were consulting a crystal ball and therefrom waxing prophetic. He said, 'Many men will die for this girl. There will be much horror and bloodshed before it is over. But when it is, I think perhaps things will be better.' And then, looking up suddenly as though he had only just heard the Leopard's question, he said softly, 'He will contact us.'

Indeed, his remark was prophetic if not clairvoyant. For the Colonel was at that very instant on his way to the bar, guiding his car down the long *Avenue de Verdun*, where for a moment he pulled up at the side of the road and stopped to contemplate the extraordinary activity of night work going on towards the completion of the new Port Vauban, and which must have fallen behind schedule to account for such an unusual beehive of after-dark and weekend overtime.

Already where his machine was parked and where two years before the waters of the bay had lapped up against the road, the sea had been filled in all along the road for half a kilometre to a breadth of more than a hundred metres and on this new soil, under overhead electrical lighting, cranes swung their loads of enormous concrete blocks for the laying of the foundations. There

was heard the roar of the concrete mixers close
to the mountainous piles of cement and crushed
rock. There was the clang of the trip hammers
driving piles into the bed of the sea and the rum-
ble of lorries dumping their loads of rock quar-
ried from inland. In the middle of the bay of
the Anse St Roch, a huge suction dredge was
syphoning up the mud from the bottom to deepen
the channels and conveying it by pipeline all the
way across the port and out to sea, to create a new
bathing beach for the public.

Overall, and distant under the electric lights,
looking like insects—beetles—in their shiny helmets, the workmen toiled and moiled except for
one static figure standing by the central control
hut, whom Colonel Roquebrun was able to recognize.

He was a short, chunky man wearing a dark
business suit which already set him apart from
the workmen in their stained clothing and safety
helmets, and on the back of his head he wore a
fedora hat. It was this hat and the angle at which
it was worn which identified him as Philippe Santoro, the proprietor of one of the biggest contracting firms on the Coast, 'Entreprise Santoro et Fils
—Cannes.'

The Colonel watched the busy figure diminished by distance. He must have been talking vol-
uble Italian because his arms were waving. The
Colonel smiled to himself for he knew the stout,
important little man by his more familiar name to
his friends as Papa Santoro and what is more, he

had known him when—when he had just started
up in business and he and the Colonel had met
and pursued an acquaintance during the War.
Papa Santoro's extractions were Italian, but this
had been some time back and his heart and soul
had been with France.

The Colonel remained parked a few minutes
longer watching the activity, then put his car into
gear and drove on.

After ten o'clock at night the streets of Antibes
become quiet and deserted. Whatever noise there
is takes place mostly indoors from television sets
blaring through open windows. Thus the four
in the bar stiffened as they heard the car draw up
outside and stop. They knew every sound connected with this; the squeak of one of the tyres,
the ratchet of the handbrake being applied and
the last characteristic roar of the engine as the gas
was stepped on to flood the carburetor before the
ignition key was turned off. It was the Mercedes
of Colonel Roquebrun.

The four men inside the room looked at one another. Wherever their old leader had been, whatever he had been up to, however he had managed
to keep his whereabouts secret for so long, he was
advertising his return as though he had broadcast
it from the top of the old Château housing the
Picasso Museum.

They heard the scuffle of feet and then his voice
as he stopped to chat for a moment with the plain-
clothes man they had known had been stationed
outside the bar ever since his disappearance. The

next moment he stood in the doorway, his stocky bulk filling it from side to side, looking his normal self, unworried, untravel-stained and extraordinarily cheerful. 'Hello, there!' he cried. 'What are you all looking so solemn for? I'm back and want a drink. Cognac. And none of your homemade stuff or tourist swill! Open a bottle of Delamain, I've been extraordinarily successful.'

The Zoo Gang were clued in. The plain-clothes man would still be in earshot, not yet trotting off to report, and the Elephant said, 'Well, and high time, too! What the devil have you been up to?'

'Seducing a Mother Superior,' replied the Colonel and the four actually looked shocked.

'No, no, no,' continued the Colonel, 'as I would expect you all have dirty minds, and still at your age. I've been persuading an Abbess to sell me the pewter plate of the convent to enable her to indulge in a genuine charity—the building of an annex to be used as a day nursery. It was a long process and I practically had to take the veil to get it. It's 16th Century and each piece bears the hallmark of Alois Blois, the great maker of his day. He dedicated an entire year of his work to the Convent of the Sacred Mother. I have it all.' He closed the door behind him as the Wolf reached lazily over to the cabinet where *Le Renard's* favourite bottle of old Delamain was kept. The cheerfulness had gone from the Colonel's face. There was something newly cold and glittering in his eyes as he looked over his old companions. He said curtly to the Leopard, 'Any bugs?'

'No bugs.'

'Sure?'

'Certain.'

The Colonel nodded, sat down, took his brandy glass and looked deeply and silently into it for almost a minute before he began to speak.

He began, 'As you undoubtedly have suspected, I have been searching for the murderers of my niece.'

There was heard the scraping of four chairs as the members of the Zoo Gang shifted with excitement and leaned closer to him.

The Tiger looked over the top of his spectacles and said, 'And did you find them, old friend?'

'Yes, and no,' the Colonel replied, and then, turning to the carnation grower he said, 'With any luck it may not be long before I shall ask to call upon you again.'

The other members of the quartet exchanged looks.

'But why didn't you call upon us to help you before?' asked the Elephant. 'What is this lone hand business and since when? You know that we would have . . .'

'Because it was more important for you to be visible. It was bad enough that I had to disappear but there was no other way.'

The Wolf said, with genuine interest, 'How did you manage. You know we were really worried. We knew that enquiries were being made with no result.'

The Colonel shrugged. 'Oh, as to that, it was

simple. I got off the train at Montelimar, braving
the stench of nougat, borrowed a car from one of
the old ones—you remember our friend Basse-
main? He is living there now—bought myself a little tent and made all my overnight stops at tourist
camps. These would be the last places anyone
would ever think to look for me, knowing that at
my age I have become one for creature comforts.'
He looked over the group with a deeply reflective
eye and said, 'Have no fear that I shall not be looking for your assistance. In fact that is why I am
here now. And perhaps when you have heard what
I shall be asking, you may not be quite so eager to
volunteer again. It's no longer like the past when
every good Frenchman was with us.' He paused
and said, 'This is a new kind of war I am declar-
ing. Some of us might well not see the ending of
it.'

The fat Leopard shrugged and wheezed, 'Wasn't
it always like that? Didn't we always know?'

The Colonel nodded. 'Of course,' he said, 'but
the odds have worsened. Then we had allies. This
time we will have none—not even the other hunt-
ers, for they hunt within the law.'

It was obvious that the four were not impressed.
They had lived now for so long away from danger
that it, and the risk of death, would be welcomed
back almost as an old friend.

Nevertheless, the Colonel added, 'It could very
well be the last caper.'

The Tiger said, 'I don't deny that prison would
be a humiliation I might not be prepared to en-

counter, but I gather, *Renard,* that you are offering us something a good deal more final.'

The Wolf sniggered and asked, 'When is this war to be declared?'

'It has been,' the Colonel retorted calmly. 'The chocolate factory of the *Compagnie Jean Latour* at Toulon.'

'My God!' gasped the Leopard, 'Was that you?'

They all remembered that it had only been three weeks since one of the largest manufacturers of wholesale chocolates and other sweets, located in Toulon, had gone up in flames during the night and been utterly destroyed. There had been some mystery connected with the place due to the fact that the unidentified remains of two bodies had been found in the ruins the next day. The night watchman had reported the blaze shortly after three o'clock in the morning, though from his confused account he must have been asleep on the job and the fire burning for some time, for by the time it was reported and the *Sapeurs Pompiers* arrived, it was raging out of control. The most likely explanation of the two unidentified remains was that they were thieves that had broken into the premises during the night and, in the course of dynamiting the safe, or with a careless cigarette, had set the highly inflammable factory alight and been trapped themselves.

'What?' asked the Tiger, 'An old and respected family like Jean Latour, handed down from father to son, involved in narcotics? I can't believe it!'

The Colonel said, 'The Company has passed on. They sold out, including the name and good will, two years ago when the eldest son died. The successors—at least some of them—have been making *dragées, langues de chats* and *pralinées* by day, and refining raw opium, coca leaves and hemp by night.'

'But the Company? The registration?' asked the Leopard, 'Wouldn't the police . . . ?'

'Oh, an unassailable front,' the Colonel replied, 'with most of the stock holders still retaining their interest. The manager who was so kind as to show me over the premises, in the belief that I was a large distributor and exporter of chocolates from Lyon, was most affable and I gather a respected citizen. He is still alive because his left hand was not permitted to know what the right hand was doing. That is to say he wasn't aware of the night-time operation.'

The wizened Elephant turned a slightly jaundiced eye upon the Colonel and said, 'I take this very ill of you, brother *Renard*. If we had been organized along the lines of a trade union, you would be expelled, and if we are to continue, as you indicated, in the near future I'll thank you not to encroach upon my preserves.'

The Wolf sniggered again but felt that the wholesale dealer in onions and garlic was not faking. For in wartime, sabotage, destruction and mysterious fires had been the speciality of the Elephant.

The Colonel acknowledged that he had crossed lines by saying, 'Seriously, my apologies, my little

Elephant. But it was so simple and besides which, there was an immediacy. For one thing, all of the ingredients for both the day and the night operations of the factory are highly inflammable. Hence there were not the kind of problems that called for your particular kind of genius.'

The Elephant acknowledged the gracious apology but added, 'And the two?'

'Small fry,' replied the Colonel, 'technicians.'

The Tiger was looking over his spectacles again, 'Then you have also been crossing my lines, friend Pierre.'

The Colonel only replied, 'Your turn will come.' Then he added, 'It was an opportunity to destroy a considerable amount of *stupéfiants* which were being prepared for distribution along the *Côte,* as well as the factory itself; and possibly to smoke out the ones behind the traffic.'

'And did you?' queried the Wolf.

'Not quite,' replied the Colonel, 'except to learn that the operation that has taken over the Riviera is so gigantic in scope that the little factory in Toulon with the two night-working cookers was considered expendable. No one has budged. The amount destroyed at Toulon is the merest drop in the bucket compared to the shipment which has come, or is about to come, across into France and the works at Toulon a mere boy scout's cookout compared to the operation contemplated to flood the Riviera with hashish, cocaine and heroin. The Coast is considered to be ripe for picking.'

The Colonel fell silent for a moment, contemplated the pale colour of his cognac, drank some of it, regarded it once more with satisfaction and said, 'We are again at war, my friends. There has been a war declared upon us and I consider myself upon a war footing.'

The Leopard, the fat electrician, said, 'I don't follow you.'

The Colonel nodded and said, 'I'll try to explain it as simply as possible. War is a condition, as you know, of society where one branch of it has unilaterally given itself licence to kill and destroy another with, at bottom, gain as a motive, however mendaciously flamboyant the patriotic posters. The drug pushers have declared war upon our society for their personal gain, except that I find them more wicked than the international adventurers since they first wreck the souls of their victims before destroying their bodies.

'As in all wars,' the Colonel continued quietly, 'we are all eventually hit personally, else we would not strike back with a savagery equal to that of the aggressors.'

His voice dropped even lower and he seemed to be speaking now, as he went on cold-bloodedly but clear-sightedly, as though the person of whom he was speaking had no connection with him whatsoever. He began, 'Madeleine Renault was a normal girl of nineteen, a university student of, I will say, possessive middle-class parents—her father, I might add, is old-fashioned and might still be living in the era of Napoleon III in his attitude towards his family. She was a diligent student and a happy enough child.

'It is normal in almost every generation for youth to be in some kind of rebellion if not against authority, then against customs or clothes, or ideologies. Madeleine's generation sees a more violent protest against authority and the organization of modern society than usual. At the university, perhaps helped along by the restrictions she had experienced at home, Madeleine joined one of those groups of self-styled Revolutionaries.

'Under normal circumstances Madeleine would have come to no great harm before she woke up to the infantilism of her companions or the vacuity of their intellects.'

The Colonel paused and looked gravely over his companions. 'Except that a new element was introduced into the situation, made possible by the temporary destruction of values through which the young were passing, the introduction of drugs, the use of which became an integral part of the rebellion. The pushers saw their opportunity and the war was on—to kill at random for gain.

'Madeleine was started on hash by a boyfriend in her group, found it necessary in increasing doses both as a stimulant and to maintain her standing with the community.'

He glanced over his friends again and said, 'You see, one of the things I have been able to do is to trace her progression from hash to heroin and cocaine; the syringe, and utter degradation. She was soiled, despoiled, debauched and abused. She was also pregnant by someone unknown when she died. As I have said they first killed the soul of an innocent girl, before her body followed. Made-

leine Renault was a victim of warfare for gain as
surely as though she had been shot or joined those
hosts of innocent civilians who have died by
bombing.'

When the Colonel had fallen into silence and
it was seen that he had no more to say, the Wolf
said, 'And so *Renard* has returned and declared
his own war to avenge Madeleine Renault.'

The Colonel looked up with a perceptible
change of colour so that the scars on his face
showed once more and said, 'Revenge, friend
Wolf? What profit for the dead from revenge?
This is a war to defend the living. It is a world
war on a scale far surpassing the last one. There is
not a country that isn't involved.' The tone of his
voice changed. 'I will, if I can, clear this piece of
France where we live of the monsters.'

'WE will,' corrected the Elephant.

'Where do we begin?' queried the Leopard.

'We will see.' The Colonel replied. 'I have found
out perhaps a little more than the agents from
the *Brigade des Stupéfiants*, the police and those
from the International Narcotics operatives who
met recently again in Marseille. By the way,' he
asked suddenly, 'does Papa Santoro still come in
here for a drink occasionally?'

'Oh yes,' replied the Wolf, 'frequently, when
he isn't too long on the port site during the night
work. You know they've fallen badly behind schedule,' and then as the possible import of the Colonel's question struck him he cried, '*Mon Dieu!*
Don't tell me that he's involved?'

The Colonel shook his head and smiled a slightly crooked smile. 'No, no, not yet. I saw him from a distance as I drove here and had the strangest feeling that he might be eventually.'

They all knew Santoro's story. During the war, as a young man he had been a small builder starting out in Cannes. His Italian extraction dated back to the era when the Riviera as far west as Nice had been Italian. But his heart was pure French. The Germans had conscripted him and his business to construct pill boxes and fortifications in the first panic of the threat of an Allied landing in the South of France. He had deliberately sabotaged his work, but unfortunately made his mixture so thin that his works crumbled too soon, even before they were attacked. The Gestapo arrested him and marked him for execution. Two days before he was scheduled to be taken out and shot, the Zoo Gang had rescued the unfortunate young contractor in one of their more daring exploits and spirited him into hiding, until the Allied landings had made the district safe. Philippe Santoro had never forgotten this and never would.

The Colonel continued to speak. 'The waging of the drug war falls into four parts. Purchase of the raw material, transportation, distribution, and it is organized by plain ordinary thugs. Does this surprise you? Well, Hitler was a thug. Scratch a communist leader or warmaker of today and you will find an ex-gangster. Do you remember the photographs of that pair arrested by the police at

Nice airport, a few months ago, wanted in five countries as heads of a narcotic ring? Mafia hoodlums. The drug traffic is even simpler than the rum-running business was in America during prohibition, because the bulk is less.'

'So,' said the Elephant, whose feelings were apparently still ruffled, 'and that is all you have to tell us besides indulging in a bit of gratuitous arson which is not your *métier* and could have ruined everything?'

The Colonel, ignoring the shaft, said, 'Not exactly. There are seven. Five of them are French or German, two probably Americans. I had it from a pusher.'

'Did you kill him?' inquired the Tiger disagreeably.

The Colonel again chose to ignore the irritation he had set up by playing a lone hand, and replied:

'No, only hurt him a little. But he didn't know anything except what I have told you, and he may have been only guessing. Like all those little chaps, he was far removed from the centre.'

'That's always the way it is,' said the Elephant, 'what do you expect?'

'He had one more bit of information,' the Colonel continued; 'he thought that one of the gang went by the name of The Magician, in the underworld. Does that ring any kind of bell?'

The Wolf reflected, 'One had heard of him. His speciality was completely confusing the police, making his crimes appear something quite different from what they actually were and making himself invisible, as though by magic. I believe they had him in their hands only once, until he vanished again and even then they were not sure.'

The Colonel nodded and said, 'Exactly, and this gang has been operating on the *Côte* now setting up the traffic for the last eighteen months. They are responsible for the death of my niece. Unless they are destroyed, they will bring about the deaths of many more. And so we will do so.'

'And how do you propose to go about this?' the Leopard inquired.

The Colonel replied coolly, 'I have made a beginning. Once more with apologies to my friend the Elephant here, through burning their factory. I have perpetrated an act, and every act calls for a reaction. The reaction to mine must be that when the huge shipment of the stuff arrives, it will be necessary to conceal it for longer than they had anticipated. I have succeeded in breaking their rhythm and, in all probability, seriously upset their timetable.'

'What huge shipment?' asked the Elephant. 'You say you know nothing, and then . . .'

The Colonel said, 'I have one more bit of information.'

The Wolf's dark eyes sparkled and he nodded. 'I thought you would.'

The Colonel said, 'Do you remember little Pignon?'

The Tiger broke in with less gentleness than was usual for him, 'Ha! Do I! The nastiest bit of work of those on the wrong side of the law with whom we had to cooperate. I never trusted him. I should have killed him.'

The Colonel said, 'Perhaps it is just as well that you didn't. I dug him up in Bormes, on the N.98, outside Hyères. He has a dirty little bar there and is his same dirty little self.'

'And he knew something?' inquired the Leopard.

'Yes, but he was too frightened to talk.'

The Wolf showed his teeth in a grin which was not of amusement. 'So you frightened him still more,' he said.

'Yes,' said the Colonel, 'but, as you know, there are limits. Only to the point where he would give me a hint or two. To do more than that, he swore was worth his miserable life. Well, they were about to import the largest delivery of raw, unprocessed drugs into France ever attempted, a big operation. When this shipment will arrive now I don't know. Nor how, nor where it will be concealed, until they are ready to cook it. It can come in by land or by sea. We are working completely in the dark.'

'What was the other hint?' asked the Leopard.

'He said only to watch the Carnival at Nice.'

All four heads turned to the fly-specked calendar donated by a shipping company that hung on the wall at the back of the room.

'But that is still four months away,' cried the Leopard.

'Exactly,' said the Colonel, 'which means that probably, and most unusual in an affair of this kind considering what needs to be done, time is on our side.'

Friday, April 9, 1971 *continued*

Scoubide looked up irritably, for his mind was still preoccupied with what he had been thinking. He said, 'Good morning, Marcel. What is it? Don't tell me that your hounds have been sniffing out another fifty-franc packet of weed from the hip pocket of some American student passing through? Actually your beasts haven't had enough work the last two or three months to be able to distinguish a rose from a coca leaf.'

The sergeant looked hurt. He was a red-faced police type, which meant that he looked like an agreeable family man somewhat out of place in a uniform. He was in charge of the kennel of four Alsatians trained to smell out the undisguisable odour of quantities of narcotics and were especially valuable in police searches of cars, vans, train and aircraft lavatories and other means of transport used by the traffic.

He replied, '*Non, mon Capitaine.* You know that I wouldn't disturb you for such a triviality and yet, perhaps on the other hand, this may be exactly what I am doing. I know that there has been this drop in the drug traffic in our area and that you are still concerned as to why. Well, I have a strange story to tell you which may lead to absolutely nothing. But, on the other hand . . .'

'Perhaps we'd better hear about it,' said Scoubide. 'Sit down.' Cigarettes were proffered and lighted. 'Well then.'

The sergeant looked concerned, now that he was going to have to actually tell something of which he was uncertain, but he began, 'You know, Captain, that I am in the habit of exercising the dogs every evening before I close the kennels and go home, following the same route behind the Promenade and through the deserted market. Well, lately the Rue de Balzac has been torn up and completely blocked off where they are laying the new sewer, and so instead of going that way we have been passing through the alley behind the Rue Danoise leading to the Place Virgile.'

'I know where you mean,' said Scoubide, 'and . . .'

'At a certain spot in the alley each time I have had a reaction, the strongest from Bruno and Dina and less so from Marco and Peri.'

Scoubide's head came up swiftly. 'Narcotics?'

The red-faced sergeant grew slightly redder as he looked more uncomfortable and had to confess, 'I wouldn't say so. Not at all a positive reaction.'

'Then what?'

'Just an uneasiness, a discomfort, a bewilderment. I would hardly know how to describe it except that I know these animals like my own children. Perhaps the best thing to say would be that something has upset them.'

'Upset them how?' queried Scoubide. If there was not a definite narcotic reaction, which he could well trust the sergeant to recognize, what was he being bothered for?

The sergeant blushed still more and said, 'Well, sir, if it weren't utterly ridiculous and I didn't know that they were animals, and as an animal trainer I have no part in ascribing human behaviour to beasts, I would say that in a way they were looking or acting like we do when we have forgotten something we are trying to remember.'

Scoubide smiled and said, 'Really, Marcel!' and then asked, 'And actually what is this spot where they behave in this manner?'

The sergeant replied, 'It is where the rear of the *Théâtre des Variétés* backs on to the alley, actually the back of the stage where are the big doors that admit the entrance of large scenery. The stage door is around the corner in the Rue Vauban, but as you know, the theatre has been closed for more than a year.'

Scoubide nodded. It was true; closed and sealed. The owners had gone bankrupt and there were still court proceedings before the property could be put up for sale. An idea struck him and he asked the sergeant, 'What was the last performance there before the theatre shut its doors?'

The sergeant replied, 'I looked it up. The *Cirque Cajou*. It was booked for the summer.'

'And ... ?'

'Everyone sees the circus, and the best of the circus, every fortnight on television, on the *"Piste des Étoiles"* programme. Why pay, then, to go? Nobody came.'

Scoubide reflected, 'And so they went broke, elephants and all.' He looked over at the sergeant and said, 'There were elephants, weren't there?'

'Yes, I believe so. A troupe of four.'

'Then they must have been introduced through those big doors opening on to the alley Ribaut.'

'Of course,' said the sergeant. 'How else, with such enormous beasts?'

Captain Scoubide smiled. 'There, perhaps, is your answer. It is known that other animals—horses particularly—are desperately disturbed by the scent of elephants. It is this, perhaps, lingering odour, which lasts for ages, if my memory serves me, that has upset your dogs.'

The sergeant, looking more embarrassed than ever, arose and said, 'I beg of you to forgive me for having troubled you, Captain. You are undoubtedly correct in your assumption.'

But Scoubide waved him back to his chair, for the Captain's hand still reposed on one of the thick dossiers through which he had been checking before the sergeant's arrival. He was remembering that most of the crimes therein had been solved not by fanciful deduction or thriller detective work, but by unrelenting attention to the slightest detail. In other words, one ignored nothing. He said, 'Nevertheless, friend Marcel, we shall have a look. Get your disturbed animals and we will check if I am right. I will arrange to have us admitted to the theatre,' and under the grateful eyes of the sergeant he reached for the telephone.

It took Captain Scoubide most of the rest of the day to secure a Court Order admitting him into the *Théâtre des Variétés,* plus the keys, as well as the services of the old watchman who had been the caretaker there during the days when it was in operation and who was now working on another job. Scoubide wanted someone who knew the place to accompany them, so that they would not go blundering about.

Hence it was nine o'clock and dark when the expedition set forth. It consisted of Captain Scoubide, Sergeant Pelissier with the four Alsatians Bruno, Dina, Marco and Peri on the leash, of which the first three were dark and Peri a gentle-faced, honey-coloured female, and the ex-caretaker whose name was Fasco.

It was only a short walk to the theatre. Fasco said, 'It was a pity it had to close. It was a good job, better than the one I have now.'

Scoubide did not reply. He was arranging his mind to receive whatever impressions would be awaiting him.

They were to enter from the front. The lobby was filthy and bedraggled. A glass covered panel on either side still advertised the bill of the *Cirque Cajou* which had never been removed, and peering through the grime of more than a year Scoubide noted Rajapoona's elephants, sixth in order of appearance. So that much of the sergeant's story tallied. A Court attendant awaited them there and ceremoniously removed the seal from the entrance doors. He would be waiting there for them when they came out to replace it. So much for the machinery of the law.

Fasco inserted a large key selected from the bunch he had been given and opened the brass and glass panelled centre doors, now stained and tarnished. One of the glass sections showed a diagonal crack from top to bottom.

The lobby itself with its filth and the cobwebs spun across the curved box office window was gloomy enough, but nothing compared to the depression that seized them all as they entered the foyer of the theatre which was shrouded, except for a dim shaft emerging from the open door, in absolute and complete darkness without a single light of any description showing anywhere.

'In the name of God,' Scoubide said to Fasco, 'turn on some lights. You must know where the box is.'

The old man said, 'There won't be any. The day they sealed it and I quit the job, they cut off the electricity.'

Scoubide and the sergeant had equipped themselves with police torches and now they flashed these on, the circles of light travelling over the empty foyer and the curtained door leading to the auditorium. The smell was close and musty but not of interest to the dogs who yawned and lay down at their trainer's feet.

'Where do you want to go? What do you want to see?' queried the caretaker.

'The stage,' Scoubide replied.

'Hmph!' grunted Fasco, 'we could have gone

directly through the stage door, if that's all you
wanted.'

'No,' said Scoubide, 'I want to approach it
through the orchestra seats.'

'Well, come this way, then.' The caretaker did
not open the centre door which would lead down
the central aisle, ending up no doubt at the barrier
of the orchestra pit, but went over to the farthest
one on the side, a swinging affair, which led them
into the auditorium where if anything the gloom
was even thicker and the smell mustier. Their
torch circles fell upon the rows of seats which
had not even been cloth-covered; the velvet was
thick with dust and beginning to be motheaten.
It was a huge theatre seating some fifteen hundred
on the floor, side boxes and three balconies which
was one reason it had gone broke. The stage was
yet too far from the rear of the auditorium for the
beams of the torches to penetrate.

Scoubide was saying nothing and hence no one
knew what he was thinking and feeling, but Sergeant Pelissier experienced a slight shiver as suddenly the tug upon his wrists increased as the
leashes of the dogs tightened.

They moved carefully down the extreme left-
hand side aisle, which it was obvious to Scoubide
the caretaker had chosen since frequently these
side aisles led to a small flight of steps up on to
the stage, which were used when performers,
stage magicians or mind readers, or even comics
wished to come down and mingle with the audience.

Halfway down the torches picked up the semi-circle of the barrier of the orchestra pit behind which lay, in the same curve, the apron.

The deep stage itself was still in darkness but all three men felt that within that darkness was something darker even than dark, and Scoubide held up his hand for them to stop. But the dogs were now pulling hard at the leather and small sounds were beginning to emanate from them.

Fasco cleared his throat and said with something of a tremor in his old voice, 'What is it? The stage was empty when we closed the theatre. It was I who made the last inspection.'

It was Captain Scoubide now who took the lead and strode forward, trying to penetrate the gloom with his pencil of light. The rear of the platform from left to right was taken up with something enormous, not yet identifiable.

'*Mon Dieu!*' breathed Sergeant Pelissier, 'Not the elephants!' and immediately realized the ridiculousness of what he had said, because through his mind had flashed somehow a picture of the four elephants left behind, having starved to death there and dried up, remaining standing like stuffed exhibits in a museum.

'No,' said Captain Scoubide, 'not elephants. But then in God's name, what? Follow me.'

He moved forward until they reached the foot of the expected small flight of steps giving access to the stage where to their horror their torchlights picked up a part of the object—the body of a woman who seemed to be floating in mid air between the stage and the flies. But the woman, who was lying horizontally on a kind of bier, was some twenty-five feet long and ten feet high. Her eyes were shut, her hair, cheeks and the flowing draperies, in fact the entire affair was made of *papier-mâché*. Simultaneously the dogs broke into high-pitched yelps of a peculiar note.

'The narcotics reaction?' Scoubide asked sharply.

'My God, yes!' replied Sergeant Pelissier, 'but . . .'

Captain Scoubide was already on stage searching the object from all over with the spotlight of his torch; the six-wheeled, rubber-tyred chassis, the tyres now flat on which the body of the woman rested. Other features included dried and scattered flowers and flower petals.

The Captain spoke. He said, 'Hold the dogs. Nobody move. So this is where Float No 19 ended up.'

Fasco looked upon the object with stupefaction, 'But that was not here when I made my last inspection. I don't understand.'

He moved towards the affair when he was brought up sharply by Scoubide who cried, 'Stand, I say! I said not to move. Nobody is to move stirring up dust until we see what we have here. And keep those dogs quiet, Marcel.'

'But there must be narcotics, Captain,' the Sergeant argued.

'Yes, yes,' said Scoubide, 'but I wish to go alone. This is the float that disappeared from the Carnival

over two months ago—supposed to be a student
rag. Now I don't want anyone messing about destroying whatever indications may remain of how
this thing got here and who was involved.'

Carefully he played his light along the float.
The gaily painted colours had not yet faded and
the other *papier-mâché* grotesqueries surrounding the recumbent figure had not yet collapsed;
the giant *Amanita* mushrooms red-topped, white-
specked, a squirrel, a deer, an owl, a fox and other creatures of the woods, paper trees, shrubs, and
flowers.

'I remember this one,' said Scoubide. 'Wait
here.' He lowered his light to the floor of the stage
where the dust lay thick and he thought of those
convenient snowfalls that were always covering
up footprints. So, treading carefully, he walked
to the side of the float accompanied by the shrill
yelping of the dogs, climbed up on to the contraption and almost fell off as some rotting material
came away in his hand. He said, '*Merde!*'

He picked his way cautiously the length of the
float and back, and then shining his torch upon
the figure, he came upon the latch of a door, over-
painted so as not to show. It was a low affair, no
more than three feet high but wide enough to admit a person. His light showed the interior wire
and lathe framework of the figure, the cavernous
space, and he was aware of a lingering sweetish
scent. The dogs were screaming horribly and
Scoubide directed the sergeant, 'Bring them, Marcel. But walk in my footsteps. You, Fasco, stay

where you are.' The dogs went scratching scrab-
bling, sniffing and shouting.

'A drugs lay-out,' said Pelissier, 'We . . .' and
then correcting himself, '. . . you found it, *mon
Capitaine*. They must be here.'

'*Were* here, you mean.' Scoubide said. 'There
must have been more than a ton of it. That's why
the scent has lingered so. Even the remnants of it
penetrated the back doors through which this
thing was brought in here and got to the dogs, but
was so faint that they could no longer fully recognize it.'

He again waved his torch to show up the vast
area where the dogs were poking their noses into
every corner, standing up on their hind legs trying to reach the upper part of the figure.

'A ton of it—what am I saying!' Scoubide said.
'It could have been two or even more, hidden
away in here and not a soul would . . .' He suddenly struck his forehead with the heel of his
hand, 'Dear gracious God!' he cried, 'What has
happened to my brains? The hole, the hole!' and
both the sergeant and the old caretaker thought
that he had suddenly gone out of his mind. 'The
load that wasn't there! It was here, right under
our eyes and noses. But then what became of it?
Where did it go? And what happened to those in
charge of it? There were seven of them.' His
thoughts went back to that dossier that had so occupied his attention all that morning and the
seven characters that had disappeared. The hole
was looming wider, deeper and blacker than ever,

for now for the first time there was evidence that
it had once been filled, that it existed and was not
just his imagination. He made up his mind.

'Marcel,' he cried quickly, 'go, take the dogs
with you. Fasco will show you out. Return to the
office and phone the laboratory. I want everyone
over here immediately—photographers, fingerprint
men, the forensic crowd, a pathologist—the lot.
And I want Georges and Nino from my own
personal staff. Tell Picot to get in touch with the
electricity company and have the lighting restored here at once. I don't care how many men
it takes, or what they say.'

At the door the Court attendant said stiffly,
'What? One of you still in there? How long am I
expected to wait?'

Sergeant Pelissier said with even more inflexi-
bility, 'You may go. These premises are not to be
resealed. The police are investigating a crime.'

Two hours later the *Théâtre des Variétés* was a
blaze of lights again; the great central crystal
chandelier, all the side brackets, and the spotlights
connected with the stage control board as well,
beaming down from the flies and the wings. The
lights burned all through the night until late in the
morning, while groups of careful, meticulous,
knowledgeable men with their instruments went
over every inch of the long-lost Carnival float and
the bare stage on which it had come to rest.

It was six o'clock in the morning. The sea and
sky visible from Scoubide's office were beginning
to yellow from the grey of early dawn. The Rivi-

era sunshine was about to grace the Côte for another day of delight for the tourists assembling for the holidays. The detective held his weary head in his hands and groaned over the pile of reports littering his desk before him. The last of the experts had departed.

The Chief of Detectives of the *Service Régionale de Police Judiciaire* now knew more about the float that had so mysteriously disappeared from the last pre-Lenten Carnival than anyone had before, and he knew nothing. The mystery was still unsolved.

To begin with, Float No. 19 not only should not have been stolen from the Carnival parade a day before the end of the celebration, it never should have been there in the first place. And to end with, some person or persons had lost their lives either inside, or in the vicinity of, the contraption hidden away on the deserted stage of the *Théâtre des Variétés*. And if the cubic contents of the giant figure on the float could be translated into bales, sacks or boxes of *stupéfiants,* there had at one time been almost two tons of illicit drugs stowed inside.

What a mess! Skulduggery and false pretense, and theft from the Carnival, murder, illicit narcotics in probably the greatest quantity ever assembled in one place, ex-convicts, mysterious disappearances. Results: so far none, no *stupéfiants,* no bodies, one float.

The President of the *Comité des Fêtes,* organizers of the Carnival, had been got out of bed not very happily as had the leading family of the *carnavaliers*, a curious industry handed down from father to son which each year manufactured the floats and the grotesque heads worn by the mummers dancing through the streets. Theirs was a profession that dated back more than a hundred and fifty years. The present head, a moustachioed *Niçois* by the name of Lacreuse had brought all his files and papers with him. Early in the autumn of the previous year, the committee had designated the theme of the carnival-to-be. Artists had drawn up sketches for floats, costumes, as well as the heads and bodies for the street dancers, and there were handed to the *carnavaliers*, where in their giant hangar at No 4, rue du Dr Richelmi, they were manufactured. One float alone would consume a tone of old paper mixed with more than 600 pounds of flour, to become the paste known as *papier-mâché*, which along with plaster of Paris materials and paint results in a grotesquerie weighing between seven and eight tons and at enormous cost.

At the same time the participants who would man the floats or don grotesque *papier-mâché* heads and figures, in which they would parade through the streets, were registered; usually the same year, *commerçants* with pretty daughters and other locals.

The theme agreed upon at the meeting of the Committee early in September 1970 for the '71 Carnival had been 'Fairy Tales of the World'. The head of the Committee had with him the list and

nature of the floats, or '*chars*' as they are called in
France, agreed upon. One of them was 'The Sleeping Beauty', but the President remembered that
there had been an argument over whether this or
a similar float from another story should be constructed. 'The Sleeping Beauty' had prevailed because of the fact that the author of this ancient
and classic tale had been a Frenchman—Charles
Perrault.

But the moustachioed Monsieur Lacreuse was
equally certain about his instructions and the
carrying out of them. Yes, he had received the instructions and the *maquettes* for 'The Sleeping
Beauty' and produced it, including a photograph
of it from the *Nice-Matin,* printed during the
Carnival. But he also had with him a *maquette*
for the Float No 19 which he had also produced
and which had been ordered by a group who had
the necessary documents and registrations from
the Committee. Was not *Monsieur le Président de
la Comité* aware of the presence of this second
float in the procession?

Monsieur le Président was reduced to some
frowning, head scratching and deep reflection.
Yes, of course he had been aware of it, but at the
time it had struck him that since there had been
an argument over which of these two similar floats
should be used, members of the Committee in his
absence—he had been away for a week attending
the obsequies of a deceased relative in Norman-
dy—had decided to use both, and since obviously
the *carnavaliers* would not produce a float without

authorization or a *maquette* designed and agreed
upon by the Committee, he simply had not given
the matter a thought until its disappearance
which, like so many others, he put down to a student escapade.

It was plain enough to Captain Scoubide. Someone had slipped *Monsieur* Lacreuse an unauthorized *maquette;* a group with forged credentials
had collected it, stuffed it full of the biggest load
of drugs ever to cross into France and boldly pa-
raded it before the eyes of the world, as it were,
the perfect hiding place, until they were ready
once more to move it.

If the plan had gone through as devised, the
stuff would eventually have been distributed, the
hiding place abandoned, the raw materials cooked,
processed, converted and the Coast, and probably
all of France and a good deal of England, flooded
by drugs on a scale that made the detective's
blood run cold to contemplate.

But it had not. Something had happened. Two
nights before the end of the Carnival, Float No 19
had disappeared and when Scoubide had questioned the President of the Committee if when
this happened he had not made immediate enquiries, the President admitted that he had not done
so.

'Do you mean to say,' Scoubide had asked, 'that
it's possible for a Carnival float that has not been
ordered by the Committee to appear in the procession and then disappear without a trace before
the finish, without someone being responsible and

intensive enquiries being instituted? I should have thought that somebody . . .'

The President replied, 'Mon Capitaine, have you any idea of the tremendous burden resting upon the shoulders of the organizers of the Carnivals? Not only the floats, the processions but the other festivities as well; the balls, the illuminations, the preparation as well as the disposal of the confetti, fireworks—everything is in the hands of the proper committees but when occasionally some of the work overlaps . . .' He shrugged. 'As you will note by the documents and the evidence of Monsieur Lacreuse here, instructions for all the floats and costumes which appeared in the Carnival are accounted for by the proper committees, and as for the disappearance . . .' and here he threw a hard look at the Captain, '. . . the celebrations were drawing to a close and in the end we simply accepted the verdict of the police that student idiocy was responsible.'

The shaft told and Scoubide did not resume the subject. But he thought to himself: *How simple and how easy. All you need is enough committees who anyway are usually at cross purposes, and nobody ever asks any questions. Each thinks somebody else has acted.*

He now turned to the reports of the laboratory boys. Here was something more formidably definite, but as was usual with this damnable affair, a total absence of anything as reassuring as even one corpse would have been, let alone the missing seven.

What complicated the problem was that whatever had happened it had taken place two months ago. It was all in the past and witnesses of any kind would be useless. One of the difficulties faced each year by the Carnival Committee was the storing under cover of the gigantic floats, some of which were more than eight or nine metres high. What passerby at night, towards the end of the Carnival and seeing exhibit No 19 driven in through the two great doors opening on to the stage of the *Théâtre des Variétés,* would have thought there was anything unusual in this, or even remembered that the *Théâtre* had been closed and sealed? One might dig up one or two of such witnesses and be no further along. As for those faceless ones who had come later, they would have entered through the stage door and attracted no more attention. The more a criminal, or anyone up to no good, goes about his business openly and as though it were completely legitimate, the less the average citizen is likely either to notice or be moved to make enquiries. The last thing people wished was to be involved with the police. But who had those others been? Who had arrived after the introduction of Float No 19 and what had happened?

Scoubide's subconscious mind suddenly screened a picture of Colonel Roquebrun, a respected antique dealer, and four of his friends, an electrician, an onion dealer, a carnation grower and a bar owner.

What made him so furious was that these people

who came popping up into his mind and had obviously nothing whatsoever to do with the affair
kept him from concentrating upon the solution
of what was probably a major hijacking job and
the only reasonable explanation in accordance
with what amounted almost unexceptionally to
the criminal pattern: one gang organizes the importation and distribution of a record quantity of
something illegal; a second gang learns of the plans
of the first, hijacks the goods and silences gang
number one.

And that exasperating void was still there. Who,
what and where were gang number two and the
prize they had hijacked? Where was gang number one, or what remained of them? For of all the
most indisposable objects on the face of the earth
and of which it is almost impossible to leave no
single, solitary trace, the human body takes the
lead. And seven? And no evidence but some fingerprints and a few stains of what was analysed
as having been at one time human blood?

Scoubide pulled the report of the fingerprint
men from the file and re-examined it. Thank
God, most major print depositories of the world
being computerized, one could obtain a photograph of loops and whorls and two hours later be
possessed of the information that the owner thereof had once passed through the hands of the police
in Vienna, Oslo, or some place in America with
the unlikely name of Pocatello, Idaho, for something more than a misdemeanour.

Four of these prints had criminal records. One

French, two American ex-convicts, and a German about whom the police had nothing good to say.

The Frenchman, however, had some interest for Scoubide for, according to information from Paris, the prints were those of a wanted criminal, one René Clamart, who went by the name of The Magician, a fellow who had been in their hands only once and then had escaped before he could be charged or tried. He had not been heard from for more than ten years and now, suddenly, his fingerprints had turned up on a *char* disappeared from the Carnival and concealed in an abandoned theatre. And after this, once more silence and no trace of him.

The prints of the other three had no criminal records, but tallied with those on file for *carte d'identité* of those unsolved disappearances written off as husbands flying from unsatisfactory matrimony; occupations, truck driver, metal worker and automobile mechanic, which of course might be so, or also could mean nothing, but where were they? Already agents were reinvestigating these disappearances.

Scoubide was disturbed in his reflections by a knock at the door, and when he cried, 'Come in' it proved to be André Picot, the oldest detective on the staff, a veteran of some thirty years' service, who was still useful in the department because of things he could remember. Behind his back he was referred to by other members, as Sherlock Picot, because he fancied himself as an expert in deduction on the order of the *littérature policière* or detective thrillers of which he was an avid reader.

He was a small, bright-eyed, white-haired old fellow from whose wrinkled face a pipe almost invariably protruded and which those who laughed at him were certain was a part of his Sherlock Holmes fancy. Picot knew as well as anyone that detective work on the Coast consisted in hard-working, hard-nosed, hard-minded, detail-sifting, and he was good enough at it to be humoured in some of his ideas, which were often so far-fetched as to be ludicrous. Sometimes, however, oddly enough, if he did not exactly hit the nail on the head, he would come strangely close to a solution.

But this was not the time for such, and Captain Scoubide looked up with irritation.

'Well, Picot,' he said, 'I suppose you have some deductions.'

'Yes, my Captain,' said the old fellow, removing his pipe from his mouth, so that he might be able to use it as a pointer to emphasize his arguments. There would be no getting rid of Picot until they were out.

'Well, then,' said Scoubide, 'let's hear them.'

'We know,' Picot said, 'that two nights before the Carnival came to an end, last February, after the crowd in the streets had dispersed, the seven operators and occupants of Float No 19 drove the affair to the rear of the *Théâtre des Variétés,* from which the seal had been removed on some pre-

vious occasion, and deposited it upon the stage.
I deduce that the seven did not remove their dis-
guises but kept them on, should they by any
chance be disturbed, for if they had taken them
off, they would have been found somewhere about
the premises.'

Scoubide said, 'Brilliant, Picot! You list the
non-finding, the absence of something, as evidence. You will have to do better than that. Besides, what difference does it make?'

'Well,' Picot replied, 'because of the oddity of
the costumes, it seems strange that none of them
has turned up.' Then, unruffled by Scoubide's sarcasm, he continued, 'Before the seven could depart from one of the many exits of the disused
theatre, they were disturbed by the arrival of a
gang of armed men, who entered the theatre,
lined them up against the wall and killed them.
For there were no signs of a scuffle having taken
place, which surely there would have been if the
seven had not been taken completely by surprise
and held immobile by the threat of at least one
firearm. I have seen the Forensic Laboratory report.'

Scoubide's patience was beginning to be
strained. He said, 'You are sure, my dear Picot,
that you are not giving us a recap of the famous
Valentine's Day massacre in Chicago?'

But Picot remained undisturbed, 'There were
similarities,' he replied.

'And,' inquired Scoubide sarcastically, 'how was
this mass assassination accomplished, since there

are no traces except one blood-stain type O, with one damaged brick and a flattened bullet from a Rashak, sub-machinegun 3.50 of modern Israeli manufacture, a new model only recently finding its way into other countries.'

'Ha,' said Picot, pointing his pipe-stem, 'they were dispatched by means unknown to us, but I deduce that while this was happening, one of the victims attempted to escape and was immediately shot through the back, the bullet passing through his body and flattening against the wall. I further deduce that the second gang acquired this weapon recently and were not acquainted with its power, and were certain the bullet had remained in the body, otherwise they would have searched for it and removed it.'

'What makes you think that?'

'The evidence. They were so thorough in everything they did.'

'God!' cried Scoubide aloud, 'one more example of this kind of evidence, and I lose my mind.' But then he was compelled to add, 'but the damn bullet is an evidence of some kind, anyway. Someone was killed or injured there.'

Picot continued imperturbably, 'When the seven were dead, the second gang of which, I deduce, there were no less than four or more than six . . .'

Scoubide said sharply, 'What is your evidence for that?'

'The job that was done there that night. If the enormous figure of Snow White was loaded with

narcotics, one man alone could never have removed it, nor could one man have controlled sev-
en, even with a gun.'

'If—if—if,' cried Scoubide.

Picot paid no attention. 'As I said, when the
seven were dead, the second gang removed the
bodies as well as the cargo concealed in the *papier-
mâché* figure, loaded them into a lorry parked
outside, resealed the stage door and the entrance
at the rear of the *Théâtre des Variétés,* and drove
off to parts unknown.'

'What makes you think it was the second gang
which did that, and not the other way round?'

'Why,' replied Picot with such sweet seriousness
that Scoubide could not be angry, 'the resealing
must have been done by the second gang, since
the members of the first gang were all dead.'

'O my God!' cried Scoubide, and his tortured
mind tried to think of the name given by philoso-
phers to arguing a *fait accompli* from a false or
non-proven premise, but he controlled himself
and said finally, 'Thank you, Picot, we will give
your thoughts some consideration.'

When the old man, satisfied, departed, Scoubide
merely muttered, 'Christ!' and buried his head
in his hands, trying to obliterate the picture which
had forced itself into his mind, because of one
of Sherlock Picot's absurd deductions.

*Friday, February 19 through
Saturday, February 20, 1971*

The annual Nice Carnival celebrated the week

before Lent goes back to the year 1294 when Charles II, King of Naples, was reported to have enjoyed the rout immensely. But of course, like all such celebrations, it is ante-dated to fertility rites that precede even the ancient Roman Saturnalia. In one respect this pageant has remained unchanged down through the centuries, namely the procession and the dragging through the streets of effigies, preceded by mummers in colourful costumes or weighed down with grotesqueries in the form of heads of birds, beasts, men or devils in *papier-mâché*, leaping and dancing.

King Carnival himself, a gigantic figure often thirty feet in height, heads the parade followed by some thirty floats, vast affairs illuminated and often surrounded by bevies of pretty girls in national costume, or dressed to fit the theme, who wave to the populace thronging the route, or exchange flights of coloured paper streamers and showers of confetti. These monsters and grotesqueries are mounted upon drays, truck chassis, or long wagons; some motorized, others drawn by tractors and others still horsedrawn.

The strange thing about them is that while they are supposed to celebrate freedom, joy and release, they are horrible, menacing, vulgar and obscene.

But there is a certain compulsion about this vulgarity and obscenity—obscene not in the pornographic sense, but in the revelation of everything that is ugly about the human form and face.

It is as though these ancient families who sculpture these monstrosities have lived so long through everything that is cheap, low and hateful in human nature that they cannot help but reflect it in their figures. They are unable to manufacture a smile that is not composed partly of a leer. Every expression is a revelation or a caricature of some phase of human venality. Whatever they reproduce, be it saint or devil, policeman, monk, soldier, clown, jester, tramp, student, male or female, animal or human, there is some kind of underlying menace connected with it. One is compelled to recognize some form of our despicableness under the guise of illumination, blaring band music, whirling dancers, young girls and all the trappings of merriment, and this is its compulsion. Whatever is spent upon it is worth it, for it attracts literally hundreds of thousands of spectators each year who pay to jam the stands built around the Place Masséna and along the Promenade des Anglais where the procession takes place twice daily —afternoon and night-time.

It is superficially gay; aggression is limited to the buying of paper streamers and bags of confetti which are then thrown into the faces of one's neighbour or used to attract the attention of a girl, and when the procession of floats has circled the Place Masséna three times before setting off down the Promenade the merrymaking, if such it can be called, fades away in a desultory manner as the crowds disperse. One looks for dancing in the streets or some kind of intermingling of the spectators, but there is none. At night there are a few private balls and entertainments, but the latter-day carnivalists seem satisfied with viewing the illuminations, the floats and then going home and trying to shake the confetti out of their clothes. It lasts for a week.

Colonel Roquebrun with his four companions sat in the stands for the fifth afternoon, not together but close enough to be able to signal to one another. The Colonel in his private war was at the end of a trail that had led to nowhere. Almost four months of intensive search by men who once were the equivalent of an underground army had brought no result. They had uncovered just as little as the police in turning up who had been behind the death of Madeleine Renault or who was planning the death of so many other young people on a vaster scale than ever before.

How often had Colonel Roquebrun regretted the burning of the chocolate factory in his rage over what had been done to his niece, for that trail was now as cold as the ashes of the incinerated bodies. Alive they might have led him to the Syndicate. He knew no more than he had before; that he had managed to throw out the timetable of the Syndicate and that somehow its resumption would be connected with the Carnival.

For the fifth day now in succession, with growing disgust, he had been observing the caricaturing of all the characters that had been a part of his youth: Hänsel and Gretel, Snow White, The Sleeping Beauty, Red Riding Hood, Pinocchio, Cinderella, Goldilocks and the Three Bears, The Snow Queen, Puss-in-Boots, Beauty and the Beast,

and all the rest of the galaxy that had once been
such an intimate part of his childhood imagination.

The dominating figure that exemplified the
theme of the Carnival, the Fairy Queen, a figure
towering some twenty feet in height, star-crowned,
wand raised aloft, had somehow been drained of
every element of tenderness, mystery and sereni-
ty, as she gazed down upon the assembly with a
horribly fixed, toothy smile.

Puss-in-Boots was a mask of contained ferocity.
The *papier-mâché* Prince in Cinderella had his
mind and his leer somewhat elsewhere than on the
glass slipper he was engaged in fitting. Goldilocks
was not Goldilocks but a caricature of a gold-dig-
ger. The Bluebeard float was a *Grand Guignol*
with enough blood to frighten the wits out of gen-
erations of children.

For the hundredth time the Colonel reflected.
Had that nasty little pigeon Pignon given him an
utterly ridiculous steer in order to save himself
and be rid of him? No, he had been too genuinely
frightened. At the moment of the interview the
menace of the Colonel had loomed far greater to
the man than the more distant dangers of being
found out at giving away secrets. Besides which,
what had he given away? What was there that
could be traced to his door? Nothing! He had said
only to watch the Carnival at Nice. Well, this they
had been doing for five days and nights, with and
without binoculars, until they were half blind
and knew every lecherous grimace of every *papier-*

mâché figure, as well as the human occupants of the *chars,* by heart.

No, Pignon had not been lying and whoever they were, the terror inspired by the Syndicate was genuine. For not even the shadowy side of the *Côte* could or would finger the identity of the seven.

The single clue, and one leading nowhere, which had turned up oddly enough, had been provided by a ten-year-old Paris police record—a photograph, front and sideview—of one René Clamart, followed by a number of aliases, then aged 27, occupation mechanic, and a criminal known to the underworld as The Magician.

His capture had been a sheer accident, resulting from one of those bumper-locking affairs, with a *Quatre Chevaux* in traffic, except that the occupant of the *Quatre Chevaux* was a *gendarme* returning home in civilian clothes after his day's work and in an irritable frame of mind. The attitude of the other driver had been so arrogant and overbearing that the *gendarme,* producing his credentials, had arrested him out-of-hand for careless driving, and taken him to the station-house of the 11th *arrondissement.*

There, a detective strolling by, had remarked, 'Hello, I have seen this fellow before, somewhere. I wonder if he mightn't be The Magician.' The prisoner had, thereupon, been held, photographed and fingerprinted. While the bureau was engaged in trying to verify the identification and tie the man up with unsolved crimes, The Magician quietly vanished one night from his cell, how, nobody ever found out.

After which, as far as the police records were concerned, the man had never surfaced again.

The Colonel had the image of The Magician burned into his brain though, but as he was forced to admit to himself, for what purpose? The photograph was of a young man of twenty-seven; he would be thirty-seven now and anyone nicknamed The Magician would be an adept at altering his looks to suit his convenience.

The Magician, however, had one identifiable and ineradicable flaw, a slight cast in his left eye but, as Colonel Roquebrun's Inspector friend in the Paris bureau who supplied him with the photo and the information remarked, it presented no problem; no problem that is, to The Magician. To begin with there were thousands of people walking the streets with casts in their eyes. There were dark glasses or thick glasses to conceal it. 'If I were trying to find him today, I should ignore that element and pay more attention to his habits. But since his escape we have no record of his having been up to any mischief.'

At one time early on, during their intense vigil at the fiesta, the Colonel had hit upon the not untenable notion of the confetti salesmen. What better way to push narcotics during this period of supposedly unbridled merrymaking than via the thousands of packets of confetti and streamers peddled through the crowds? The five had sampled dozens of packets of these bought in every area and from every salesman, approaching them with winks or knowing gestures and receiving exactly what their one-franc piece called for—confetti, with no traces of drugs nor anything else concealed therein.

The Elephant then had been commissioned by the Colonel actually to try to buy whatever drugs might be available in the area, with results that were practically negative. In a small tobacconist's shop just off the Place Masséna he had been able to procure fifty-francs-worth of highly inferior weed, and a hippie whom he had pressed for information where he might be able to find a fix, had cheerfully and for one hundred francs, parted with half his own supply of cocaine in powder form, which he said he had been able to pick up in Aix. A handful of illicit cigarettes turned up, but whatever the caper was which, according to Pignon, the terrified stoolie, was to take place during the Carnival, retailing on a large scale was not yet a part of it.

The brass band blaring into 'Who's Afraid of the Big Bad Wolf?' crashed into the Colonel's consciousness and gave him a headache. All the members of the band were dressed as pigs and preceded the float of 'The Three Little Pigs and the Big Bad Wolf.' The mask-makers had outdone themselves. All the pigs resembled people, a change from other confections in which the people looked porcine.

Through the Colonel's weary head sang the line, 'I'll huff and I'll puff, and I'll b—l—o—w your house down!', and he thought back for a moment to all the fairy tales he remembered from his childhood.

The float of *'La Belle au Bois Dormant'* came by and his tired mind rapped him sharply over the knuckles for having diverged for a moment. A massive figure asleep on a pallet, practically surrounded by the recumbent figures of her court, girls and boys in 18th Century costumes. What was her story? Oh yes, of course! The evil fairy at the christening, the curse of the pricked finger, the hundred years' sleep, the awakening kiss of the Prince . . .

He shuddered at the *carnavaliers'* version of the Prince and wondered why the Committee had chosen two stories and two floats in a way so similar. For three or four down from The Sleeping Beauty the figure of *Blanche-Neige et les Sept Nains* was approaching, and he knew every lineament of that one because he had seen it some twenty-five times already: the thirty-foot-long body of the supposedly dead girl, her breast rising and falling at the instigation of some internal clockwork which made it rather revoltingly lifelike, and the capering figures surrounding her.

Blaring bands, noise, colour, the float passing by and out of the confusion, the voice of a little American girl nearby with her mother, 'Oh Mommy, look! It's Snow-White and the Seven Dwarfs. But She's not dead really, she's only got the poisoned apple caught in her throat.'

The English word 'snow' struck the ear of the

Colonel who had been thinking in French, caught his mind completely off guard and yanked it back to the miserable, unhappy and so far unsolvable problem of linking up the Carnival with narcotics.

Snow, snow! Snow, the American slang name for the white powder of heroin.

Snow-White and the Seven Dwarfs. Snow and the magical number seven.

'Mommy, what makes Snow-White breathe like that? She's not real, is she?'

Her mother replied, 'Of course not, darling. It's probably someone inside.'

The Colonel's mind suddenly let him off the hook and something clicked. Snow! Snow-White and the Seven Dwarfs—seven capering figures, there they were. Grown men with tasselled caps, dwarf suits, flowing white beards and moustaches on wires hooked over their ears, but dwarfed by the size of the gigantic figure of the unconscious girl draped on the bier. Because her eyes were closed, she was less depressing than the others and the word 'inside, inside' hammered through his consciousness. Was it possible? If one wanted to conceal the biggest load of drugs ever, nobody would ever think of looking inside the figure of that epitome of innocence, Snow-White.

For one instant which might have blinded him forever, the Colonel violently rejected that any drug Syndicate composed of even the most limited brains would have the stupidity to tease and thumb their noses at the authorities by deliberately incorporating a charade in their hiding place offering the clue of snow. This would have been so utterly senseless that, as said, the Colonel came close to missing the clue. The float passed by but would come around again. It was followed by the gigantic figure of Jack-and-the-Beanstalk and the Colonel had a glimpse of something, or rather his mind once having entertained a seemingly absurd idea, tackled the problem from an entirely different angle, and he signalled to the four members of the Zoo Gang to come to him, to collect about him in the stand.

It had only been the first procession; Snow-White and the Seven Dwarfs would be coming around again and for the first time Roquebrun had an idea as to the possible reason for the similarity of the two fairy-tale reproductions—The Sleeping Beauty and Snow-White. Practically all of the other floats consisted of conglomerations of grotesque figures standing upright and calling for a strong, internal construction to keep them erect. What the narcotic smugglers needed was space, and space was what the two fairy-tales of the unconscious but horizontal Princesses provided.

Snow-White or The Sleeping Beauty, the cubic space inside the figures was enormous. Which, then, which one had been ordered by the Carnival Committee? Which had been intruded into the procession, how and by whom? The nickname 'The Magician' came into his mind. The Sleeping Beauty with the Prince come to awaken her and the court surrounding her couch? Or Snow-White and the Seven Dwarfs? Which one was it?

Seven of the Syndicate . . . Seven Dwarfs . . .

Snow-White . . . again snow, the deadly white powder of heroin thrown in their faces.

And then, with a great sigh, the scales fell from
the eyes of the Colonel as resolution flooded his
mind. The gangsters were not clever; they were
not deliberately taunting the authorities and daring them to guess. Oh no, it could be more simple
than that. Compelled by the fact that the Carnival Committee would have chosen the Perrault
story, the mob had needed another with a huge re-
clining figure and naturally turned to Snow-
White, but the connection simply had never
dawned on them. Or perhaps just because of the
subconscious use of the word for heroin, they had
hit upon using Snow-White and then promptly
forgotten all about it.

When the four had gathered about him and
joined in flinging confetti about, the Colonel said
curtly and out of the side of his mouth, '*La Belle
au Bois Dormant* and *Blanche-Neige*—put your
field-glasses on them next time.'

Around and around went the hideous procession. The Sleeping Beauty drew abreast. The Colonel asked sharply, 'Any of you recognize any of
those girls there?'

The Tiger said, 'But of course. The third from
the right is Mademoiselle Lisieux, the controller's
daughter. Very social. Always getting her picture
in the *Nice-Matin*.'

The Wolf suddenly snickered, 'I know the one
on the extreme left. Not quite so social.'

'Forget it!' snapped the Colonel, 'Not a chance
then.'

The Snow-White float was approaching and the Colonel ordered, 'Get ready!'

The Leopard asked, 'What are we looking for?'

'I don't know,' said the Colonel. 'Anything we might recognize or that would give us a clue. I may be wrong but . . .' But by now he had not the slightest notion that he might be wrong. He was convinced of his theory. It was the only one that fitted.

The Snow-White float was preceded by a revolting caricature of a band in which the bodies consisted of violins and cellos and the heads lunatic faces with insane eyes and twisted mouths, with the mummers incorporated inside. The faces were like those of men in death agonies and the Colonel shuddered and wondered what a float would look like with King Death instead of King Carnival as the theme. And was King Death riding the Snow-White float, now abreast?

The Elephant exclaimed sharply, and so at the same time did the Colonel. 'The second one!' cried the Elephant. 'But the cast is in his right eye,' and then quickly he corrected himself, 'No, it's the left, of course, because he's facing us.'

Alphonse Cousin, the Wolf, stated nasally and flatly, 'It's The Magician.'

The Colonel still had his field-glasses on the second Dwarf. 'It's in the left eye,' he repeated, 'Blast! He's turned his head. Alphonse, are you sure?'

'Certain!' replied the Wolf. 'Remove the beard and you have him.'

The Colonel lowered his field-glasses and said,

'Then that's it.' No one thought to question the positiveness of the Wolf. Of the four he was the most intelligent and had a photographic memory.

The Tiger had been silent through all of this but he had missed nothing of what had passed between the others, and in his soft voice he enquired, 'Tonight, perhaps?'

The Colonel, looking at him, saw that into his eyes had come that curiously glazed look that turned them from human into something he had never been able to compare, except perhaps the eyes of another killer, and he was glad when a blonde girl threw a handful of confetti into his face and blotted out the sight. He spat out the bits of paper that had got into his mouth, smiled genially at the girl and said, 'Yes, I think so. Since we don't know what their plans are, we'd perhaps best make things begin to happen in accordance with ours.' He said to the Tiger, 'You understand, of course, that we must be absolutely certain? A mistake would be a catastrophe from which we could never recover in our consciences.'

'Quite,' sighed the Tiger.

They did not wait for the float to come around a third time but elbowed their way out of the crowd, went into a nearby café and made their dispositions. There would be time to carry them out, for the procession would take place again that evening. One of them would follow the *char*.

It was going on towards one o'clock in the morning when the Elephant's largest truck from his wholesale garlic and onion warehouse, back in the hills, drove up with the Elephant himself at the wheel and the Colonel beside him nursing an Israeli Rashak 3.50 sub-machinegun in his lap. As they passed the corner of the Rue Danoise they came upon the fat figure of the Leopard standing there. He nodded. The Elephant slowed down and he swung himself aboard the back of the truck where the Tiger was already concealed.

They passed the mouth of the alley leading to the Place Virgile and turned into the Rue Vauban where the Wolf was waiting, gave the same nod, and joined the others in the truck. They could not, however, draw up at the stage door of the *Théâtre des Variétés* because of the huge moving-van with double doors already parked there, on the side of which was inscribed, the legend, '*Giraudin Frères. Transport. Nice-Lyon-Paris.*'

The Elephant drew up behind it.

'Are we too late?' queried the Tiger.

The Colonel said, 'No, I don't think so. But perhaps just in time. They must be moving the stuff tonight.'

There was no driver in the cab of the van and nobody on watch at the stage door.

'Being a little careless, aren't they?' remarked the Elephant.

'It's such a normal operation, if you happened to pass. Scenery being loaded for transport,' the Colonel said.

'If you don't happen to remember that the theatre has been closed for over a year,' the Wolf added.

'People don't,' said the Colonel. 'Whereas a man on watch outside the door might look suspicious, this doesn't. Shall we proceed?'

None of them had lost their cunning at seeing that this part of the game, the 'proceeding', was accomplished soundlessly. They were all armed now. The Elephant, the Leopard, the Wolf and the Colonel carried their machine-guns so that there would be no clink of metal. The Tiger had no visible weapon. He had a long parcel wrapped in newspaper under his arm. All five were wearing thin, silk gloves and carried torches. The streets were deserted. They moved in a leisurely manner to the entrance of the stage door which was unlocked and went inside, past the short passage that led directly into the wings and on to the stage.

And thereafter the operation was classic and reminded the Wolf of the night that they had wiped out an entire German communications centre just west of Marseille, in 1944, leaving not so much as a trace of what had happened to the dozen or so men manning it.

Now the Seven Dwarfs were, still in costume, tasselled caps and beards, working by the light of electric lanterns set up in a semi-circle so as to throw their beams upon the open doorway, into the body of the recumbent figure of Snow-White. A number of packages and parcels wrapped in burlap and tarpaulins had already been removed and were piled on to the stage where one of the dwarfs was checking them on a tally pad. The

Dwarfs, however, were fullgrown men. The Colonel thought that it was intelligent of them to retain their costumes, for any possible intruder, even a policeman checking, would have accepted that they were engaged in shutting down their float in preparation for the next day. The quiet, efficient entry of the five took them completely by surprise.

With extraordinary agility for one who was getting on, the Wolf was up on to the float and had rooted out the two men who were inside handing out the cargo.

The Colonel said, 'Please remain very still, and don't under any circumstances make any sudden moves. Perhaps you had all best line up facing the wall until we have completed our investigation.' He was taking no chances on a quick break to kick over the lanterns. A free-for-all was not on the programme.

The men obeyed. Four machine-guns made up the difference of seven people against four quite conclusively. The movements of the men behind the guns and the voice of the speaker were decisive and they did not know yet what they might be up against.

The Tiger laid his parcel on the stage and made the examination of the packages, ripping open several, feeling, tasting and smelling. He was, after all as a carnation grower, a horticulturist and something more besides. He disappeared inside Snow-White and when he reappeared he said, 'Indian hemp, raw coca leaves, bulk raw opium.

There must be a couple of tons. It will take us three or four hours to shift it. We had better be quick.'

The Colonel said, 'Thank you, Antoine. You're sure?'

The Tiger laughed a most unmusical laugh and pushed the block of a dark grey, sticky material up against the Colonel's nose. 'Here, smell!'

'Peuh!' said the Colonel, 'Unprocessed death.'

The Tiger said, 'As pretty as a field of poppies.'

The Leopard queried, 'How the devil did they get all that in?'

The Tiger tapped one of the tarpaulin-wrapped packages and said, 'Waterproof, with still traces of salt. They have been dropped into the sea.'

'That's neat,' said the Wolf. 'Probably from a cargo plane at night.'

'No, I think a steamer more likely. Thrown overboard, marked by flashing buoys. They go out by boat, collect them, land them at any appointed place on the coast, transfer them by lorry, and then load them into *mademoiselle* here, and the job is done. Even should there have been any kind of slip-up in the transfer, or anyone suspicious, once the stuff was inside *Blanche-Neige* it was safe.'

The Colonel sighed, 'One can always learn, can't one? No two capers are ever alike. I hadn't thought of throwing the stuff overboard, far enough out at sea, so as not to attract attention.'

One of the men spoke up in a flat, angry American voice. He said, 'What are they? Cops? Find out how much they want. It'll be worth it to pay.'

The Colonel, who theretofore had spoken in French, now replied in English, 'Not cops.'

Another American voice then put in, 'It's a hijack job. Listen, you bastards, you'll never get away with this. We've got too many connections. What about a split?'

'Not a hijack job, either,' the Colonel said and then, turning to the Tiger said, 'I think yes, Antoine. There can be no mistake.'

'If it ain't a hijack job,' said the second American, 'then what the hell do you want?'

'Cauterization,' said the Colonel.

The Leopard asked, 'Do you want to see what any of these fellows look like?' and prepared to reach for a beard.

The Colonel for a moment stood contemplating the weird scene. The float with the part of the gigantic figure of Snow-White shown up by the yellow light of the electric lanterns, and their own torches which occasionally illuminated the first few rows of the seats of the theatre beyond the apron; the seven men lined up with their faces to the rear wall of the huge stage; their hands in the air; the shadow of the muzzle of the raised sight of one of the Rashak guns thrown upon the plaster of Paris breast of the figure. The Colonel replied, 'Is anyone really interested?'

The Wolf said, 'Perhaps we ought to make certain of The Magician, then we'd be sure.'

The Colonel said, 'You may be right. Go ahead.'

The Wolf went to one of the seven, whirled him

around and twitched off the ridiculous beard. The others picked out the pale face with their torches concentrated like spotlights would have done during a show on that stage. It was unmistakably the man of the photograph, off-centre eye and all.

'Very good,' said the Colonel. And then to The Magician, 'You may turn around again.' And when he was slow about it, the Wolf assisted him to jam up against the wall.

The Colonel for one instant more looked upon the faces of his four companions. They were implacably expressionless. He nodded to the Tiger who replaced the lump of raw opium on to the floor of the float, and went and unwrapped his parcel of newspaper. It contained seven long, thin-bladed, razor-sharp butcher's knives. He walked quietly to the head of the line of seven men standing against the wall and, poising the blade at his back where the space between the third and fourth rib would be, slid it home. The man fell to the stage without uttering a sound.

The fellow next to him turned his head to look in surprise to see what had happened and as he did so, collapsed himself, the haft of the knife sticking out from his red flannel costume. The Tiger, in accordance with the practised usage of the war days, was leaving the knives there. Thus there would be very little blood and what there was would not seep through the clothing for hours.

When the third man died, the fourth turned and began to yell. He was one of the Americans. 'Hey! Help! They're mur . . .'

The Colonel shot him through the heart. 'I said nobody was to move.'

'What did you do that for?' cried the Tiger angrily, and for a moment the Colonel entertained the thought of the absurdity of the Zoo Gang's touchiness when their preserves or specialities were intruded upon.

'To acquire equal guilt,' replied the Colonel. 'Also to keep him from making a fuss.' The others understood Roquebrun. If it ever came to a murder charge, he would stand with them.

'But now there will be blood,' complained the Tiger, almost in the manner of a child who has had his game spoiled.

'Well, let the laboratories analyse it then,' the Colonel remarked. 'It will give the police something to do if they ever get this far.'

The Tiger was still upset. 'Supposing someone heard the shot?'

The Colonel was unruffled. It was again the old *Renard* of the war days in action. He said, 'Muffled by the walls. Let's hope they'll take it for a backfire. Get on with it.'

The other three men, paralyzed with fear, never moved. They did not know what had happened to the others and the violence of a death by gunfire and the prospect of the crash of a bullet into their bodies petrified them. The Tiger neatly slid in the last three of his four remaining knives.

Voices were heard from the street. The Colonel said, 'Go and see.'

The Leopard laid down his machine gun, hoisted a huge, burlap-wrapped package that must have weighed more than a hundredweight on to his shoulder, and marched to the door. He saw a group of late revellers, four boys and three girls, passing on their way home.

One of the boys emptied half a packet of confetti over a girl who cried, 'Oh, François! You're a beast! I'll never get this out of my hair.'

The Leopard calmly opened the rear doors of the van and dumped in his package and then returned. 'All clear now,' he said. 'Some kids. They paid no attention. The van is empty.'

'The bodies first, then.'

'Where?' queried the Wolf.

'Their van, I should say,' replied the Colonel, 'since through my carelessness there will be some blood. We can't leave it here anyway, as it would lead to questions being asked.'

'*Giraudin Frères* won't like that,' remarked the Leopard. 'They will most certainly be making enquiries.'

The Colonel gave a short laugh and said, 'Don't be naïve. There will be no *Giraudin Frères* or the van will have been stolen. It had been prepared. It can also be unprepared. Some paint, a change of licence plates, a different body and you, brother Elephant, will have acquired an addition to your fleet.' Then he added, 'And who's to make any enquiries?'

The others followed his glance towards the seven heaps on the floor of the stage. Their expressions did not change and the Wolf suddenly found himself going back in his mind to a scene during the war, in a village on the banks of the Durance, where one day the body of a German sergeant come floating by, face down, while some of the villagers had assembled there to watch it. There had been a murmur from one of the women. An old, old man with a white beard halfway down his chest had turned upon her, removed a pipe from his mouth, in his eyes was the knowledge of the suffering that had been imposed, and in a voice of thunder he had cried, *'Pas de pitié!'* The Wolf thought to himself: *Indeed no pity either, for such as these*. This, as the Colonel had explained, was a war.

The rear of the theatre was in an area of warehouses and small factories. There was nothing there of interest to thieves or night prowlers. The Colonel kept watch but no one came by, not even the police who might normally be expected to pass on patrol. During the Carnival, of course, they had been shifted to other posts to control crowds and traffic.

The bodies were quickly loaded into the van and covered with the parcels of narcotics. Emptying the cavernous interior of Snow-White took longer. Boxes, bags and cases were piled to the roof. This, then, was the expected load that would have inundated the Riviera with drugs; the big caper and death and disaster for how many young and their families?

By four o'clock in the morning the transfer was finished. Snow-White was empty of all but the clockwork that had made her bosom rise and fall. The mother of the little American girl in the stands had been right; it had been something 'inside' which had caused this, and the Colonel again blessed her for giving him the clue.

They had found the key that had been manufactured to open the stage door and the Government seals that had been on the back doors that gave entrance to the stage, and through which the float of Snow-White had been driven. For a moment they stood looking at the small pool of blood on the floor where the shot man had fallen.

'Leave it,' said the Colonel, 'it will dry.'

They locked and sealed the stage door and went around behind in the alley and resealed the other as well.

The Elephant went to the wheel of his truck but the Colonel himself chose to drive the transport van of *'Giraudin Frères, Nice—Lyon—Paris'*. There were several passers-by as each slid behind the wheel but none of them thought even to look, much less to question, as the drivers switched on the engines and drove off into what remained of the night and was beginning to turn into morning.

Friday had turned into Saturday and by ten o'clock the disposals had been made at the warehouse of the Elephant, in the valley of Piol behind Antibes, where he stored the tons of onions and garlic brought in by the local farmers until he transported them to his depots in the town for distribution in the market.

The van of the non-existent *Giraudin Frères* had been dismantled so that it was no longer recognizable; licence plates had been changed, the sides stripped so that only the frame remained,

the cab altered and the engine number filed. Later the Leopard would replace it with a new one,
one of his handier little tricks. The haul of narcotics had been stowed beneath the heaps of un-
sorted onions and the five men were dog tired.
Twice in a period of eight hours they had shifted
some two tons of material.

There remained only one thing left undone
and, as they all knew, the biggest problem; the
seven corpses laid out face down upon the floor of
the huge warehouse. The Colonel was seated on a
crate of garlic, mopping his bald head and
streaming face. The others were disposed about
on sacking, puffing at *Gauloises*. Only the Tiger,
expressionless, stood looking down upon his
handiwork. He had carried out his assignment as
he had always done, with despatch, efficiency and
no remorse. What happened to the remains had
never been his problem. The others had always
disposed of the residue of his labours which in
wartime had not been too difficult. No one
looked into new graves, or bothered about bodies
drifting downstream or blocking drains. But he
recognized that these were different times and the
matter more grave.

With a slight nod of his head he indicated the
seven and asked gently, 'Well, and what now, my
friends? For how long are we to have company?'

Friday, April 16, 1971

But a week later, after the discovery in the *Thé-*

âtre des Variétés by Captain Scoubide and his staff, the ridiculous reconstruction by Adjutant Picot was looking better, or at least was as good as anyone, including experts from the *Sûreté* as well as the *Brigade des Stupéfiants* who came beetling down to help with the investigation, could determine.

Now, with the hindsight possible through having the float of the Seven Dwarfs in his hands, Scoubide cursed himself for not long ago having made more of a connection of the affair of the seven missing men: seven disappearances in a week, though none of the big brains from Paris blamed him for this—men were disappearing all the time, all over France as well as in other countries. Unless there was some kind of political crisis or the men themselves were known agitators, criminals or political figures, there would be no inclination to try to link up the disappearances.

But Scoubide was still angry with himself, for if he had thought of it at the time, he might have solved the mystery then and there before the trail was such dead cold ashes, and have received credit for it. Now the Riviera was positively crawling with agents and not only the local experts but men from narcotics bureaus of the United States, France, Germany and Switzerland as well. One of them would surely stumble upon some clue and crack the case, leaving Captain Scoubide, the dull witted local *flic*, who had had it under his nose all the time and failed to see it.

By now they had photographs of all seven of the

vanished men, including the fellow who had not
been drowned in his sailboat at all, but simply disappeared. The dinghy itself had been located tied
up at Port Gallice.

It was one of those cases that up to a point having been cracked, went along swimmingly and
without a hitch. All seven of the men had been
identified by one or another method as having
been involved in the narcotics racket, even to the
point where the man behind the chocolate factory
of the *Compagnie Jean Latour* had been traced
to the missing owner of the non-missing sailing
dinghy.

Photographs of the Carnival float of Snow-White
with the Seven Dwarfs, taken at the *Place Masséna*
during the festival, had littered Scoubide's desk.
Police artists had painted out the beards and
showed up enough to match with the snapshots
and cabinet photos they had secured of the seven.

When Captain Scoubide had taken the pictures
to the head of the *Carnavaliers* he had readily
identified two of them as having come to him with
the order for the Snow-White float, all properly
signed and sealed. A costumier had remembered
another as having rented the outfits for the Seven
Dwarfs, and a farmer with a tractor figured yet
another as having hired him for the duration of
the Carnival to drive the float. His interrogation
drove Scoubide to new heights of frustration when
he asked the peasant, 'And when the procession
was over, what did you do?'

'Why, we parked it, of course.'

'Where?'

'In a vacant lot where some of the other *chars* were.'

'And at night?'

'Oh, we left it there too. The weather was fine, you know.'

'Every night?'

The farmer scratched his head and repeated the question. 'Every night? No. Now that you mention it, there was something curious. Two nights before the end of the Carnival, they said they thought it might rain, and so they gave me directions and I drove it down the street where there was a big place, you know . . . It looked something like a warehouse and we put it inside. We could just get it in.'

'Did you know what that place was, that it was the rear of the *Théâtre des Variétés* which had been sealed up by the authorities?'

The man looked blank and replied, '*Non Monsieur,* how would I know? I have never been there or to any theatre, for that matter, except a cinema. I did think it curious that they paid me off and said they would not need me any more, since there was still two days more of the Carnival. But then I said to myself, "Mathieu, mind your own business". A man who sticks his nose into other people's affairs could lose a bit off the end of it.'

'And you never read in the newspapers about the stolen or missing *char,* which did not appear the last two days?'

'*Monsieur,*' said the farmer, 'I have no time to

read the newspapers.' And then, suddenly anxious, 'Why? Have I done something wrong?'

'No, no, no,' Scoubide had said, 'forget it. But if you ever see any of those men again, you are to notify me immediately.'

But that was the point at which the case came to a halt. No one ever saw any of the faces again. They were published in the *Nice-Matin,* side by side; seven nondescript mugs of what had been organized as the biggest narcotics importing, cooking, distribution and pushing Syndicate in the history of the French traffic.

The pictures were reproduced in Paris, Lyon and in Marseille as well as the London and Zurich papers and an international hue and cry had been raised with police handbills and rewards for anyone reporting a sighting of any of these men.

Nothing turned up. Adjutant Picot had not made life any happier for Scoubide by saying, 'But it's as I told you, *mon Capitaine.* They are all dead.'

'Dead, dead, dead!' Scoubide had screamed at him in a complete loss of temper. 'Where are the bodies, then, you bloody fool? Find me something —a tooth, a bit of bridge work, a button, a bone. It's impossible to destroy seven cadavers completely so that nothing remains, so that nobody comes forth with any evidence of hearing graves dug, or a patch of newly turned earth somewhere. You know this as well as I. And where is the stuff? There could have been two tons of it, the experts calculated. I didn't dare mention your deductions to them. Can't you see that we must have something which we can hold in our hands or put under a microscope, or analyse in the laboratory? Of course any idiot, and the experts as well, have been able to figure out that the gang was planning to shift the shipment and we have even turned up a group of young people who think they saw a transport van outside the *Théâtre des Variétés* one night, during the Carnival. But they couldn't remember which night it was and paid no attention to the van. I tell you that seven men and two tons of raw drugs cannot disappear into thin air.'

But against all precedent they apparently had. The experts having done all they could in the line of identification and research, departed with their files for Paris, London, Zurich and Washington. The handbills yellowed on police bulletin boards and in the end Captain Scoubide was left with his hole unfilled to balance against the satisfaction that it had become difficult even to pick up so much as a packet of marijuana cigarettes, or a couple of ounces of heroin. Supplies had simply dropped far below what had been the normal expectancy of the Coast trade and, what was more, there seemed to be no indication of a replacement. No one was filling the void. Captain Scoubide's underworld contacts were very quiet. They were also very frightened because for the first time they knew no more than he did.

Saturday, February 21, 1971, continued

It was the Colonel who replied to the Tiger's question. He said, 'I think we shall be able to an-

swer your, I'll admit, most pertinent question
very shortly. In fact I suspect almost immediately.'
For he had cocked an ear towards the door of the
barn to the sound of a car arriving which they all
heard. He arose and went to the entrance as Papa
Santoro drew up alongside and climbed out of his
car.

The contractor looked exactly what he should
have looked like, a stout, comfortable, Italian family man with greying moustaches and a friendly
eye. A heavy gold watch chain travelled across the
paunch beneath the waistcoat of his neat, dark
business suit and of course, his particular signature, the fedora hat clinging to the back of his
head.

He shook hands cordially with the Colonel,
gripping him by the forearm as well as the hand
in a gesture that showed his affection, and then in
the Italian-accented French of so many of the in-
habitants of the *Côte,* enquired, 'Well, where are
they? Let's have a look at them.' He followed the
Colonel into the warehouse where the others welcomed him with surprise, with the exception of
the Wolf whose eyes flashed in remembrance of the
Colonel's query long ago as to whether Santoro
was still an *habitué* of his bar and around.

'Oh ho,' murmured the Wolf, 'old *Renard!* So
that's why you wanted to know . . .'

Papa Santoro pushed his hat slightly back and
regarded the corpses. He said, 'Aha!' and then he
said, 'Well, well', and finally, 'Of course. I remember these chaps. I took my family to see the Carnival.'

He stared down at the seven dead men who, dressed in their Dwarf's costumes, were like something out of a grotesque *avant-garde* film. He said, 'They didn't have time to change their clothes.'

'It wasn't convenient,' the Colonel said.

Papa Santoro grunted again, and then enquired, 'When did you say . . .'

'Last night,' replied the Colonel, 'or rather early this morning.'

The contractor said, 'Hmhmm . . . Very neat, very little blood, except for that dead one there,' and he flashed a glance of appreciation at the Tiger who said nothing.

'Yes, I see.' Papa Santoro then said, with one hand covering a double-chin. He walked about the seven, estimating them with his eye, exactly as he would have judged a piece of construction before putting a measuring tape upon it.

'Yes,' he mused to himself, 'it certainly could be done,' and it was evident from his manner and his remarks that he and the Colonel had had a chat upon the subject at some time prior to this visit.

'Yes,' he repeated, 'it would work with sufficient reinforcement. For instance, this tall one here—just as well *rigor mortis* hasn't set in. We'll double him up.'

The Tiger looked shocked. What became of the corpses after he had rendered the designated victims into that category was neither his job nor his business, and he did not care to hear about it. He had no qualms about the transmogrification but did not care to look further upon the change that had taken place. Evil, he always felt, when destroyed should vanish as did the demons in medieval days, leaving no trace behind them but a slightly sulphurous smell.

Papa Santoro noticed the expression and said, 'Well, what would you do with a long lout like that?'

The Tiger replied stiffly, 'It's none of my affair.'

The others remained silent.

The Colonel stepped in quickly to mollify his comrade, knowing of his idiosyncrasy and said, 'Yes, yes, of course Papa, one or more of us will see to that. And once we know the size . . . But I confess that I am worried as to how you can accomplish this. I have no doubt that you will, else I should not have sent for you. But I'm wondering if we have not set you too much of a problem,' and with his toe he touched the boot of the one who had once been known as The Magician. 'Even this clever fellow here might have been stumped. How do you propose to go about this?'

Papa Santoro, who was still estimating sizes and quantities of material, replied, 'Tomorrow night.'

'Tomorrow!' echoed the Leopard, in a kind of horrified disbelief. 'But tomorrow is Sunday night and nobody works on Sunday. It would take more than two dozen men even to do a halfway job.'

Papa Santoro nodded and said, 'It's true that tomorrow is a day off, but we have been working actually on alternate Sundays, since we are behind schedule, and it will not take two dozen men. The six of us, I can assure you, will be adequate. And you, my friend, who are an electrician, must surely know that we have progressed from the days when a strong back and a weak mind were the chief qualifications of a workman, to the point where everything is done for us by the marvels of mechanics. I will show you what buttons to push and the machinery will obey. You will all be given one to operate. The Colonel and I will do the rest.'

The Wolf enquired, 'But won't the passers-by notice the work going on on a Sunday night, and be curious?'

'But of course they will,' replied Papa Santoro. 'They have been noticing work going on on various Sunday nights for the past six months but have never been curious, because we shall be doing it out in the open, under the brightest lights —so bright and open that not even a passing policeman on a bicycle or patrolling on foot would be inclined to give it a second thought.'

And so, the work was done the next night which was Sunday, under the glaring arc-lights that formed a canopy over that part of the port, toward the centre where the work of dredging, pile driving and the pouring of the foundations for the new moorings was still under way. As Papa Santoro had predicted, nobody paid the slightest attention to what was going on, not even the usual fascinated small boy, since the work was going on into well past midnight, and the small boy was in bed, asleep. It so happened that the watchman who ordinarily would have been on duty to keep any small boy away and out of trouble, also was asleep, owing to the fact that a glass of beer which he had drunk with Papa Santoro when he had come on duty earlier in the evening, had been carefully laced with an adequate dose of soporific.

At two o'clock in the morning, the Colonel mopped his face wearily and said, 'But must we go on now?'

'But of course,' said Papa Santoro. 'Do you wish, in case of a slip-up, to advertise to the whole world what has become of your seven friends?'

The Colonel looked shamefaced, and said, '*Mon Dieu,* Papa, how you are right! I am getting old, not only physically but, I believe, mentally, and am no longer fit to command such a team as this. Very well then, let's get on with it.'

Two hours later, after the contractor had seen that every piece of equipment and material had been left shipshape and in its proper place, exactly as his foreman would have seen the area cleaned up at the completion of a night's work, the six changed from the work clothes they had borrowed, stowed them in the proper lockers and dressed.

Papa Santoro, standing by the work they had done, removed the fedora from the back of his head with something of the reverence of one arriving at a graveside and said to Colonel Roquebrun, 'Would you perhaps wish to say a few words, *mon vieux?*'

The Colonel kept his hat on, regarded the twelve gigantic wooden forms with the utmost malevolence and said, 'May you all rot in hell, as you will rot where you are.'

It was the Wolf whose sardonic sense of humour could not restrain him from murmuring, 'Amen!'

But the Colonel did not even notice.

They then made a quick examination of the watchman, saw to their satisfaction that he was still blissfully snoring and turned off all the illumination, leaving only the normal watchman's lights burning. They shook hands, climbed into their various vehicles and departed for their homes.

And that would have been that, and the end of this story, except for one of those completely unforeseeable circumstances, or rather accidents, resulting neither from carelessness on the part of the Zoo Gang or Papa Santoro, nor from the following up of clues by Captain Scoubide.

As a matter of fact, the Captain had locked the case away in his 'unsolved' file, and had managed to put it out of his head as well, and was carrying on with his normal business of making it unhealthy for the usual run of burglars and hold-up men to operate in his area.

And then, three weeks before the grand ceremonial opening of the new Port Vauban by the Mayor, an affair that would bring Ministers from Paris, honour guards of the various services, groups of war veterans, trumpeters, as well as red, white and blue bunting decorating the special stand, flags, parachutists descending from the sky, interminable speeches, and all that human beings could whip up to congratulate themselves, Captain Scoubide received an invitation and paid a call.

Sunday, May 23, 1971

The visit of Captain Scoubide, paid on that par-

ticular Sunday, had, as said, nothing whatsoever
to do with this particular story, narcotics or even
any other branch of his work, though it did stem
from one of his earlier successes some years back,
when he had been fortunate in securing the return of an invaluable Renoir stolen from his
friend, American millionaire Joel Howard, while
at the same time extricating his daughter from a
dangerous position.

Since the new port was practically completed,
many of those who had purchased berths were already moving their yachts into the new moorings
and those luxury craft were beginning to come
from England, Italy, Belgium as well as France,
for the summer season. Amongst these was Howard, who had arrived in his 150 foot yacht 'The
Lone Star.'

Upon the occasion of 'The Lone Star' putting
into port at Antibes, it was the custom for Howard
to ask Captain Scoubide and his wife aboard for
lunch, at least once during his stay.

This then was the invitation which Scoubide
and his wife were enjoying on the detective's day
off, dining with Mr Howard and his daughter Sarah and her husband, for the girl had, since, happily married.

When around four in the afternoon the Scou-
bides made their farewells; Madame Scoubide
hoping that her slightly spinning head would not
betray her as she walked down the gangplank of
'The Lone Star' to the concrete mooring platform, the Captain himself felt more relaxed than

he could remember in months. There were certain unexpected rewards to his job which seemed to make it all worth while and especially so upon this particular day.

They were watched going ashore by the usual group of tourists as well as natives wandering the moorings for a goop at the wealthy aboard their palatial craft.

Captain Scoubide, his mind still on a superb repast and the pleasant companionship of the afternoon, had his wife gallantly by the arm, guiding her through the crowd. But it must be remembered that the Captain was a veteran detective and never at any time found himself mingling with a large group of people without instinctively using both his eyes and his ears.

Thus, penetrating through the after-effects of a brandy that might actually have been drunk if not by Napoleon himself, then certainly by one of his descendants, came the voice of a small boy who with his sister and parents were sightseeing along the quay. And what the little boy was saying was 'Who was Madeleine Renault, Papa?'

Captain Scoubide had already taken two further steps on his way before the shock of the name and the incongruity of the question penetrated wholly, and he turned back to observe that the two children were bending over a spot in the concrete of the mole, opposite and some little distance from Joel Howard's 'The Lone Star', where smaller craft would be berthed. They had been examining something.

Time suddenly stood still for the Captain, and he felt as though he were locked in a frame of a motion picture in which the action is stopped and all the characters are frozen into immobility.

Then the father bent down, looked and said, 'I don't know. Probably someone who had to do with the building of the port, perhaps.'

The mother also leaned to see. She remarked, 'It's probably for some little girl who lived on a yacht, perhaps that . . .' and here she looked up to note that the moorings were vacant and alertly changed what she had been going to say to, '. . . a little girl, who lived on a yacht that was going to be moored here, and died. How very sad.' They passed on.

Madame Scoubide suddenly cried, 'Claude! What is the matter? You are so pale—are you ill? That brandy was terribly strong. I'm not feeling too well myself.'

'No,' said Scoubide in a voice that his wife hardly recognized as his own, 'it wasn't the brandy.' He had bent down and with a cold knot at the pit of his stomach examined the elegantly designed, bronze plaque no more than eight inches square, on which in raised lettering he read, 'IN MEMORY OF MADELEINE RENAULT. 1951-1970'.

Madame Scoubide now also examined and read the plaque and said, 'Oh, it's that that's upsetting you? Isn't that the name of . . .', and she searched for the memory, ' . . . of the niece of Colonel Roquebrun, that poor girl who . . .'

'Yes, it is,' said the Captain, and inwardly cursed

luck, chance, coincidence, timing or whatever it was that had caused him to be within earshot of that piping voice demanding, 'Who was Madeleine Renault, Papa?'

But for this luncheon the brazen challenge he was now examining might have remained there unknown to him until a million feet of a million transients had obliterated it. Now it called for a visit to Colonel Roquebrun and he did not wish to visit the Colonel. Suddenly the case which had quietly gone to sleep was wide awake; the mystery of the vanished men and the great narcotics importation was once more there to tantalize him. What had made him so good at his profession was that by nature and character, Captain Scoubide was a man who hated mysteries. There was an explanation for everything and even if not set down in a dossier, he liked to have things tidied up in his mind.

Monday, May 24, 1971

But first, before the Captain drove himself up into the hills outside Vence, close to Tourette sur Loup where the Colonel had both his home and his antique shop, he paid a call at the working office of Papa Santoro, in the heart of the great port to which the finishing touches were now being applied, which meant that Santoro was engaged in doing six different things all at the same time.

However, with the announcement of Captain Scoubide, Santoro cleaned out a gaggle of fore-

men, inspectors and accountants from his office,
invited the Captain inside, shut the door, offered
him a cigarette, an *apéritif,* shoved his hat further
onto the back of his head and after the usual
amenities of the honour of this visit enquired what
he could do for him, though he knew very well.
He himself had been strongly against the Colonel's
insistence upon the insertion of that plaque at his
mooring, but then the Colonel was a stubborn
man, the mooring was his and he could do what
he liked with it, and also he was a friend. Papa
Santoro too was very well aware that Scoubide
knew of his friendship with the Colonel, the affair
from which it stemmed and in fact his entire early
connection with him and the Zoo Gang in the old,
brave days when a man's life hung upon chance,
luck, timing and courage.

Captain Scoubide began by saying, 'I'm calling
upon you quite unofficially, Monsieur Santoro, in
the hopes that you may be able to help me in the
matter of some difficulties in a case I have been
investigating for some time. Quite by accident
yesterday I came across a bronze 'In Memoriam'
plaque, inserted into mooring number . . .' and
here he consulted a notebook, '. . . number 218.
It is unoccupied at the moment. I wonder, could
you tell me who is the owner of this?'

Papa Santoro reflected for a moment and came
to a decision. He said, 'For this you should enquire at the *Bureau de Vente et Renseignements,*
down the road, where they have all the maps and
records. However, they have furnished us with a

duplicate of the list of purchasers for our own use, in case of complaints, etc., and I will look it up for you.'

From a desk drawer he produced a thick file of names in numerical order, ran a stubby and somewhat grimy finger down the list until he came to No. 218 and looking up said, 'That's owned by the *Société de La Tourette.*'

This name, of course, completely confirmed the link of suspicion which had formed in the Captain's mind at the first sight of the plaque, but he gave no indication of this and merely repeated as a question, 'The *Société de La Tourette?*'

'Yes,' replied Papa Santoro and let Scoubide see enough of the page to note that there were a number of these *Sociétés*. He said, 'Many of the moorings are in the name of *Sociétés Anonymes*—something to do, I understand, with taxes or renting, or re-selling. This kind of business is not my line.'

'And do you not know who is the *Société de La Tourette?*'

The contractor took a sip of his *apéritif* and Scoubide noticed that his hand did not shake in the slightest as he replied blandly, 'Of course not. But they would naturally know at the *Bureau de Vente*. However, I doubt very much whether they would tell you, unless you made the demand official with the proper authority. The whole purpose of the name *Société Anonyme* is that the proprietor remains exactly that—*anonyme.*'

Scoubide nodded and had a small sip himself

and hoped that *his* hand was not shaking. 'That
makes sense,' he declared. 'And the plaque, with
instructions for insertion? Came from where?'

'From the *Bureau de Vente*.'

Captain Scoubide now changed his subject. He
said, 'Tell me, Monsieur Santoro—though the
question is too much of an encompassing one,
considering the gigantic nature of this operation
—were you aware at any one time during the
construction of any outstanding irregularity?'

Papa Santoro took a normal time to reflect upon
this before he replied, 'None. We have had difficulties with one or two workmen. They have been
dismissed. We had a threatened strike. The
Union steward had, I think, a little blackmail in
mind. He was dissuaded,' and here Papa Santoro
smiled at the memory and Scoubide had to smile
with him, for an echo of the affair had reached
him.

Santoro was known to be thoroughly fair with
his workmen and on good terms with the Union,
but blackmail he did not like. He was a very tough
old bird, was Papa Santoro and Scoubide gave a
moment's thought to wondering just how the
Union shop steward had been dissuaded. But then
he turned his thoughts to a more important problem—how to get the conversation around to what
he wanted to know, when the contractor himself
solved this for him by saying, 'Perhaps if you could
be a bit more explicit with me about your problem I should know better how to try to be of assistance.'

'Willingly. It concerns the disappearance of seven men—all at one time.'

'Seven men,' Papa Santoro repeated, 'People of importance?'

'Seven scum,' the Captain replied briefly.

'Approximately when did these disappearances take place?' the contractor enquired.

'Around the time of the last *Mardi-Gras* in Nice.'

Papa Santoro sipped again and remarked, 'That would be last February, then. And they are still missing?'

Captain Scoubide said, 'They are unquestionably dead.'

'Then in what manner could I be able to assist you?'

'Every other avenue of investigation having been exhausted,' replied Captain Scoubide, moving to the direct attack, 'I was wondering whether the seven might not at this very moment be wearing concrete overcoats.'

Papa Santoro retained a serious mien, saying, 'An American custom, I believe, but not yet, as far as I know, widely imported into France. I fail to see the connection.'

Captain Scoubide said, 'It has been obvious to anyone who has observed over the past eighteen months the marvellous manner in which you have built this new port which, I might say, will be a monument to you as well as progress in France, that as well as dredging and pile-driving, the construction has consisted of the formation of enor-

mous blocks of concrete, and I was merely wondering whether it might have been possible for
the missing seven somehow to have managed to
have inserted themselves into these.'

There, it was out now, the question that had
been burning at his brains ever since he had come
upon that confounded inscription, 'IN MEM-
ORY OF MADELEINE RENAULT.' It ought
to have hung between them like something living, and it ought also to have caused some kind
of consternation if there was any truth in it, but
it failed to do so and only caused the old contractor to repeat, 'Our concrete blocks . . .' and shake
his head, 'I should hardly think so. That would
be something of a difficult feat for anyone to
perform, voluntarily or involuntarily, without my
knowledge.'

'I see,' said the Captain, 'then there would have
been a record kept of the pouring of all these
blocks used, for whatever purpose?'

'My dear Captain,' replied Papa Santoro, with his
first indication of anything that might approach
indignation, 'in an operation such as this there is
a record kept of every single, solitary item from
split pins to the exact tonnage of rocks used in the
construction of the breakwater. Well, as for example, you are interested in concrete blocks—shall
we have a look at the tally sheets?' He picked up
an internal phone and said, 'Tell Jean Prevot I
want to see him, and to bring along his tally
sheets.'

In a few moments a workman entered carrying
two large books under his arm. 'This,' said Papa

Santoro, 'is Jean Prevot, foreman in charge of the concrete blocks. He will show you in his books that they were constructed of various sizes, each one recorded and numbered. About how many were there, Jean?'

The foreman replied without even consulting his books, 'I can tell you exactly, *mon patron,* the total came to 3,740.'

The Captain shuddered inwardly. He asked, 'You produced what ... a norm per day?'

'This was our objective, since to have made too many at one time would have taken up more space than was available, and to have had too few on hand would have thrown the foundation men out of gear.'

'So how did you manage to maintain this norm?'

The foreman hesitated for a moment, but Papa Santoro said, 'Tell him, Jean, We have no secrets from Captain Scoubide, who is here unofficially.'

'Overtime,' said the foreman. 'It added to the cost, naturally; nightwork at double the pay and men idle the following day while the nightwork was drying. It sounds inefficient but ...'

Papa Santoro said smoothly, 'Captain Scoubide understands perfectly that on a project such as this one cannot always be one hundred-per-cent efficient.'

'And you were present during this nightwork?'

'Oh no,' replied the foreman, 'that's not my job. I go off about five o'clock, but in the morning I note the number of extra blocks that have been made and control the day's work.'

Scoubide asked, 'Would you for instance be able

to say whether there was much such overtime around the period of, say, the Carnival at Nice this year?'

Again the foreman hesitated and looked at the contractor who said testily, 'Tell him, tell him, Jean! Unless there's something wrong with your tally sheets that I don't know about, in which case you will have to deal with me afterwards.'

'No, no, *patron*,' said the foreman, 'but it just happened to be a bad time for us, with supplies of cement coming in unreliably due to the rail strike.' He opened one of his tally books and read from it: 'The time of the Carnival—the two weeks. Of the fourteen days, on nine of them there was overtime work at night: nine blocks; twelve blocks; fourteen blocks; then twice six, and again eighteen. I tell you, I was at my wit's end. It was not until the end of February and into March before we really got back on schedule again. You remember I advised you of this at the time.'

'And I said that the Port authorities would not be pleased,' Papa Santoro reminisced.

'Was there any record kept of where these blocks were used?'

'Good God, no!' said the foreman. 'That would have complicated our work beyond management. What we were interested in was the amount and their cost. They were numbered in accordance with their manufacture but the construction crews came and fetched them when, where and as needed. Our job was to see that they were there.'

Papa Santoro said, 'Thank you, Jean,' and the foreman left. The contractor gave his hat another shove so that two-thirds of his ostrich-egg head now showed and said, 'If you are thinking of looking for your friends . . .'

Captain Scoubide felt frustrated and a fool, for peering over the foreman's shoulder he had seen that the tally sheets had not been fiddled with. He had been hoping for the magic number '7' to appear during that period. Well, it had not, and there was an end to that lead, even though a visit to the Sales Office of the port would reveal what he already very well knew, namely that the owner of the *Société de La Tourette* was Colonel Roquebrun. He had been barking up the wrong tree with Papa Santoro since the Colonel whose shop was near La Tourette had not even bothered to disguise the name of his company.

The Captain finished his drink, wiped a few drops delicately off his small moustache and said, 'No, no. It was just an absurd notion, that is to say a routine investigation. I am sorry to have troubled you and thank you for your cooperation. I shall be present at your opening. It will be a proud day for you.' He shook hands with the contractor and left. There was nothing for it now but the dreaded visit to the Colonel himself.

Wednesday, May 26, 1971

Having put off the unpleasantness for one whole day, Captain Scoubide further postponed his call

upon Colonel Roquebrun at his antique shop outside La Tourette until late, six o'clock, though it
was light—light enough to observe any changes in
the colour of Colonel Roquebrun's face. The Colonel, when angry, indignant or embarrassed, was
known to flush rather easily, nor could he keep the
blood from rising to his bald skull. Also, Captain
Scoubide was hoping that by then the last customer would have left and he would have had the
Colonel to himself.

However, there were still two Belgians in the
shop, a husband and wife, the latter who rather
fancied herself as having some knowledge of the
Louis XIII—Louis XIV period, and they were
examining two commodes with beautifully carved
doors, one being slightly heavier, more solemn
and less airy than the other.

Captain Scoubide busied himself with looking
into the display cabinets that contained that portion of the Colonel's private collection of ancient
Greek, Roman and Cretan jewellery that he was
unwilling to sell, this being his personal hobby,
while the Belgian woman said, 'But why is this one
cheaper when it is so much prettier, and the better piece?'

'Because,' replied the Colonel, 'I will grant you
it is more attractive in design, but it is not the
better piece. It is made up. At least as far as I am
concerned it has been tampered with; most intel-
ligently and artistically, I will say, but yet fiddled.
If you will look at this leg, here, you will see the
slight difference. It has been added later. A mat-

ter of another generation of workmanship, that's all, and the style is perfect. It is this strip at the corner I have my suspicions about. The other is untouched, as it came from the hands of the original maker. It has actually stood in one place, in one château, all those years.'

The Belgian woman was put out that her own knowledge was being questioned and said, 'Well, if one is real and the other is false, why did you buy the fake?'

Captain Scoubide turned from the contemplation of a gold Cretan hairpin that had once been used to hold one of those pyramidal, piled-up hairdos affected by the ladies of that age to watch the Colonel colour slightly.

The antique dealer said, 'I did not say it was either false or a fake, Madame, I merely said that it had been tampered with. If in your home a visitor of too large girth sits upon one of your fragile chairs and breaks it, you call in a cabinet-maker to repair it. He does so; the chair is as good as new, but it is no longer the original chair, is it? I bought it because it was pretty, and since it was pretty I felt certain that someone would wish to own it.'

Captain Scoubide thought to himself: *An honest man, and how I love him for it. How many in this day and age and in this slightly rotten business would so tell the exact truth? Now if I were in that position I would double the price of the not-so-authentic one and sell it to the bitch who thinks she knows it all.*

'Well,' said the husband, 'which do you think you would like, my dear?'

The woman pointed to the prettier one which the Colonel had just so mildly denigrated and said, 'That one.'

Colonel Roquebrun turned away to hide a smile and Captain Scoubide once more interested himself in the ancient artifacts, because the way she said it, it was obvious that she did not believe the antique dealer, still thought she knew more than he, and was getting a bargain.

The deal concluded and the commode loaded into the station wagon of the pair, the two men were now left alone in the antique shop and it was Colonel Roquebrun who spoke first, and frankly. He said, 'Well, my friend, it's a long time since you have paid me the compliment of a visit; not, I think, since you came to make enquiries from my wife as to my whereabouts during one of my absences. If I'd known you were interested I should have sent you some postcards. I will next time.'

Captain Scoubide's heart sank for he remembered those misleading postcards that Madame Roquebrun had received during that time.

'And furthermore,' the Colonel continued, 'I understand that some of my friends had been placed under surveillance—a waste of the taxpayer's money, if ever I heard of one. I suppose you have stayed away because you were ashamed of such pranks. Well, you need not be. You and I have known one another long enough to understand that business is business, and in the end honesty is the pay-off.'

Captain Scoubide said, 'Like the sale of that piece.'

Here the Colonel laughed heartily and said, 'Well not exactly, for if I had told her that this genuinely authentic one, here, had been diddled about a bit, she would have bought that one. She was that kind of a fool. But the ending is not unsatisfactory, is it? I still have my good piece and she has her illusions.'

After which there was a silence. Captain Scoubide did not know where to begin. Roquebrun decided to help him out.

'Are you still on the trail of whatever it was that was biting you that time I was away, stealing that magnificent set of 16th Century pewter from the Convent of the Sacred Mother?' And here he pointed to the shelves of plates, salvers, drinking cups and pitchers, all with that exquisite glossy sheen that exists only on the oldest of this metal. 'For I assure you at the price the Abbess sold it to me it was a steal, though I gave her what she asked for the purpose she wished. Or has there been some new mischief abroad which either has or hasn't reached my ears and about which you would like me to look into my crystal ball?'

Captain Scoubide now felt himself colouring slightly and it was with anger, for he considered that he was being played with and did not like it and this gave him the courage to come to the point. He said, 'Did you know that Joel Howard's yacht was in? I had lunch aboard her last Sunday. You remember his daughter, Sarah, who was almost in such trouble here a few years ago? She is

married now—charming fellow. They all wished
to be remembered to you.'

Scoubide would have sworn that the colour of
the various visible parts of the Colonel's epidermis
had not changed by so much as a fraction, and yet
he was also sensible to the fact that the Colonel
had suddenly grown slightly wary. There was
nothing about his demeanour to indicate this, but
Captain Scoubide was a detective and a policeman. This made him at times a very delicate instrument.

'What pleasant news,' said the Colonel, 'I must
go and call upon them.'

'As my wife and I left the yacht we happened,
quite by accident, upon the touching bronze
plaque let into the concrete of a mooring nearby:
"IN MEMORY OF MADELEINE RENAULT
1951-1970". The mooring has been purchased in
the name of the *Société de la Tourette.*'

The Colonel's scarred face suddenly increased
every line and wrinkle as he grinned widely and
said, 'Brilliant, my dear Scoubide, and you have
made the connection between the *Société Anonyme* and myself. Don't tell me that you are now
also working for the *Ministre des Finances,* and
have come to put the handcuffs on me for a bit of
toying with the tax laws? Come, come, Claude!
How naïve can you be? Who, in France, personally owns anything any more? But I don't see in
which direction this discovery of yours could be
leading you.'

'Well,' replied the Captain, now having the

bull's horns firmly in both hands, 'it just seems to me an odd place for a memorial.'

'Does it?' asked the Colonel. 'You didn't know my niece very well.' He paused and lowered his naked head and for a moment Scoubide bled inwardly because he knew that the whole past was being raked up and that the Colonel was once more suffering the girl's death. But time had also worked its healing; the instant passed and he said, looking up, 'She was a water sprite. She swam, she dived and on skis, like a nymph, she danced upon the waves. She was like a daughter to me who am childless. In the summer I am taking delivery of a thirty-foot cabin cruiser for the enjoyment of my wife and myself as we grow older, and I intend to give myself more free time. She will be named the "Madeleine Renault".' Suddenly and quite sharply the Colonel added, 'See here, Claude! What the devil is eating you? Do you think I have buried someone I consider responsible for the child's death beneath that plaque? If so, go and dig it up and leave me alone!'

'*Mon Colonel! Mon Colonel!*' stammered Scoubide.

'*Mon Colonel! Mon Colonel!*' imitated the Colonel, 'Whenever you have perpetrated a particularly embarrassing piece of idiocy in my presence I become "*Mon Colonel*" to you! You are trying to connect my grief at the loss of a loved person with some problem you are unable to resolve. Continue to do so, if your official conscience compels you to such nonsense, but I beg of you not

in my presence? Or, are you expecting me to
confess?'

There was no question now about the change
in the Colonel's colour. His choler had risen.

Captain Scoubide felt such an emotional up-
heaval; a sense of frustration, anger with himself
for his clumsiness, shame and at the same time his
deep affection for this brave and honest man that
he was on the point of tears.

And indeed one or two did gather at the corners of his eyes as he pleaded, at the same time
folding his hands together in his anguish, 'Pierre!
Pierre, dear friend, forgive me! I am a fool! I am
weak! I am stupid! I am nothing but an *idiot flic*
whose job has grown too big for him, but I cannot
help it when I am haunted by something that
happens on this coast, on my beat, that I cannot
explain. And the worst is that I don't wish to solve
this, for all that happened is so much for the best
—and yet . . .' and now he rapped his temples with
one set of knuckles, 'it goes on, here. It goes on; it
goes on! What am I to do? I am a policeman,
and not even a very honest one.'

There was genuine sympathy in the expression
on Colonel Roquebrun's battered countenance.
The choler had passed and he placed both his
hands upon the shoulders of the unhappy detective. 'I understand, Claude,' he said, 'and I think
if I were in your position I would feel the same.
Sometimes, really all one wants is no more than
to *know* beyond any peradventure of a doubt. It
can be maddening. Don't give up; continue your

investigation and someday perhaps the solution
will come to you.'

What really made Captain Scoubide wish to
weep copiously now was that his friendship with
the Colonel had been made up and would remain unimpaired. When there is genuine asexual
love born of respect and long acquaintance between two men a lasting quarrel is something almost unbearable.

To control and hide his emotion Captain Scoubide turned to the artifacts cabinet again and said,
'Did that golden hairpin really at one time hold
up the dark hair of some Cretan beauty?'

The Colonel replied, 'A princess, probably. It
came from the vicinity of the Palace at Knossos.'

Captain Scoubide said, 'My wife has hair like
that. I know it would give her pleasure. What is its
price?'

The Colonel began, 'Would you permit me to
offer it as . . .' but saw the expression on the detective's face and said, 'I beg your pardon. That
would not be right, would it? What I do for all my
friends, then—dealer's discount. If you really
wished it, it would cost you six hundred francs.'

Captain Scoubide reached for his chequebook.
The Colonel wrapped the hairpin in tissue and
placed it in a box. The two men shook hands and
parted.

Monday, June 14, 1971

One thing you may count upon on the Côte

d'Azur, particularly on a *fête* day, is the sunshine
and those blue skies reflected in the Mediterranean
from which this famous coast takes its name. Even
if there is some rain about it will hold off or drop
its shower and then go away in time for the festivities.

But there was not so much as a cloud to mar the
ceremonies attending the opening of the finest
pleasure harbour on the Riviera, the newly built
Port Vauban.

The majority of the yachts that would be permanent occupants of its more than six hundred
moorings were there, from speed boats, tall-masted
seagoing sailing yachts, cabin cruisers of every
size and, of course, the palatial oceangoing yachts
of the billionaires, dressed overall in their gay signal flags, putting down a patch of colour at the
edge of the sea when seen from the sky, like a tu-
lip field in Holland.

The tribunal draped in red, white and blue
bunting for the dignitaries had been set up in the
centre of the port. The organization had been excellent. There were some rows of benches immediately in front of the speaker's stand for slightly
lesser dignitaries, then a semi-circular grandstand
divided into sections: one reserved for the workmen who had collaborated on the construction,
looking highly picturesque in their protective helmets; another for the townspeople—first come,
first served; yet another for the yacht owners, and
one for the wives and families of the workers, pro-
viding another pretty patch of colour; and then,

to round out the circle, a vast area of standees who would hear the speeches from loudspeakers attached to temporary poles bedecked with tricolours.

By the tribunal one huge, permanent flagpole of concrete had been erected, to the top of which the tricolour would rise at the proper moment of dedication.

There were three bands, a boys' bugle, fife and drum corps and an entire covey of drum majorettes, and when all these were compelled to pause temporarily for breath, canned music emerged from the public address systems interspersed with the thunderous concussion of aerial bombs thrown up from mortars. Parachutists suspended from gaily coloured chutes floated down from the sky. French history has a long record of producing impressive pageantry.

On the tribunal the principal speaker and guest of honour was an important Minister who had flown down from Paris for the occasion, flanked by the *Préfet* of the Alpes-Maritimes, the town Mayor and brother mayors from Nice and Cannes, as well as city officials, councilmen, politicians and people of importance. Amongst these, to the credit of the organizers, was Papa Santoro resplendent in a shiny, dark blue suit and a new fedora to replace his battered old friend.

It was because of his one-time Resistance command as well as his personal notability in the area that Colonel Roquebrun, with an impressive number of decorations including the British O.B.E.

lining his left breast pocket, was there, not far
from the central cluster of dignitaries. And on the
outskirts and at the highest point, his uniform also resplendent with various tributes to his bravery
in his service, sat Captain of Detectives Scoubide.

He, however, was there not only as a guest, but
for the special reason that, being charged with a
portion of the security made necessary by the
presence of V.I.P.s, he was able from this vantage
point to have an overall view of the agents, uniformed as well as in plain clothes, he had interspersed amongst the crowd.

Captain Scoubide's sensitive nervous system
was a jangle of mixed emotions. Pride was one of
these, for like all Frenchmen he was vastly engaged with the prestige of his country. Anxiety
was another, even though he knew he had made
his dispositions well and no rumours of any kind
of troublemaking had reached his ears. He was
still slightly raw from the encounter with Colonel
Roquebrun.

And finally, he was still worried by his problem,
his unsolved mystery which if the truth be known
had never given him really a moment's absolute
peace since it had developed. Seven creatures of
flesh and blood, villains and monsters though they
might be, two tons of narcotics to the value of an
astronomical number of francs, vanished into
thin air, or—and here his small dark eyes ranged
over the vast area of the port with its forests of
masts and floating pennants—into something
somewhat more solid?

The opening ceremonies and minor speechi-
fying and introductions were scheduled for two
o'clock, but the main event, the address of the
Minister to be followed by the cutting of the ceremonial ribbon, was set for three. The ever-roving
eye of Captain Scoubide, wandering over the
crowd in the stands, on the benches and the standees to check upon the circulations of his agents,
would occasionally light upon people he knew and
thus it was that he saw sitting in the stand reserved for the townspeople, but not together since
apparently they had become separated in the rush
for the best seats, the four members of the once
celebrated Zoo Gang: Antoine Petitpierre, the Tiger, the executioner; Jean Soleau, the Elephant,
genius of sabotage; Gaston Rives, the Leopard,
wizard of communications, and Alphonse Cousin,
the Wolf, for whom such a thing as an unsolvable
lock or an unenterable premise back in the days
of the war had not existed. They were all in the
front row, but cut off by from one to three persons
intervening between them.

Oddly, the first moment that Scoubide discovered them, his thoughts turned to quite another
affair in which as a game to amuse themselves on
a Sunday afternoon, they had—at the behest of
their one-time captain, Colonel Roquebrun—in-
vented a method by which it would be possible to
pull a stick-up of the charity Gala Ball and make
away with the fabulous amount of jewellery that
would be worn there. This had come so close to
reality that the Captain still shuddered as he re-

membered that by being forewarned of how they
felt it might be done, he had been able to prevent
a catastrophe. He owed them and Colonel Roquebrun a lot. There they were, those four simple fellows—a carnation grower, a garlic and onion
wholesaler, an electrician and the owner of a bar.

But how simple? And again he was aware of
that niggling maggot at the base of his very being.
Growing older they might be, but combined with
and under the leadership of that bald-headed, ex-
hero with the tortured face and body, the man
with no fingernails—Colonel Roquebrun—they
were quite capable of anything.

Time passed with the drone of voices, the blaring of music and when Captain Scoubide looked
again, the Tiger and the Elephant had managed
to exchange and secure seats next to one another,
as had the Leopard and the Wolf, so that they
were two and two, but still separated by a family
of four unwilling to make a trade.

Promptly at three o'clock, following a series of
shattering aerial detonations, the massacring of the
'*Marseillaise*' by the massed bands, the *Préfet* introduced the Minister and he arose to speak.

As became a representative of the Republic of
France, he was a tall, handsome, impeccably
turned out man with a noble head and an exquisite voice. He spoke as an important official should,
from memory and from his heart with only a few
notes to assist him.

He began, as indeed his sense of form dictated,
at the beginning, that is to say with a backwards

look at the ancient port of Antipolis, located upon this very site where they were now gathered. Here once the triremes of the Phoenicians, the Greeks and the Romans had landed to conduct their commerce, unloading their stone amphora of wines and olive oil in exchange for the products of the Gauls. Coins, pottery and artifacts, already in the museum of Antibes before the port had even been begun, proved the antiquity of the site as having been bustling with commerce before the birth of Christ.

He built up his speech logically and fascinatingly: how the port had developed, how Vauban—military engineer for Louis XIV—with his ramparts and four-sided Fort Carré, had made that part of France's coast impregnable, and from there he moved up to the present where France now at peace with all her neighbours, had been able to construct upon this ancient site one of the great pleasure harbours and yacht basins of the world to attract tourists and visitors by air, land and sea from every portion of the globe. Antibes, a name already well-known, would become famous throughout the world.

'And should,' he now said, 'all those assembled here perhaps not be aware of the gigantic nature of the operation which has been taking place before your eyes the last eighteen months, I am prepared to tell you.' And here he took to the small sheaf of notes which had been supplied to him. 'Millions of cubic feet of silt has been dredged from the bay, the Anse Saint-Roch, to transform what had been a shallow inlet to a deep-water port. Half a million tons of rock have been dumped into the sea to form the series of breakwaters which are making Antibes the safest and most protected yacht harbour between Menton and Marseille. Five thousand piles have been driven into the floor of the sea, and some 3,740 gigantic concrete blocks, ten to fifteen feet square, have been poured to provide the enduring foundations of this grand venture.'

He went on about the cubic yardage of the piping used for drainage and the miles of plastic tubing, copper sheathing and electric wiring that had gone into this construction so that each individual vessel, no matter how small, would have water, electricity and telephone communication at his mooring. He then revealed the cost of all this, a figure so enormous that it brought a gasp from the crowd, even though they could not quite encompass it in their minds. And finally, in his peroration the Minister neatly tied up the threads of his speech with his opening by making the public address system resound to his dramatic conclusion: 'And, my friends and fellow citizens, two thousand years from now I promise you that our descendants will still find these foundations standing as evidence of what our civilization was on this day of June 14, *Anno Domini 1971*.'

And amidst the roar of applause and acclamation, why he did not know and never would be able to figure out, the eyes of Captain Scoubide were drawn to that portion of the stands where the members of the Zoo Gang were sitting. And what he saw was the Leopard and the Wolf leaning forward around the intervening family and giving the thumbs up sign to the Tiger and the Elephant, who smugly returned it.

He saw, too, that their gaze was pinned upon the tribunal, their thumbs still elevated. He turned to look at where Papa Santoro was sitting. The contractor moved his new fedora hat slightly further on to the back of his skull, while hooking his own into the armholes of his waistcoat thus preventing them from the danger of twitching a reply to his co-conspirators. But it was obvious that he had got the message. Captain Scoubide glanced quickly at Colonel Roquebrun, but his face might have been poured of that same concrete for all of the expression there was on it. But the Detective well knew the panache and Gallic pride that would lead him to write '*Finis*' to his work via the little memorial plaque to Madeleine Renault.

And now Captain Scoubide suddenly found himself caught up once more in a violent mixture of emotions: rage, jealousy, humiliation, admiration and relief. Angry that he had been taken for a fool, violently jealous that the situation should have been cleaned up by someone else, deeply humiliated for the same reason, grudgingly admiring at what had been done. It would be, as those telltale thumbs had indicated, two thousand years before some enquiring archaeologist would find and crack open from one to seven concrete blocks, each containing a human skeleton, and wonder-

ing how ever they had got there, and what curious
burial custom of the long-ago Twentieth Century
they represented. Perhaps even like the hair that
remained on the mammoths of the glacial age,
clothing would still adhere to these bones to reveal
how they dressed in those times. And that would
be still more baffling if the skeletons were wrapped
in the red tatters of the clothing of the Seven
Dwarfs of Snow-White.

And again in a sudden fit of blind rage, Captain
Scoubide vowed, 'I'll dig them up! I'll have every
block of this port up and opened! Crime is crime,
and justice is justice!' And justice belonged in
the hands of the people through their police, their
courts and their judges.

There was no question in his mind now. HE
KNEW! They had made a fool of him, the Colonel, Papa Santoro and those grinning four. And
he had been a fool himself. Of course there would
have been no record on the tally sheets of *seven*
concrete blocks manufactured overtime. Santoro and the Colonel would have been clever
enough to have poured more than seven blocks.
His mind went back to the interview. Once twelve
had been poured, another time fourteen. The sev-
en would have been amongst one or the other. As
for the work itself? The Zoo Gang and Roquebrun had all been able at one time to turn their
hands to practically anything. Under the direction of Papa Santoro and with his help on the modern machinery they would have quickly mastered
the pouring of the blocks, seven of which would
contain . . .

And again he was blinded by what he felt was his humiliation and he muttered, 'I'll tear it apart, block by block until . . .'

The approving roaring of the crowd was making his ears ring and his head hurt, and caused him to look upon the Minister who was standing with his arms outstretched in a graceful gesture, acknowledging the ovation and in his right hand still holding the small sheaf of notes containing the statistics that he had read out.

Until what? Until two hundred and fifty kilometres of electrical wiring had been torn up, twenty kilometres of piping unearthed, 3,740 separate concrete blocks drilled, dynamited and craned from their foundations at God knew what expense, not to mention the complete wastage of that incalculable sum which the Minister had just revealed the port had cost? And all this on the say-so of one unimportant little Captain of detectives who had a theory that a respected antiquarian, aided and abetted by four ostensibly simple townspeople of Antibes and a building contractor, had contrived to murder seven purveyors of narcotics and bury them and their product in seven of the gigantic concrete blocks scattered over fifty acres. And suddenly from raging he began to laugh. He had to laugh so silently, so as not to attract attention to himself, that it almost choked him. But as he did so he found that the laughter was also filling his heart with even greater love for that rock of a much-decorated ex-Colonel and *antiquaire,* sitting a few paces away from him, and his companions who, at least for an ap-

preciable time in their own way, had, in the process of avenging a poor and innocent young girl,
spared the Coast a danger greater than war.

And he found that with this silent laughter and
affection, peace had descended upon him as well.
For the great narcotics gap was a mystery no longer and, as everyone in the department as well as
his friends knew, if there was one thing that Captain Scoubide could not abide, it was mysteries.

Le Snatch Double

ON A SOFT warm August evening at dusk, three men who had an appointment arrived almost simultaneously shortly after seven o'clock at the table which had been reserved for them on the Carlton terrace, on the Croisette, in Cannes. They shook hands, one introduction had to be made, after which they sat down and ordered drinks, each drink in a way characteristic of the man. *Un Scotch,* a double dry Martini on the rocks, and a Jack Daniels.

The bourbon drinker was named Henry Fairchild, who owned a string of newspapers in five key American cities. The other American—the Martini drinker—was a film producer by the name of Arnold Salmon, and the third was a Frenchman, Colonel Pierre Roquebrun. He had acquired his taste for Scotch during periodic visits to Britain towards the end of World War II, when his work as a leader of the Resistance in the South of France had called for him to arrange for *rendezvous* and parachute drops of men and supplies into the occupied areas.

Fairchild was the most prepossessing of the three, a handsome six-footer with that characteristic massive, greying head and interested blue eyes of the well bred American who has become a commander of men, properties and ideas; in short a powerful personality. Salmon was a good two inches shorter, running somewhat to fat but striking, too, younger than Fairchild so that his hair was still dark as were his eyes; he was slightly overdressed. He had a cigar ready to clamp into his mouth and yet he was far from blasé. If one could combine alertness to all that was going on about him with the world-weariness of one who had seen it all, that was Mr Salmon.

Fairchild had already noticed that except when he sipped his drink, the Colonel kept his hands beneath the table, and had observed the missing fingernails. He was not aware of the Colonel's past.

However, this had nothing whatsoever to do with the meeting of the three which was quasi business and social, the business having already been concluded. Fairchild had bought Colonel Roquebrun's collection of 16th Century pewter acquired from the Convent of the Sacred Mother, and out of satisfaction at finding and possessing this collection, which would most certainly gladden the heart of his wife when he presented it to her as a gift, he had invited the Colonel and Madame Roquebrun to a drink and dinner in Cannes. Madame had begged off, like a good French consort who knows when it is only men who wish to get together.

Fairchild said to the Colonel, 'I hope you don't mind, I've brought Arnold along. He wants some advice from you on buying a bit of jewellery as a present for his wife.

Salmon said, 'She doesn't go for that antique stuff the way Fairchild here, does. She's sort of got bigger ideas.'

Neither Fairchild nor the Colonel felt inclined to suggest that if Salmon were to spend on his wife what it had cost Fairchild to buy the Sacred Mother pewter collection, she would be getting quite a trinket.

Instead the Colonel said, 'I should be delighted to be of any assistance I can.'

Salmon then explained, 'She's got her heart set on one of those Florent pieces, but I dunno. I'd like to have your ideas.'

The Colonel nodded and said merely, 'To the best of my ability,' but involuntarily his eyes turned to the left of the terrace where across the street on the corner, even from that distance, the glitter of the display in the window of Florent, the jeweller of the Croisette, was fracturing the lights that were beginning to come on along the seafront.

It was the hour when cocktails on the terrace of the Carlton was a 'must' for anybody who was anybody; the famous, the near famous and the infamous liberally sprinkled with the most exquisite assortment of hetaerae assembled on the Coast, sat at too small tables, jammed elbow to elbow and looked out upon the enchanting view.

The palm and flower-lined boulevard that paralleled the Mediterranean from the Palm Beach Casino to the old port was known as the Croisette. White, incandescent globes made an endless string of pearls the length of the avenue. Two-way traffic of expensive cars flowed through the streets. The sidewalks were jammed to the curb with tourists, vacationers and pleasure-seekers. This was the playground of the millionaires and the Carlton terrace, for that hour or two until the drinkers scattered for dinner, was its heart.

That portion of the scene that it overlooked was embraced by two arms: to the east the Cap d'Antibes and to the west, overlooking the port with its millions of dollars-worth of parked yachts, the old fort. Straight across lay the Iles de Lérins, where the fugitive St Patrick was supposed to have served his missionary apprenticeship before his call to the Irish.

Anchored offshore, directly in front of the Hotel Carlton, lay one of the great new Italian liners, an exciting sight, every porthole and deck ablaze with yellow glow, searchlights playing upon its weird-looking funnels wearing their flat, silver hats in the modern style. The beauty of the giant liner at night took one's breath away and filled one's heart and mind with the longing for adventure. Sailed out of Genoa for New York, she was putting in at Cannes for a few hours to pick up passengers, as she would at Barcelona and Lisbon.

Overhead a Caravelle letting down for its descent at Nice airport a few minutes later, against the darkening sky was a silhouette, its red and green navigation lights blinking on and off; bright yellow showing at the cabin windows as at the portholes of the liner. There was no mistral. The air was soft and on that corner of the terrace, just above the parked Rolls, Daimlers, Jaguars and Mercedes, fragrant with the smoke of the finest Havanas and most expensive perfumes, champagne and whisky. The clatter, the chatter, the blending of voices male and female talking in many languages could have been a recording from the monkey house.

Occasionally figures would pop up from a table or come out from the bar of the hotel to join the throng and then there would be individual cries, 'Hey, Jake! When did you get here?' . . . 'Hello, Mollie, come over here and join us! Bill's just got in.' . . . 'Who are you looking for, Frank? Can I buy you a drink?'

The men were clad in slacks and vivid sports shirts, some with scarves at their throats. The women were dressed in the most expensive couture that the Paris houses could provide. The tarts sitting by twos until 'joined' were exquisite, their clothes carefully chosen to invite exploration.

There were two sitting close by the table of the three men, one a natural blonde with terrifying lustrous violet eyes; the other a fox-coloured redhead, hazel-eyed and shatteringly seductive, her long green chiffon evening gown was tight to her throat to suggest everything that was bursting to escape.

The blonde was noticing Henry Fairchild who, after a cursory glance, was paying her no further mind but he was making her sit up with parted lips. Arnold Salmon had observed the redhead. In fact their eyes had already met and sent out their first signals like ships exchanging code by blinker light.

'Of course,' said the Colonel, 'if that's what Madame Salmon has her heart set upon, you couldn't go wrong with a Florent piece. The gems are all of first quality and the originality of their designs well-known.'

The Colonel's recommendation had been delivered in a manner that could only be described as flat, polite and disinterested, but Arnold Salmon was no fool, having fought his way up from a studio errand boy to studio chief, and his clever ear caught that unvoiced nuance of, well . . .

'But,' said Mr Salmon.

'Only,' the Colonel answered the implied question, 'if the article is really for your wife I should be careful to declare it to the American Customs at your port of entry.'

'Oh—oh,' said Salmon, 'somebody snitches?'

'And collects half the fine,' completed Fairchild with a grin. 'I have a friend who got nicked that way once. Bought it from one of the big Paris jewellers. They not only knew he had it, but also where to look for it. Boy, was he mad!'

Mr Salmon was not yet satisfied and it was the question which the Colonel had managed to raise *en passant*, so to speak, that little 'if' that niggled him. He took a draw upon his cigar, studied the Colonel carefully and said, 'And if it was not for Mrs Salmon?'

The Colonel took a sip of his Scotch and said, 'Then you would be ill advised to pay the price they ask. You should bargain for at least twenty-percent reduction. Ten percent off is normal anyway.'

Here it was that Salmon showed that though he was astute about men, he was naïve about Europe, for he cried, 'What? You mean you can *handle* . . . I mean bargain with an outfit like Florent? I thought . . .'

The Colonel smiled and said, 'The bigger the outfit, as you call it, the more outrageous the profit margin, hence the more room for negotiation. Mr Fairchild did not pay me the original price I asked him for my pewter collection. I didn't expect he would. One reaches an amicable understanding.'

'But I don't get it,' Salmon said. 'Why if it isn't for Mrs Salmon shouldn't I pay the asking price, and why shouldn't I bargain for Mrs Salmon as well?'

'Oh, you can,' said the Colonel, 'and I am advising you to do so, except that when one buys something for one's wife, one is disinclined to cheapen it.'

Salmon insisted, 'But you said if it *wasn't* for my wife.'

The Colonel withdrew within himself slightly and said, 'I apologize, I shouldn't have brought the matter up. But since I have, let's put the explanation on a hypothetical basis. The hypothesis couldn't apply to you, since you have just arrived. This, as you know, is a playground for wealthy men. Often they are fortunate in the Casino, or are grateful for the companionship that has been granted them during their stay, and reward the lady involved with a valuable trinket. They then leave, let us say, for their native Sweden or Brazil. A week after their departure that piece of jewellery will be back in the window again.'

Salmon said, 'I don't get it.'

The Colonel said, 'The girl sells the piece of jewellery back to the jeweller from whom it was purchased, at a discount of something approaching the wholesale price, since she isn't interested in precious stones, but money. The proprietor of the shop has his piece back, his profit as well and the girl has the cash. Everybody is happy.'

'Oh boy!' said Salmon, 'you French can think up rackets we never even heard of.' He was wondering whether Roquebrun had caught him dating up the girl with the fox-coloured hair at the adjoining table for later.

The Colonel was wondering whether Salmon knew that he had caught him making connections. The sudden silence that fell upon the table made the chatter and the clatter and the noise around them all the more audible. Three long-haired men in filthy jeans, wide-brimmed hats and hippie beads, accompanied by a pretty, bare-foot girl with tangled, dirty dark hair passed by and stopped to regard the smart crowd on the terrace, their faces smug with the self-satisfaction of the state of being and appearance they had chosen.

Looking at her, Salmon felt a sudden stirring of desire but it was simply because of her availability to the men she was with and involuntarily he turned his eyes and met those of the red-headed prostitute. They said, 'Message received. Don't worry, I'll manage whenever you are ready.' He thought that in all probability in the end she would wheedle a piece of jewellery out of him and do exactly what the Frenchman had said.

Fairchild's antennae had picked up practically all of the emanations and to cover the suddenly awkward silence he said, 'Florent? Florent? Weren't they involved in that kidnapping case recently?'

The Colonel nodded carefully. He had been drinking in the beauty of the evening and the view from the terrace and wondering how many of those there appreciated it. Directly in front of them in the harbour, a small boat was making its way out to the giant liner that itself lay like a piece of the most exquisite jeweller's art displayed upon a black velvet cloth. *Oh, my beautiful, fascinating, wicked Riviera,* he thought. He then replied, 'Yes. They had their nine-months-old baby stolen from them.'

'My God,' said Salmon, 'are you fro . . . Frenchmen,'—'frogs' had almost slipped out—'importing the American snatch as well as all of the rest of the mess we're making of things?'

The Colonel said, 'Shall we say, a French adaptation?'

Fairchild had turned around for an instant, almost idly and had been caught by the pleading expression about the eyes and mouth of the blonde girl who was looking straight at him, and felt a second's stirring followed by the stern self-admonition, 'Not on your life, sister! Not when you hunt in pairs.'

'They are German girls,' the Colonel said. 'Some of the most beautiful *poules* who come to the Riviera these days are German.'

'Clients of Monsieur Florent?' Salmon asked, deadpan.

The Colonel only smiled.

Fairchild asked, 'I don't remember the details of the Florent kidnapping, except that there was something particularly horrible connected with it.'

'The mother is his second wife,' the Colonel said, 'and it was her first child aged nine months—a little girl. He is much older than she, you know; sixty, I believe, and she twenty-five. The child was spirited away in broad daylight a few yards from here and disappeared, it seemed almost as though by magic. One moment it was there and the next it wasn't.'

'Get-away car?' Fairchild queried.

'None. There was no get-away, at least at the time of the kidnapping. Up to this moment it still is not known how it was done.'

'But the child was returned, I seem to have read,' Fairchild said.

'Yes, it was.'

'Ransom paid?'

'Yes.'

'How much?'

'Never disclosed.'

'But what was the horror?' Salmon enquired, his curiosity now seized.

The Colonel looked reflective and said, 'The Florents proved difficult. Monsieur Florent refused to pay the ranson.'

'What?' said Fairchild, 'But he's wealthy! And in view of what must have been the mother's anguish?'

Colonel Roquebrun looked far back into the years of his mind and replied, 'Monsieur Florent is known to be a difficult man.'

'But what happened?' Salmon reiterated.

'The kidnappers sent an ear to the Florents.'

'Oh, my God!' cried Salmon, and Fairchild showed his disgust by the curling of the lips in his handsome face. The two birds at the next table were forgotten.

Roquebrun said, 'The proposal was that unless the ransom was paid immediately, the kidnappers would return the baby to the Florents piecemeal.'

'So he paid?'

'He paid,' replied the Colonel, and they were both so interested in what he had been telling them that they failed to note the grimness with which the last remark had been endowed.

'And the baby was returned?'

'The baby was returned.'

'But wait a minute,' Fairchild said, 'the one thing I do remember—for my wife, like all women, was upset by what she'd read of the kidnapping—according to the story, the baby was returned intact.'

'That's true,' agreed Colonel Roquebrun. 'It was.'

'You mean with both ears?' Fairchild demanded incredulously.

'With both ears,' said the Colonel coolly.

Salmon burst out, 'But how the hell did they manage that?'

'I told you,' said the Colonel, 'it was the snatch, French style.'

Fairchild was regarding the Colonel deeply, earnestly and quizzically, and thinking: *By God, I'd give a lot to know what's under that naked skull. You know a hell of a lot more about this Florent business than you're letting on and, what's more, you're teasing me, my friend. One minute the baby has only one ear, and the next it has two. The snatch, French style, hell!*

The Colonel read his thoughts and said, 'I'm afraid there's no story for you, my friend, or at least not yet. Though perhaps . . .' He did not finish the sentence, for in the passing throng he had caught sight of Captain Scoubide, head of the *Service Régionale de Police Judiciaire* for the area of the Alpes-Maritimes, strolling in the crush on the sidewalk and threading his way past the cars parked now so chock-a-block in front of the hotel that they extended out into the street, interfering with the flow of foot traffic.

Scoubide was in his usual disguise which was no disguise at all, since he was so insignificant that he needed nonc. The criminals all knew his face very well; the non-criminals would never have noticed it, narrow as it was with an insignificant little moustache—a thin face upon a thin body. His uniform was a pair of neutral-coloured slacks, a short-sleeved white sports shirt, and a camera and light meter slung about his neck. Like the rest of the crowd he was moving casually between the parked motor monsters and, too, like them he looked up upon the elite of several continents gathered upon the terrace and for a fraction of a second he discovered the Colonel. Roquebrun caught the practically imperceptible nod before Scoubide passed on and the old Resistance fighter said to himself, '*Oh, ho! So it will be tonight, then. And tomorrow, friend Scoubide, you will be eligible for yet another ribbon to string across your chest and I shall have to hide from your effusions. Perhaps then, if this is how things are, I can satisfy my client, here to whom I'm indebted for a really excellent piece of business, and he is the kind of man one could rely upon.*'

Fairchild said, 'I'd give a lot to know how the trick was worked.'

'So would I,' said Salmon.

Roquebrun said, 'If I tell you the story, Mr Fairchild, have I your word of honour not to pub-

lish anything in any way, shape, form or manner
—no hint of it to any reporter; no searching out
of things on your own until . . .'

Fairchild said eagerly, 'Yes. For how long?'

'Well, shall we say,' replied the Colonel, 'until
it is quite obvious that there is no longer any
need for not publishing it.'

'I promise,' said Fairchild quietly, and Roquebrun knew he would never break it.

Salmon said eagerly, 'If I promise, too, would
there be a film in it for me?'

The Colonel reflected. 'Yes, I should think a
most excellent one, almost everything for which
you could ask.'

'Girls?' queried Salmon.

'Girls,' the Colonel answered him and his eye-
balls never wavered the fraction of a millimetre.

'What's the yarn?' Fairchild asked impatiently.

'Well, you see,' the Colonel replied, 'there was
not one, but two kidnappings.'

'Two kidnappings!' exclaimed Fairchild incredulously, 'I don't get it. What was the other?'

'On an evening like this, some three weeks ago,
during the course of a party given by the de
Merseraux family at their villa Rose d'Or,'— (and
here Roquebrun turned politely to Salmon who
he knew spoke no French and translated, 'The
Golden Rose', and added, 'The golden rose has
been in the de Merseraux crest for centuries.')
—the de Merseraux grandchild was kidnapped.'

This bit of news, rather than forcing exclama-
tions from the two other men stunned them into

silence, for this was a name that not only they but, practically everyone in the civilized world knew, because of the de Merseraux cars. Almost every other car driven in France was a de Merseraux. They were exported all over the world; half a dozen airlines had the famous de Merseraux jet engine in their nacelles. It was reputedly one of the richest as well as most aristocratic families in France.

The newspaper publisher was the first to recover from his astonishment for the very good reason that he was a newspaper publisher. 'But,' he said, 'there hasn't been a line in the press. A story like that . . .'

'It was one of the conditions set by the kidnappers. If so much as a single word of the crime were to reach the press the child would be killed immediately.'

Salmon remarked, 'That's a new one in the snatch racket. What was that for?'

'Shall we say that the French style is slightly more subtle?' said the Colonel.

The waiter came by and looked at their empty glasses. Fairchild signalled with a wave of his hand for a refill.

'Intelligent,' the Colonel continued. 'They didn't want strangers intruding. Do you remember in your own Hauptman case how many outsiders, who had nothing to do with the Lindbergh kidnapping and didn't have the child, attempted to collect the ransom?'

Fairchild, now thoroughly fascinated, sat up

and said, 'Come on, Colonel, give! You say it was the de Merseraux grandchild?'

'Yes,' said the Colonel, 'As you know, Giscard de Merseraux is the head of the enterprise. His eldest son, René, is following in his father's footsteps, a serious and talented young man who married a young and beautiful girl of an excellent French family several years ago. The baby, a boy, François de Merseraux, eight months old, was their first-born. The young de Merserauxs, who own the villa where they came for the summer, are a very popular couple on the Riviera.'

Fairchild wanted to get down to cases. He snapped, 'How was it done?'

'The de Merserauxs gave a party; one of those Saturday night affairs. Everyone was there.'

Fairchild interrupted and then was sorry he had, 'What do you mean by "everyone"?'

The Colonel regarded him with some astonishment over the rim of his second Scotch, and then realized that even so sophisticated a man as the American publisher might not be acquainted with the *mores* of the coast. He said, 'Well, there are roughly two kinds of parties given here; the intimate, for a few selected friends—usually twenty-five to thirty people—and the other kind which includes everyone, and by everyone I mean anyone who is somebody; that is to say, well-known for being at the top of his or her field, profession or business. There are mystery millionaires and their mistresses, if the latter are sufficiently beautiful; titles, genuine and assumed; painters, writ-

ers, musicians, lawyers, heads of firms who are
socially acceptable or because they breed horses
or race ocean-going yachts, and of course, the
usual aviary of acceptable deviates. Say between
seventy-five and a hundred. You would have been
asked, if you had been here. They would have
known somebody who knew you.'

'I get it,' said Fairchild, 'Sorry. Please go on.'

'The Rose d'Or is a sprawling villa cresting one
of the hills behind Cannes, with a glorious view,
extensive grounds and is reached by one of those
winding, mountain roads which you may or may
not have encountered, that go up into the hills
overlooking the sea. The child's bedroom was on
the ground floor. It was a hot night; the window
was open. When, after the last guest had departed,
and the nursemaid went into the baby's room to
check that it was sleeping and not in need of anything, she found its cot empty and a note.'

Salmon did not want to be left behind Fairchild
in savvy and said, 'Why the hell wasn't the woman
in the room with the kid all the time?'

'Because,' replied the Colonel, 'she was helping
out in the kitchen, assisting with the women's
wraps and generally making herself useful.' He
then, under the perplexed stare of the two men,
felt constrained to explain, 'You see, in France
no matter how rich you are, you are also practical
to the point of wholly unnecessary penurious-
ness. On the night of a party like that, even though
if they wished they could hire a full catering service, all the regular staff in the house fall to and

do double duty. I gather that the nanny did the checking of coats, then she cut bread in the pantry, then she did a bit of needlework when a shoulder strap broke, or a woman needed some other kind of attention. She also helped out at the buffet and the washing up. From time to time she, of course, did pop in to have a look at her charge, satisfied herself and returned. But towards the end of the evening as the guests began to depart, she was busy for a longer time with their coats and no doubt collecting tips. When she finally went to the room, there was only the note.'

Fairchild said, 'Do you know what it said?'

Although every word of the message was burned into the brain of the antique dealer, he replied, 'It said in effect that they had the child; that the police would never find them; that the family would be hearing from them and added a secret code word which would identify them as the kidnappers.' The Colonel paused for a moment and then said, 'And they added a grim warning. If so much as a single word of this affair were to be leaked to the press, or appear published in any form, the baby would be destroyed immediately. They wrote, "There is nothing more simple than to snuff out the life of a baby and dispose of the small remains".'

Arnold Salmon said, 'Jesus Christ!' and shuddered, for since he was a picture-maker, he thought in pictures.

'Yes,' the Colonel nodded, 'there is actually nothing more difficult to dispose of without a trace than an adult, human cadaver. But a tiny baby

... no bigger than a dog ... ?'

Fairchild thought to himself: *My God, you're tough! I'll bet you didn't get those scars for nothing.* And then aloud he said, a word so that it stood alone in quotes: 'They.'

'Yes, of course. The police noted this at once. "We" in the kidnappers' note; more than one person—perhaps a gang.'

Salmon was puzzled, too. He said, 'If they made the kid's life a condition of keeping it out of the newspapers, why didn't they make the same condition for keeping the cops out of it?'

'Intelligence,' replied Roquebrun. 'Affairs can be kept out of the French press. Nothing can be kept from one or more of the various departments and services of the French police, of which there are at least six. Besides which, on the night of the kidnapping the place was swarming with *gendarmes* and plain-clothes men.'

Salmon cried, 'What? You mean right under their noses?'

The Colonel said, 'The plain-clothes men were not looking for a kidnapping. They were there to see that no one got off with any jewellery or summer furs.'

'And the *gendarmes?*' queried Fairchild.

'Parking cars and checking that no uninvited or unauthorized guests entered the premises. On loan from the Cannes *Commissariat*. In France, you know, when you give a big party, you may hire off-duty policemen and pay them to function at your affair.'

Fairchild said, 'Footprints?'

'Ambiguous. The grass leading from the window disturbed, but by the time the crime was discovered the blades had resumed most of their original position and only indicated that one person had actually removed the child.'

'With the rest of the gang waiting in the get-away car,' Salmon concluded, since he was familiar with the plots of a number of films he had produced.

'Uhuh,' grunted Fairchild. 'Then a get-away car? Tyre tracks?'

Colonel Roquebrun laughed. He said, 'There were fifty-three cars parked there. You could have your choice of tyre tracks, my friend: Rolls Royces, Bentleys, de Merserauxs, Mercedes, Jaguars, B.M.W.s, Daimlers, Citroëns, Peugëots . . .'

'All inside the grounds?' asked Salmon.

'No,' the Colonel replied, 'just to make it more difficult, strung out for half a mile either side of the entrance. Actually the parking space in the driveway to the villa and down by the garage is limited. On that night it was reserved for the special V.I.P.s. There were two ambassadors, a Cabinet Minister and the *Préfet*. That's what the *gendarmes* were for. The cars strung out along the avenue; the early guests close to the entrance, the late-comers, as I said, often more than a quarter of a mile away. As they arrived the *gendarmes* would direct them to put their machines on the side of the road, examine their invitations; purely a formality, since practically every arrival was known to them—and the guests thereupon proceeded up to the villa on foot. Upon departing they returned in the same manner. Thus, ten minutes after the discovery of the snatch the biggest manhunt in France was under way, involving every agency of law enforcement—and we have many—including the army, the navy and the airforce.'

'My God!' said Salmon, 'You should have turned up something with all that, and considering the kidnappers couldn't have gotten very far.'

'But . . .' put in Fairchild.

'There wasn't a trace,' said the Colonel. 'Not a hint; not a clue. And the odds were all on the side of the police.'

'What do you mean by that?' Fairchild asked.

'It's a curious fact which has a particular bearing upon the number and nature of the crimes committed in this region, but the Côte d'Azur— let us say what we understand by that, the Riviera stretching from St Tropez to the Italian border— is a most difficult area from which to escape, if the authorities are made aware in time of the commission of a serious misdeed. To begin with, there are only two major roads paralleling the sea: the coast road and the new *autoroute*. To the east lies the Italian border with all its controls. The *autoroute* can be closed off at its entrances and exits. There is no problem setting up road blocks on the main coastal arteries. The point is that there are very few main roads leading off at right angles into the centre of France where miscreants might lose themselves. We can winkle any stranger out of a small mountain village. No private aircraft can take off either from the little airfield at Man-

delieu or the airport at Nice without a checkout.
And, of course, in any case of alarm, the airport
police will instantly double check-out every pas-
senger on commercial flights.'

Fairchild grunted. 'You must have ten thousand yachts, cabin cruisers, speedboats, fishing
smacks or dories strung out in the dozens of ports.
What about them?'

'The simplest to control,' said Roquebrun.
'Every harbourmaster knows the tenants of his
port. We have maritime police patrolling, riding
the fastest boats in the water, as well as helicopter
observation. From the moment the alarm went
out not a craft moved in or out of a harbour without being stopped, and even small vessels spotted
at sea between St Tropez and San Remo, which
must have been under way hours before the kidnapping took place, were stopped and interro-
gated, with the co-operation of the Italian police.
A regiment of alpine troops were flown in and
scattered through the hills. Technically and theoretically it was impossible for that child to have
been removed from France. And yet it was.'

'How did they know?'

'They didn't know,' replied the Colonel. 'I did.'

Salmon gaped and Fairchild cried, 'You? Why?
I don't understand.'

'Because,' said Roquebrun, 'the night after the
kidnapping I saw the kidnappers, with the de
Merseraux child and the get-away car removed
from Cannes and thence from France.'

Both men were now regarding the Colonel with
utter amazement and even some dawning disbe-

lief. Was the man out of his mind? Was this a fairy-tale? Hallucination of a fellow who had obviously at one time or another been battered about the head, and retailed to make an impression?

'And you didn't do anything about it?' Fairchild snapped.

The Colonel remained composed and even allowed himself a drink of his Scotch. 'At the time,' he said, 'I wasn't aware of what I was seeing.'

Taking in the antique dealer's words and his manner of speaking, Fairchild's suspicions were dispelled. The man was not fabricating. He asked, 'Where were you when, as you say, you saw this happening but were not aware of what you were seeing?'

The Colonel set down his glass, the noise of its making contact with the table drowned out by the hubbub all about, and replied, 'Sitting right here where I am now.'

It was Salmon who broke the stunned silence that followed by his plain, unvarnished statement of what was unquestionably a fact. 'Brother,' he said to Roquebrun, 'if you ever want to stop selling pewter piss pots and write suspense scripts, come and see me.' And then the words came tumbling forth from the film producer, 'Was the ransom paid? Was the kid returned? Have they got them yet? Was the kid killed?'

The Colonel suppressed a smile and said to Salmon, 'You are obviously the kind of man who would read the end of the script before the beginning. I will satisfy your curiosity. No ransom was paid. François de Merseraux is safely back with his parents and in excellent health, the last time I saw him.'

Salmon cried, 'You call *that* ending my suspense?'

Fairchild took a long, deep draw at his bourbon and sighed, 'My God, and you've made me promise neither to print nor pursue this story you've got in your system?'

Roquebrun's eyes twinkled. He said, 'Your promise is still good?'

'Obviously.'

The Colonel nodded and then said, 'Well, then, let me think how best to make it clear to you what happened and how it was done.'

As soon as he had used the word 'think' the Colonel thought, and thoughts exceed the speed of sound, the speed of lightning, the speed of astronauts rushing through space, even the speed of light on its centuries of travelling from the most distant star. A whole sequence of events can rush through a man's mind while he is drawing a breath to continue speech; a week, a month, a year can pass by during the lighting of a cigarette. The Colonel now drew a packet of *Gauloises* from his pocket, offered one all around, was refused and extracting one, placed it between his lips, picked up a match book with the Carlton of Cannes monogram on the cover, and lit it.

The bell attached over the doorway of the entrance to Colonel Roquebrun's antique shop outside Vence, on the road to Grasse, put there to herald the arrival of any customer, jangled so violently just before six o'clock when the Colonel was rearranging some of his objects preparatory to closing the shop for the day and had his back to the door, that for a moment he thought that he might be under surprise attack from some marauder and grasped for the nearest weapon which happened to be a Spanish 15th Century, bell-mouthed blunderbuss. There was, of course, no charge in it, but the heavy iron of the barrel would make an excellent bludgeon, and the Colonel knew something about wielding such.

However, as it turned out, the Colonel was not in need of it for the impetuous visitor was Captain Claude Scoubide. The Captain was in a state, his usually smoothly combed hair was dishevelled, his open-necked shirt was in disarray, and his face as pale and strained as ever the Colonel—who was his friend—had seen it.

Before he could so much as open his mouth, Scoubide cried, '*Colonel!* Pierre! My friend! You must help me! They've stolen the de Merseraux baby! A clean get-away—but not a trace. A threat to kill in deadly earnest. We are at our wits' end. It is the crime of the decade. It is unequalled in its scope and impudence. You will have heard something, surely? You, or perhaps one of our . . .' He hesitated here for a fraction of an instant, '. . . our friends. If so I beg of you do not keep even the slightest hint of information from me. It is a matter of the life or death of an innocent child.'

If the Captain had not been in such a complete state of shattered nerves the implication that he

would withhold criminal information from him
would have annoyed Colonel Roquebrun to the
point where his friendship for Scoubide would
not have prevented a cold rebuke. For if there was
one thing the Colonel stood upon above all, it was
his dignity and his honour. But in this case it was
obvious that the Captain of Detectives was not
himself and besides which, Roquebrun had heard
nothing whatsoever of any such crime. He said,
'Come, hold on! Pull yourself together, friend
Scoubide. I don't even know what you're talking
about. Give me the details.'

The Captain secured control over himself and
did so, although it was obvious that the rehearsing
of the inexplicability of the affair was once more
bringing him into agitation.

The Colonel, having digested the information,
was silent for a moment and then his instincts of a
gentleman made him feel that even though he was
in grave trouble, somehow Captain Scoubide's
precipitation was in a way an affront to him, even
though it appeared to be no more than an an-
guished cry for help. And so he said, 'Well, and
why have you come rushing to me in this manner, almost as if . . .'

The implication ought to have been plain to
Scoubide but he was too far gone to recognize it
and replied, 'Because I am convinced it is the
work of a gang, a brilliantly planned and executed crime, clever, thorough, experienced, dev-
ilishly cruel, uncompromisingly brutal.'

'And so,' the Colonel concluded for him, 'hav-

ing reached the end of your own resources without having found a single, solitary lead or idea
as to the manner in which this might have been
carried out, you are therefore compelled to con-
clude that because of its very cleverness that my
four friends are concerned . . .'

Here Captain Scoubide was able to comprehend,
even through his agitation, the horror of what he
had implied and cried, 'No, no, no! I meant only
whether you might have heard something. Twice
before I have come to you for assistance because
of your former connections during the war, of
which we are all so proud. Your ear to the ground,
your knowledge of the *Côte,* and . . . well . . .' and
here he shut himself off before he put himself into
worse trouble than he already was.

It was now the Colonel's turn to be somewhat
embarrassed, for he knew very well that the Captain was thinking of the episode of the picture
thieves in which his friends, the Zoo Gang, had
not been exactly innocent, even though their mo-
tives had been noble-minded and charitable. But
this was something else; a kidnapping, the most
cruel crime that can be visited upon human beings. The stealing of an infant child, a first-born,
was not to be thought of.

And so he put off his choler and said, 'Up to this
minute I have heard nothing, not so much as a
whisper or a rumour, nor I am sure have my
friends.'

'But you have not spoken to them or heard from
them?'

'No,' replied the Colonel, 'I have not.' He then said, 'Who was there at the party? Have you followed up that line?'

All of Scoubide's despairing agitation returned as he clapped the heel of one hand to his forehead and cried, 'Who was there? Why, as I told you, *everyone* was there. Do you expect me to be interrogating the Duc de Vallauris, the Marquis de Belgrade, Professor Laurent, the discoverer of Lymphard and a Nobel Prize-Winner in science? Or Monsieur Halle the Academician? Or Madame Richards, the wealthy American lady whose charities and foundations here on the Coast are a byword? Or the Cotards, the Florents, the Besalliers, or the Vinsaints? Or would you have us waste time upon the usual assortment of queers who were present, on the theory that one of them might suddenly have succumbed to a yearning for the motherhood denied him? Besides,' Scoubide added irritably, 'they had one and all departed and were either at home or on their way there when the loss of the child was discovered. Naturally we have kept them under a certain amount of discreet observation but I can assure you there is nothing to be gained from that source. A gang that for audacity and organization has not been matched since . . .'

'Have you a full list of the guests?' the Colonel queried.

'But of course,' and producing it from his pocket, Scoubide handed it over.

The Colonel let his eyes run quickly down the page. The Captain had been right, 'everyone' had been there and in his first perusal no one upon whom so much as a breath of suspicion might rest; no bogus Counts, or unidentified foreigners.

Scoubide, as though he had been following the Colonel's line of thought, said, 'We know every one of them. The majority have been living here on the Coast, or as you will have noted, on the Italian side for at least the last twenty-five years.'

The Colonel asked, 'May I keep it?'

'Yes, of course,' Scoubide replied, 'but the gang . . .'

'Yes,' agreed the Colonel, 'quite possibly a gang. Well, sooner or later they must surface somewhere, somehow, when there's a ransome note . . .'

'*Mon Dieu*, Pierre,' cried the unhappy Scoubide, 'can you not see here that sooner or later will not do? That it must be practically immediately? I must find them! I must have news! They have said that if this breaks into the press they'll kill the child. They will do so. How long do you think we can keep the newspapers away from this one? Rumour, gossip, a careless servant? They will kill the child but they will still demand the ransom and the parents will never know. They will have to pay, hoping the child is alive and receiving a corpse in return. Can't you see the absolute fiendish impasse?'

The Colonel nodded carefully, for he was now thinking of the mother and father of the lost infant and what they must be suffering and was moved. He said, 'Yes, I can, Claude. As I told you I have heard nothing. But I will ask all my friends whether so much as the faintest of whispers has reached them, though it is probably too soon.'

Due to this state of nerves Captain Scoubide's gratitude was as shattering and embarrassing as his agitation had been and he took his friend by the arm, crying eagerly, 'You will do this at once for me? You will perhaps contact them immediately . . . Oh, but of course, discreetly . . . You will see them? You will let me know within the hour? You will . . .'

The Colonel said, 'I will, I'm afraid, do what I was about to do when you came bursting in here, which was to close the shop and keep an appointment on the Carlton terrace with my friend Joel Howard who has arrived here unexpectedly on business and has invited me to join him there for drinks and dinner afterwards. Perhaps later in the evening I will be able to contact one or two of my friends.'

'And you will tell me at once if you hear anything?' Scoubide completed. 'It isn't for me that I ask, but these miserable, unhappy parents. I have seen them; you have not.'

'I know them,' the Colonel said, 'I have that much imagination. I will do what I can.'

'And it was on that night,' put in the quick-witted Fairchild, when the Colonel had reached that point in his narration, 'when you were sitting with Joel Howard—who, incidentally I know— where you say practically you are sitting now, that you saw the de Merseraux child removed from France?'

'Yes,' said the Colonel, 'that is so.'

But it was the equally shrewd Salmon who asked the pertinent question. 'Just exactly what was it you saw, Colonel?'

But before the Colonel could reply an interruption occurred which could not but help engage their attention. A pair of typical Riviera playboys, their coloured scarves perfectly and artistically tucked into the throats of their shirts to match their expensive slacks, their hair slicked back, slipped between the crowded aisles and tables to stand before the two girls nearby, one of them to remark smoothly, 'Would there be any objection to our joining you ladies?'

The three at the neighbouring table fell silent to watch the byplay. It was the golden-haired one who, in an alluringly throaty voice replied, 'I am sure you will excuse us, *Messieurs,* but we already have an engagement.'

One of them said, 'Of course. *Pardon.* Perhaps another time,' and they turned away, not at all put out.

Fairchild could not help himself. His eyes were caught up in those of the blonde who had spoken and he saw the soft, tremulous lips and said to himself in admiration: *'By God, she's got nerve! She gambled even though I have been ignoring her,'* and then again, too, he said to himself, *'Oh, what the hell! You only live once. Except I don't like Salmon knowing. However . . .'* His eyes returned her pleading signal accepting the rendezvous. She smiled like an angel.

The Colonel said in almost a far-away voice, 'The blonde one, Ilse, has a baby. Hanne-Lore, the

other, is reputed to be an excellent cook as well
as . . .' He did not finish that sentence, but then
added, 'They both come from the Rhineland, near
Mainz.'

Fairchild was startled. 'A baby?' he said. 'I
thought—well—I mean, that girls like that knew
how to take care of themselves.'

'They do,' replied the Colonel, 'but sometimes
they are known to fall in love before the man
walks out. I doubt if the father, a wealthy South
American, even knows that he has a child.'

It was all Fairchild could do to keep from turning around to look once more at the blonde girl,
for somehow what Roquebrun had told him made
her even more desirable. So they could fall in love
. . . All his male vanity was stimulated and excited
to the point where he did not even think it odd
the Colonel's bringing up the subject in such a
manner.

But Arnold Salmon said, 'You seem to know all
about everybody and everything around here.'

The Colonel looked out over the scene of the
teeming Croisette. The crowds had now increased.
A young artist paused to hold up a number of
wholly execrable paintings he was trying to ped-
dle. Further down the street somewhere a beatnik
was playing a mandolin, accompanied by a slat-
ternly girl who sang.

'It is a village,' he said, his intonation somewhat
far away. 'In fact the entire *Côte* is just one main
street strung together.'

For during the interruption the speeding film of

his mind had been unreeling the next portion of his narration.

'No gang,' said Antoine Petitpierre, the Tiger.

'No gang,' said Jean Soleau, the Elephant.

'Hmmm . . . Well, perhaps a gang—but an extraordinarily clever one,' said Alphonse Cousin, the Wolf, owner of the Bar-Restaurant *'Le Perroquet Rouge'*, where the old Zoo Gang were now meeting with their ex-leader in a back room, with the Pernod and brandy bottles on the table.

'No gang,' said the Leopard, Gaston Rives.

It was in this manner that they replied to the query of Colonel Roquebrun as to their opinion of the de Merseraux kidnapping.

'So,' the Colonel said. He addressed the Tiger, 'Why do you say no gang?'

The carnation grower answered, 'Too many police about. Gangs don't like to operate in the presence of so much law.'

'And you, friend Elephant?'

The little man replied, 'Outside of us, I can't think of any gang that would have the brains to pull off something so perfect. There is too much intelligence in the job. Besides which, as we know and even learned in the old days to add to our problems, the escape routes from the coast are strictly limited. I should think one would have heard something, some rumour, if nothing but an uneasiness amongst the legitimate criminals who wouldn't be sympathetic to this sort of thing. The police must be rooting amongst them like wild boars.'

The Colonel turned to the Wolf and said, 'You voted for a gang. Why?'

The Wolf idly fingered the guest list and said, 'No motive here. One knows them all; or at least something about them, for I have not yet had the honour of entertaining Academicians at the *Perroquet Rouge*. By the way, what are the checks against a number of these names?'

The Colonel replied, 'Information supplied by Scoubide. Those who are known to have left the Côte d'Azur within twenty-four hours of the party.' He took the list and said, 'The two Academicians, Professor Laurent and Monsieur Halle returned to Paris, as did the Minister of Culture and Monsieur Gaillard, the racehorse owner and his wife. Madame Richards flew to Boston; the Roderigos, the ex-Spanish Ambassador, returned to Madrid; and the Florents went to Lisbon to visit Madame Florent's mother to show her their infant girl. Monsieur Cotard had business in London, banking; the Conte di Salerno and the Contesse flew to Rome; the Marchesa Respigi was chauffeur-driven to Florence; and the rest of the Italians scattered back to Mortola, San Remo and Portofino. Oh yes, and Monsieur Chagres, the owner of the Chagres Gallery has gone by train to Munich ostensibly to buy some German impressionists.'

'Was there a border check?' the Elephant enquired.

The Colonel nodded, 'Most discreet, but thorough. Scoubide is no fool, though I gather that if he doesn't soon get some kind of a break on this miserable crime, he'll blow his brains out.' The Colonel then turned to the fat man and said, 'Well, and then, friend Leopard, that leaves you with your vote of "No gang"—Why?'

The Leopard thought upon his reply for so long that the silence in the back room of the bar had to be broken by some of its members filling their glasses again, and when he did reply his answer came as a shock to them all. What he said was, 'Do you remember the Antelope?' The stillness that followed upon this was thicker and heavier than that which had preceded it and there was even a feeling of outrage and indignation upon the faces of the others, for by agreement the Antelope was never referred to by any of them. His name was connected with heartbreak and one of their worst failures. It was over and done with; each one had had to bear a certain responsibility in the fiasco and they did not wish to be reminded of it. For he had been loved for himself as well as his contribution to the underground warfare of the famous Zoo Gang.

The Antelope had been the sixth member of the Zoo Gang of which the Tiger, the Elephant, the Leopard, the Wolf and the Fox had survived. He had been a boy of twenty-two, a cripple due to a bout with poliomyelitis, the dread disease before the days of Salk, and hence of no interest to the Germans as a labour conscript. His cover name of 'Antelope' had been awarded him because of his extraordinary speed of mind. He was the son of a well-to-do family, wore steel leg braces and was able to get around by virtue of a specially

constructed car. Hence he was invaluable to the
others as a courier as well as for his brilliance. In
addition to which he was a handsome boy, an en-
dearing fellow and the pet of them all.

But even his ability to think quickly did not
save him when betrayed by a collaborator, he was
arrested by the Gestapo. The Germans suspected
his affiliation with the Zoo Gang, although they
did not know who the others were, and so
they questioned him. He did not talk and when
they were finished, he was no longer a cripple; he
was dead.

The elaborate plan evolved by the other five for
his rescue failed. It was one of those bitter catas-
trophes which the law of averages often imposes
upon those who are too uniformly successful, one
of those things where at the appointed moment
none of them were where they should have been,
or did what they ought to have done. The boy
was killed and they never forgave themselves. His
name evoked the most terrible guilt feelings, aug-
mented by the fact that they had never been able
to lay hands upon the man who had betrayed him.

The Colonel said bitterly, 'In God's name, why
do you bring that up? I thought it was agreed between us never . . .'

A stubborn look came over the round face of
the Leopard and for a moment only his asthmatic
wheezing filled the room before he said, 'Forgive
me, but—well—because of something which occurred the other day, about which I was trying to
make up my mind whether to speak to you or not.'

There was still hostility in the eyes of the others as they waited for him to go on.

'As you know,' the fat man said, 'I was there when they came into Mauro's restaurant in Aix, when they took the Antelope and with him one other—a man I did not know. I was sitting, if you remember, several tables away, having not yet received the signal from the Antelope to make contact with him. The Germans came in in force, and since our boy could walk only with difficulty and the aid of underarm crutches, they simply picked him up bodily. The other fellow they hustled away roughly and with considerably more violence than necessary. I was convinced then that I was looking upon a collaborator who had betrayed the Antelope.'

The Colonel said, somewhat testily, 'Yes, yes, you told us of that at the time, and your suspicions that the Germans were using too much violence upon a man who was offering no resistance appeared justified.' It was often a trick of the Gestapo to arrest the betrayer as well as the betrayed so as to divert suspicion from the former and after a period of time he would be released. 'We looked high and wide for the fellow of your description and never found him. He might have been a *collaborateur,* as you said. He might also have been one from the British section unknown to us, equally betrayed and swallowed up by the Gestapo.'

'Yes, that's true,' wheezed the Leopard, 'as I admitted at the time. But remember, I am the only one who saw him. I should not have brought up the subject except, as I say, for something which happened the other day.'

They were all on the alert now. The Leopard continued, 'You know that big houses as well as big commercial establishments all have their own electricians, or large electrical contracting companies that have a number of workers who are familiar with the lay-out and who can be called in immediately when there is some kind of failure. But sometimes there is a short and a fuse blown, or the current fails due to some more major problem at an hour when everything in the electrical line is closed, or the man familiar with that particular lay-out is sick or away, or in some way unavailable. In the emergency you then call up electricians right and left, trying to find one who will come and at least do a temporary job and restore power and light. Afterwards you say to your friends, "We were fortunate, we were able to get a little man to come over at that hour and he fixed it." Well, the other night, about a week ago, I was that little man. I was called in where all the lights had gone out to the great embarrassment of the people involved. It did not take me long to find the trouble, construct a temporary bridge, restore the current and the light . . .'

He hesitated for just a fraction of a moment during which time the Colonel was able to get in an intense 'Yes?'

'And in that light I saw, or thought I saw—no, I'll swear to it—the collaborator, *my* collaborator, whom I saw arrested that day with the Antelope and who has never been seen since. He was thirty years older, but it was the same man.'

The Tiger, in the gentlest of voices that contained the most unutterable menace, said, 'You mean I can get my hands on him?'

The Leopard shrugged and said, 'It was a long time ago and yet I feel sure that I am right.'

The Colonel asked harshly, 'Do you know who it was?'

The Leopard nodded quite unmelodramatically in the direction of the paper lying on the table before them and said, 'His name is on that list.'

'Holy smokes!' Salmon cried. 'The Kraut with the picture gallery!'

The Colonel did not reply.

But Fairchild, leaning across the table towards the Colonel, said, 'Was there a check mark against that name?'

'Yes,' replied the Colonel, 'there was.'

'So you had him.'

'No, we did not,' replied Roquebrun, 'All we had was the possibility that one of our old group had re-identified a man who could have sold out the one of us we loved best. But there was nothing to connect or add up that an old collaborator with blood on his hands, who managed suddenly to surface as an important citizen on the *Côte d' Azur,* would become a kidnapper. And I put this to my group to receive the reply from the Elephant that a man capable of such a deed as to betray a crippled boy to his death might very well add up to anything.'

'But,' said Fairchild shrewdly, 'he was on the

short list of those who left town, wasn't he?'

'Yes, he was on the short list.' The Colonel hesitated.

'The Dutchman went to Munich,' Salmon said excitedly.

'A number of others left France at the same time as well, so . . .'

'Yes—and . . . ?' put in Salmon, now breathlessly involved.

'So,' said the Colonel, 'I put my friends to checking them all. They're very good at that.'

'And . . . ?' This time the query came simultaneously from both men.

The Colonel replied, 'They made one slip—one move too many.'

'They? The kidnappers? So there *was* more than one?'

'Yes.'

'So you knew who had kidnapped the de Merseraux child?'

Salmon started to say 'The Kraut . . .' but Fairchild waved him to silence.

'Yes, we knew, and also we knew where the child was,' the Colonel replied.

'My God,' said Fairchild, 'and you didn't do anything about it?'

The Colonel said quietly, 'We had not a single iota of proof. We knew and it brought us no nearer to the baby who, we were now aware, at any moment stood within a hair's breadth of death if there was a single wrong step. A ransom equivalent to five million dollars had been demanded.'

The dilemma reduced the two other men at the table to a bewildered silence which was only broken by Salmon who said, 'By God, and then on top of that came the Florent kidnapping. How was that done? Was it the same gang—I mean, the one you suspected . . . ?'

'No, no, not at all,' the Colonel replied, 'I told you that the de Merseraux snatch was not a gang. The Florent one was. Classic, I should say: broad daylight total surprise, confusion, get-away car and all.'

Fairchild had a good look at the Colonel and then said, with a new note in his voice, 'You saw that one, too?'

The Colonel replied, 'If you sit long enough on this terrace you will see not only everybody you have ever known, but a great many strange things happening.'

Salmon said, 'Okay, Colonel, give! How was it done?'

The Colonel cleared his throat with just a hint of suggestion and Fairchild immediately signalled for another round.

'It was shortly after the Florents were reported returned with their child from Lisbon. They had driven back. The miscreants had observed that it was the habit of Madame Florent towards evening, before returning to their penthouse, pushing the baby in its pram, to leave it outside the Florent shop for a moment while she went inside and had a word with her husband. The jewellery shop, of course, has all sorts of devices within to guard

against smash-and-grab robberies, or plain ordinary stick-ups, but nothing outside to give an
alarm and with, as you see, the crowds passing by
it was no problem for the kidnapper to pluck the
child out of its pram.'

'You mean, just like that?' said Salmon. 'Where
was the rest of the gang?' he queried.

'Nicely distributed,' was the Colonel's answer.
'As you can see, the Florent shop is on the corner
exactly opposite from where we are sitting. In the
side street was a large, wholesaler's lorry with the
wholesaler making a delivery of sacks of onions
to a tradesmen's door of the hotel. Parked in front
of him was a smaller van belonging to a florist,
likewise engaged in delivering carnations by the
hundreds to the Carlton for their table decorations and other floral requirements. And in front
of the Florent shop was stationed an electrician's
van, and the electrician was just engaged in pack-
ing his tools into a large box, preparatory to entering the hotel here.'

Fairchild, who had been listening with his chair
tipped slightly back, looking down into the amber
of the bourbon in his glass, now raised his eyes to
the Colonel and in them was bewilderment and
behind the bewilderment, the beginning of a
dawning horror.

'So when Madame Florent emerged from the
shop,' the Colonel continued, calmly, although he
was aware of his host's scrutiny, 'she screamed;
there was a hubbub; a passerby cried that a man
had taken the child and entered a car; another

pointed to a blue Peugeot identifiable by a luggage rack on the roof and said, "There, I think it
was that car." At that moment fortuitously, but
apparently just too late, a police car happened by.
You can imagine the shouting and pointing. The
police car took off after the Peugeot, and the
Peugeot went tearing down the Croisette. Monsieur Florent emerged from the shop; more policemen gathered with, of course, spectators, getting in the way. As I say, a classic.'

'The cops chasing the get-away car?' queried
Salmon.

'They caught up with him just below the Casino. Of course there was no baby. When the police questioned the driver as to why he had fled
before them, he replied quite sensibly that hearing
the sirens, and with the heavy traffic on the
Croisette, cars parked all along the kerb and a
slow line of gapers crawling down one lane, he
had speeded up to get out of the way of the police,
until he could find an opening to the right, to
give them free passage. And besides which,' the
Colonel added, 'it turned out that the man was a
local, well-known in the district. The police immediately blocked off the area and searched every
car and vehicle parked there, but no baby. A disappearance quite as complete, and to the poor
police as baffling as that of the de Merserauxs.'

Fairchild asked, and for the first time there was
a grating note in his voice, 'So where was the
baby?'

'Why, in and out of the Hotel Carlton three

times during the searches. You are familiar, I am
sure, with the game of Rugby—it is very like your
American football, is it not? The passing, I mean.'

'Oh, Christ!' Salmon almost yelled.

'The man who picked up the child had a small
piece of sticky tape prepared which he applied to
its mouth so that there would be no cries, passed
it safely to the electrician who popped it into his
empty box and entered the hotel, while the first
man decoyed the police car out of the area. By the
time the other police were searching the vehicles
the baby had been passed from the electrician to
the florist, from the florist to the merchant of onions. By this time the original kidnapper in the
Peugeot, freed of suspicion, had driven back and
around by the hotel, received the final pass from
the onion dealer, and drove off with the child to
its hiding place.'

Salmon's mind, ordinarily quick, did not make
the connection simply because he was seeing the
scene in pictures: the baby stuffed into the electrician's repair kit, thence into one of those long
boxes of carnations characteristic of the region,
and finally into a sack of onions. He said, 'My
God, they could have killed it!'

The Colonel said, 'Actually, you have no idea
how hardy babies are and what they can take. Besides, the men were very gentle and apparently
care had been taken so that there was no chance
of stifling the child.'

The horror had now fully displaced any bewilderment that the newspaper publisher might have

felt and he said coldly, 'Are you trying to tell us, Colonel, that it was you and your friends whom you call the Zoo Gang, who were actually involved in this ghastly crime?'

The Colonel appeared quite unperturbed by the icy tone and said, 'I was certain it would be obvious to you that this was the case.'

The penny had dropped with Salmon, too, now and his eyes were popping, and it seemed to him the ground was shaking under his feet with what he was hearing. 'You? You did that?' He stammered, 'Y-y-you?'

'Yes,' the Colonel replied. 'A child, another kidnapping was needed to—well—as you Americans put it, to take the heat off the de Merseraux affair. I told you that we knew the de Merseraux baby was a hair's breadth from death. We had to give the newspapers something to write about.'

Fairchild spoke again, his voice still cold, 'And your choice of the Florent baby?'

The Colonel nodded, 'You've guessed it, sir. Since it was only to be a temporary measure, doesn't it strike you as perhaps a particularly fortunate choice, in view of the fact that at one time Monsieur Florent had sent the Antelope and God knows how many other noble and self-sacrificing Frenchmen to their death by his treachery?'

Fairchild, now quite pale, was far ahead of his companion and his voice sank almost to a whisper as he said, 'My God! The cops haring off after the wrong man; the carefully timed searches of the three vans while the baby was in and out of the hotel—You don't mean to tell me that the police . . . ?'

The Colonel nodded carefully and said, 'You see, of course, why that story, or at least that part of it, is not publishable. I had some difficulty in persuading a friend of mine.' And with that extraordinary, extra-dimensional speed of thought, even as he raised his Scotch once more to his lips, his mind was back to the evening he had summoned Captain Scoubide to his shop a week after the detective's original visit.

'Captain Scoubide,' the Colonel said, 'I have begun to take a serious interest in the case of the de Merseraux child.'

It was close to midnight and they were sitting in the far corner of Roquebrun's antique shop where he had a small desk which he used for as much of an office as he needed. It was illuminated by a single green-shaded lamp and the blinds of the windows were drawn. There was a bottle of brandy on the table for the Colonel and Pernod for Scoubide. They could not have been more isolated had they been alone on the moon.

'*Dieu!*' cried the Chief of Detectives, 'then you have heard something at last! For God's sake tell me! I'm about to lose my reason.' The little man had lost eight pounds, his face was grey and his eyes red from lack of sleep.

'You must hold on to your reason,' Roquebrun said, and poured his friend a large *pastis* to help him do so, 'particularly in view of what I am about to ask of you.'

'Ask of me anything that you will!' Scoubide cried, 'Anything! If only you can help me.'

The antique dealer regarded his old friend with something like pity as he thought how soon the Captain would backtrack on that statement. He said, 'I'm going to ask you to co-operate in a crime—the worst crime, in my opinion, on the books.'

The pleading had gone out of the detective's face. He took a long draught of his Pernod and now looked upon the Colonel with something like suspicion. He knew him well. 'A crime?'

'Yes. A duplicate almost of the one you are trying to solve. I'll tell you now that we are actually capable of perpetrating this without your assistance, but the danger to the de Merseraux baby is so great that we prefer not to take chances. Therefore I take you into my confidence.'

Scoubide cried, 'The danger to the baby? Then you've found out something? You know?'

The Colonel said, 'We know how the child was spirited out of France, and we know where it is.'

Aided by the jolt from the milky liquor and his fatigue forgotten, the words came tumbling from Scoubide, 'You know? You have found it? And you've not told me before—you've not moved? Knowing the anguish, knowing the danger, knowing all? In God's name, Pierre, why haven't you . . . ?'

'For just the reason of this outburst. You would go rushing in like bulls in china shops. Don't you understand that this is not a usual kind of kidnapping, where you descend upon some house in a field, or in the woods, surround it and take some Godforsaken idiots who thought they could get away with it? Here are brains! Make a single wrong move and the de Merseraux child is dead. Of this I can assure you.'

Scoubide stammered, 'Then w-what ...'

'We need time.'

'Time! Time!' echoed the detective harshly, 'We have no time! You know that if the press gets wind of the de Merseraux kidnapping the child is dead as well.'

'Yes, that's why we must buy time,' said the Colonel, 'with, as I say, another crime.'

'But this is impossible!' Scoubide cried.

'And yet just a moment ago,' Roquebrun said quietly, 'you were saying I might ask of you anything, anything at all, if I could help you.'

'But ...'

Roquebrun leaned forward, his brandy glass in his hand, and interrupted. 'You actually have no choice. You are between whatever you choose to call it: the devil and the sea, the frying pan and the fire. You want the de Merseraux child back alive, as I do. I am telling you that to move precipitously is to court final catastrophe. Yet the longer the search is delayed, increasingly greater are the chances that the press will get onto the fact that the de Merseraux heir is being held for a five-million-dollar ransom. My crime will put a stop to that.'

'How?'

'By giving the press an almost equally sensa-

tional story on which to concentrate. As long as
they are writing about mine with all their forces,
they won't be available for yours. Nor will they
be likely to discover it.'

The Detective said, '*Nom de Dieu!*' and took a
large gulp of his drink. Pernod is a liquid known
to expand the human afflatus, sometimes to the
danger point if taken in too large quantity, but it
will also bolster courage when needed. '*Nom de
Dieu,* Pierre!' he repeated, and looked helplessly
at the Colonel.

Roquebrun knew he had him. The combina-
tion of the situation, the drink and the fact that as
Chief of Detectives covering an area such as the
Riviera, Scoubide could not afford to be wholly
honest.

'It is not,' the Colonel soothed, 'as though it
were a genuine kidnapping. We would merely be
borrowing a baby for a short while.'

Scoubide said miserably, 'And whose do you intend to—well, as you say—borrow?'

The Colonel was wise enough not to reply immediately but set his glass down and tapped the
table meditatively with one of those fingers of his
on which there were no fingernails. He thought
that in all probability the same man who had
brought the poor Antelope to his death had betrayed *him* as well to the Gestapo. He seemed to
be meditating upon choices and finally said, 'Well,
we have thought perhaps the Florents'.'

'The Florents'? The jeweller's? My God, Pierre,
are you out of your mind? Why the Florents'?'

The Colonel ticked off his reasons, holding up
one nailless finger after another. 'They are rich.
They are world-prominent jewellers. They have a
child of approximately the same age as the de
Merseraux baby. It is easier to make off and conceal an infant than, say, a boy or girl of reason-
ing age. It will be the press sensation of the year
and it will turn the trick. Besides which,' the Colonel concluded and Scoubide was not too over-
stimulated or too tired to note that here the Colonel's mouth closed like a trap, 'besides which, I
don't like Monsieur Florent.'

And somehow it was this last statement and the
way he made it, and the way he looked which
practically decided Scoubide to go along with
him.

'How do you propose to do this?' he asked.

The Colonel told him.

The sheer audacity of it made Scoubide waver
again. He said, 'Pierre, I understand everything
you say, but I am not certain that we ...'

'Claude,' the Colonel said, 'if I promise you on
my honour as a Frenchman that, say, within four
days from the creation of my diversion you will
have the de Merseraux child safely back in its crib,
will you trust me?'

Scoubide heaved a long sigh. The milky Pernod
told him that either way he could be finished. If
the de Merseraux child died, his career was over
and he would be out of a job; if his connection
with the Colonel's scheme ever came to light, he
was equally done for. But the Colonel had spoken

of the word of honour of a Frenchman. It seemed his only hope. He said, 'I'll trust you, Pierre.'

The anger and horror had drained out of Fairchild and he found himself now looking upon the Colonel with an astonished admiration, for even as he had listened to the plot that the Colonel had hatched with a Captain of Detectives, he realized that actually the story was over and that both parents had their infants back safe and sound. True, the Florents had suffered, but it would seem that the Colonel and his friends had settled a legitimate vendetta, one that might otherwise have ended in a murder, and if there had been police connivance in this, well he, Fairchild, was in a different country from his own, and he also reflected that police were police in any country. The Colonel just was one tough cookie and so obviously were his friends. He did not like to think what it must have been like when back in the 1940s a member of the Gestapo had fallen into their hands. He murmured, 'All's well that ends well. Both babies nicely tucked in where they belong. No ransoms paid. Everybody happy. And your story, friend Roquebrun, is still as full of holes as a Swiss cheese or, to say the least, it isn't finished, is it?'

'That's right!' exclaimed Salmon, excitedly, 'The ear! The ear! That goddam ear! What about that? We've got you there, Colonel, and like Fairchild here says, a lot of other things you ain't told us.'

He was so agitated by the thought of the ear
that was and was not, that Fairchild was able casually to turn and steal a look at the girls behind
him. The blonde whom the Colonel had named
as Ilse was gazing dreamily into her glass of champagne from which bubbles were rising, caught by
the illumination of the terrace in a pretty ballet of
light. Fairchild thought that later on he would
be paying for that champagne in some manner or
other, but did not mind, particularly when she
looked up from her glass and smiled her delicious
invitation. She was an exciting creature and he
was excited. He turned quickly away, lest he be
observed by Salmon. He was not certain how he
would make connections later without the film
man knowing, but assumed that when cocktails
were over they could break up; the two girls
would remain there; Salmon would come back and
fetch his fox-coloured dream and Ilse would be
there, waiting for him.

'Yes, yes, the ear,' repeated the Colonel and
thought how close that had come to wrecking the
entire affair.

This meeting with Scoubide had taken place in
the back room of the bar *Le Perroquet Rouge,*
with the proprietor thereof, the Wolf, and the
three other members of the Zoo Gang in addition
to the Colonel present. It was the second evening
after the Florent kidnapping. In the presence of
the five men Scoubide looked even thinner, more
worn and miserable and cowed, somewhat like a
starved terrier. He was not a happy man and the

first sentence spoken by Colonel Roquebrun did nothing to ease him.

For the Colonel said, 'I won't beat about the bush as to why I have asked you to come here, Claude. We are in need of an ear.'

The detective's cry of 'What?' must have reached through the walls and into the main room of the bar-restaurant where the Wolf's wife was serving, but fortunately was drowned out by the clatter of glasses and dishes and talk. 'What are you saying? An ear? What kind of an ear?'

'A baby's ear,' replied the Colonel equably, trying by calmness to keep his friend from falling to pieces.

'A baby's ear? Scoubide repeated, mounting horror now replacing his first shock. 'In God's name, if one had such a thing, what are you proposing to do with it?'

'Post it to the Florents,' the Colonel said. 'Monsieur Florent is being difficult about the ransom.'

The Zoo Gang members thought that Scoubide's eyes would truly pop out of his head and his face was whiter than his accustomed open-necked sports shirt. 'Pierre! Have you gone completely out of your mind?' And then he said, 'Do you mean to say that you have really made a ransom demand upon the Florents? I thought . . .'

'Come, Captain,' said the Colonel, 'what is a kidnapping without a ransom demand? People might not believe it.'

'But what have you asked for?' Scoubide cried, his voice now hoarse with dismay.

'Something that Monsieur Florent apparently is

not prepared to grant, hence the ear.'

'Pierre, the sheer abomination of it!'

'The sheer sensation of it,' said the Colonel, 'The story will appear in every newspaper in Paris and London, and in New York as well. As you say, the sheer abomination of it.' And now the Colonel was aware that suddenly his old friend Scoubide was looking upon him with a certain loathing.

The Captain said, 'You, Colonel Pierre Roque-brun, whom I have looked up to for so many years with admiration and as my friend, a hero, a gentleman, a man of honour, would cause such needless suffering as actually to send them an ear of their child? Oh, no, no! It must be I who am losing my mind.' He rose from his chair and said, 'I think I must get out of here,' but found the bulk of the Leopard barring the door.

'I didn't say an ear of their child,' the Colonel said, 'I just said "an ear".'

'In the name of God, what do you mean by "an ear"? Is an ear to be had just like that?'

'With any luck, yes,' said the Colonel. 'We are coming into the weekend which is, particularly at this time of year, used by the French drivers to slaughter one another with their vehicles. The dead and the wounded over that period reads like a battle statistic from Vietnam. Somewhere in one of those crashes, I'll gamble fifty-to-one, there'll be a dead and mangled baby.'

'*Jésus!*' murmured Scoubide and closed his eyes for a moment.

'That's where you'll find me what I need.'

Scoubide muttered '*Jésus!*' again and then added, 'To send to innocent people? That I will not do!'

The Colonel, never raising his voice, said, 'I have told you that I don't like Monsieur Florent.'

And now Scoubide, opening his eyes, looked into the faces of the four members of the Zoo Gang: the Leopard, the Elephant, the Wolf and the Tiger, and what he saw there gave him a sudden and mysterious chill as though he were in the presence of something deadly of which he did not know, and yet because of that very deadliness, somehow a strange kind of justice was being done. This was what is known as the policeman's sixth sense.

'Never forget, Captain,' said the Colonel, 'that I have given you my word of honour that the de Merseraux infant will be returned unharmed.'

With a tremendous effort Scoubide recovered himself, looked once more around the room and then said to the Leopard, 'You may take your fat carcass away from the door. I will try.' He went out through the opening like a man half blind.

'Will he do it?' queried the Elephant.

'In for a penny, in for a pound, as my British friends used to say when I was over there,' the Colonel replied.

'And so,' concluded the Colonel, 'the Florents were persuaded to arrange for the return of the de Merseraux baby unharmed and in exchange received their own back, equally undamaged.'

It took at least ten seconds or more for what the Colonel had just said to penetrate to the two men. First they thought they had not heard correctly, and then that the strange antique dealer was really out of his mind and the story he had told them made up out of whole cloth. And finally, when they realized that he was serious and in full possession of his faculties their cries of 'WHAT?' blended, but the questions that would have followed were cut off by the fact that the Colonel had half risen from his chair and was looking the short distance up the street to the corner block where the Florent jewellery shop was located. He exclaimed, 'Ah! I thought so.'

For there came from that direction three shrill whistles, after which things began to happen in rapid succession. A large Black Maria drew up in front of the shop and disgorged a dozen armed police who quickly cordoned off a space outside and around the shop where four entered, and simultaneously the two German girls at the nearby table arose; their eyes wide with panic, their mouths no longer seductive but twisted in terror as they reached for their wraps. But it was too late.

Three big men in plain clothes were forcing their way through the crowded aisles as the guests on the terrace craned their necks to see what the excitement outside the Florent shop meant. They blocked the way of the girls and had them by the arms, though quite gently in deference to their beauty. One said in French, most politely, 'The *Mesdemoiselles* will be so good as to accompany us, and may we beg without a demonstration of any kind to indicate that they are under arrest.'

They went quietly and only Fairchild heard the sob of the exquisite Ilse.

Down by the shop matters had moved with equal speed. The four police who had entered now emerged with a man and a woman who had been handcuffed. The three on the terrace caught no more than a flash of them: the man, perhaps in his sixties, tall, powerfully built and even in handcuffs holding himself with an arrogance; the woman young, attractive and, Fairchild felt, attractive strangely in the sense that the two girls on the terrace had been. A kind of absurd, *non sequitur* thought flashed through his head and he wondered whether she too was German.

The two in handcuffs were hustled into the Black Maria. Police went into the shop again and emerged with an exodus of frightened customers and the sales staff consisting of three men and a woman who were allowed to go. The Black Maria drove off, leaving one policeman armed with a sub-machinegun standing on guard in front of the shop.

The guests on the terrace had settled back into their chairs again before Salmon managed to articulate, 'What the hell was that all about? A police raid? What was going on there—a stick-up?'

'The end of the story,' the Colonel said. 'I told you that if you remain sitting here a sufficient length of time you would see some strange things. You will have deduced by now that it was the Florents all the time.'

Fairchild had thought of it but rejected it as impossible. 'Are you trying to tell me . . . that the Florents were actually the kidnappers of the de Merseraux baby?'

'Yes,' said the Colonel, 'They were in desperate financial difficulties and in another few weeks would have lost all they had. As you will have gathered from what I have told you of his earlier reputation, Monsieur Florent was an expert in treachery and to have survived for so long the efforts of those who since the war have been hunting him, a clever man.'

Salmon was still catching up. He said, 'I don't get it. How could they have pulled the actual kidnapping part?'

The Colonel smiled. 'Since no one actually saw it, we shall have to conjecture until perhaps the Florents, in an attempt to save their necks, will tell us. The Florents waited for an appropriate moment when the party was not too much breaking up to make their farewells, and left. Then, I would have thought that the husband remained in the path leading to the entrance of the estate while his wife removed her shoes, slipped around the side of the house out of sight, crossed the lawn, snatched the baby after sealing it with a strip of adhesive tape over its mouth, hid it under her stole and left the note.

'The chance they took would have been if other guests had come out of the house to leave, but the husband who was lookout would then have signalled to his wife, probably saying loudly something like, "I've lost my wife. Have you seen her?

I thought she was following me. She must have stayed behind." But this did not occur and so they simply marched past the hired *gendarmes* who helped them extricate their car and drove away.'

Fairchild's eyes were now shining with excitement and wild for the parts of the rest of the story which were now publishable. 'But the get-away,' he cried, 'with the strange baby, with every border watched and, as you say, there are only two exits from France!' He had a flash of memory and exclaimed excitedly, 'And you say you saw it, but didn't realize ...'

'There is a third exit from the *Côte,* which is under the nose of everyone but nobody ever sees it, really, or thinks of it—not even our clever police.'

'And that is ... ?' queried Fairchild.

The Colonel did not reply. Instead they saw that he was looking out over their heads, looking across the Croisette to the ink-black Mediterranean. They turned to see what was engaging his attention. Halfway out of the harbour, diminishing in size, a pretty sight still illuminated from stem to stern, its flat funnels showing up under the lights, the huge transatlantic liner which earlier in the evening had been lying at anchor, broadside to the gay boulevard of Croisette, was heading out to sea.

Salmon at last became articulate, 'Oh, for God's sweet sake!' he said, 'And you saw them?'

The Colonel said, 'What I saw was the Mercedes

of Monsieur Florent arrive at the shop, stop for a
moment and then drive past where I was sitting,
with Monsieur and Madame Florent in it. Slung
in the back of the car was a carry-cot and there
was some luggage visible; not an unusual sight. I
returned to conversation with my friend. There
was an Italian liner anchored off Cannes in the
manner you have seen. Later I saw a lighter make
its way out to the ship and two cars hoisted aboard.
Finally the tender which takes the passengers also
went out to the ship, and a few minutes later the
vessel raised anchor and just as prettily as you are
seeing now, sailed away from France, with the
get-away car, the Florents and the stolen de Merseraux baby. As I say, people forget that just below the winter Casino, at the beginning of the port,
is a maritime station where, if you know the
schedules and have made the arrangements, you
can board an ocean liner proceeding in either direction: towards Italy, or towards Portugal which
is the last stop before it crosses the ocean to the
U.S. That particular ship would make its next
stop at Lisbon where, as it was generally known,
the mother of Madame Florent lived.'

Fairchild shook his head like a boxer who has
just managed to get up off the floor and is still
dazed. He said, 'I don't get it yet. You still haven't
plugged up any of the holes. Surely they had to
pass some kind of exit formalities—immigration
police?'

'The carry-cot,' said the Colonel. 'It was the
carry-cot which played a major part and which

in the end did them in. They went to too much trouble to establish it.

'The Leopard was certain that he had identified Florent, even though he had greatly changed in his appearance, as the collaborator responsible for the death of our friend. That made him Suspect Number One. When we checked the offices of the Italian line here, we found that when the Florents had booked a cabin to Lisbon and made arrangements for the transport of their car, they had their baby in the carry-cot with them and Monsieur Florent explained that he would appreciate it if he did not have to bring his car to the maritime station at the usual early loading time, but just before the lighter was to sail, and they would then board the ship with the baby. The officials agreed to this. Thus, when the Florents showed up to board the liner there were no problems, no suspicions and no questions asked. One seven or eight-month-old infant bundled up in a carry-cot, with just a mouth, eyes and nose showing, looks like any baby of either sex. And that's how the de Merseraux child left the country, to be taken over by some equally desperate men in a hide-out in Lisbon where nobody would ever think of looking for it. It needed only a telephone call from Florent, if things had gone wrong, to have the child killed, the body disposed of, the men dispersed and that would have been an end to that story, with God knows what repercussions in the Government and the police, since the grandfather—old man de Merseraux—is a power. It certainly would have ended my friend Scoubide.'

Salmon had been thinking hard through all this. He said, 'But I remember your saying that shortly after the Florents returned from Lisbon by car with their baby, it was kidnapped . . .' He stumbled over the words, '. . . Y-you kidnapped . . . They took the baby out by boat and brought a baby back by car.'

'The carry-cot again,' the Colonel said, 'slung from the roof of the car. A rich-looking Mercedes with expensive luggage and a lady and gentleman in the front seats with nothing to declare at the border at La Junquera, who is going to look into a carry-cot in which there is ostensibly a sleeping child, to find only a bundle of bedding in the shape of a baby? The carry-cot was, of course, empty.'

Fairchild who had been watching the affair with considerable bewilderment suddenly had an idea and asked, 'You said that both kids were back safely and the fuzz was on to the Florents. Why wait so long for the collar?'

'Evidence,' the Colonel replied. 'What you call the tidying up. The fellows in Lisbon. The Portuguese police have them. Then the men from the Department *Judiciaire* under Scoubide had to re-check all that we had established, not to mention the uncovering of the other machinations of the Florents which drove them to the desperation of the kidnapping.'

The excitement had died down. The drinkers

on the terrace were once more concerned with their own affairs. Fairchild said, 'What I don't understand is why the Florents didn't blow while they had the chance. When they had to swap babies they must have known their number was up.'

Colonel Roquebrun reflected for a moment. Then he replied: 'How was it that famous English writer Orwell put it? "Big Brother is watching you." They didn't dare. They didn't know who it was had defeated them. Arrangements for the exchange of the infants were made privately and anonymously with no police involved and they were confused and like so many criminals hung on just too long. Now all the credit will go to Scoubide.'

'And the bastards will never know who gave them the . . .' Salmon began when the Colonel interrupted firmly.

'Oh yes they will. This I have promised the Tiger and in return he has given me his word that his long knife will remain in its sheath. He was very fond of the Antelope. The Florents will receive explicit information as to who was responsible. They will have time to reflect upon this until their reflective apparatus is removed from them.'

'Removed?' Salmon repeated.

Fairchild grimaced. 'Our friend here is referring to that particularly Gallic piece of machinery known as the guillotine. The French are not as long-winded or squeamish about disposing of kidnappers as we are.'

'It is a most black crime,' the Colonel pro-
nounced and both men gave him a quick look, but
he was serious.

The grim words, almost as something tangible,
hung there between them. Then Fairchild who
had been thinking hard said, 'So this pair snatch
the child; they take it out of the country as their
own; stay a week and . . . Hey!' he cried, 'What
did they do with their own kid while they were
gone? Supposing someone had come to their house
and found it was there, or it had been seen?'

The Colonel replied with his eyes again. He was
now looking over his shoulder to the empty table
behind them. The two men's heads jerked about
as though yanked by a cord and Salmon said,
'Jumping J.C.! You mean the tarts?'

Fairchild had a terrible sinking feeling in his
stomach at the manner in which Salmon had used
the word 'tarts', and it was not eased by the memory that he had practically arranged a rendezvous
with one of them, that his appetite had been
aroused.

'Yes . . . Ilse. You see, she had a baby.'

'I don't get it,' said Salmon.

'It's really reasonably simple and boils down to
a matter of squalls, nappies, the actual physical
presence of an infant . . . In a house where there
is no baby, it is practically impossible to conceal
the presence of one. In a house where there is a
baby, and this is known in the neighbourhood, it
is an easy matter to hide a second since no one is
looking for it.'

'But these girls?' Fairchild said, still shaken by what might have been a narrow escape, for all kinds of thoughts including blackmail were shooting through his skull.

'As companions of the evening,' the Colonel replied, 'they were trustworthy and recommendable, I believe. No one has had any trouble with them and as you see, Ilse had her baby without ever bothering the father. But they were in with the Florents on their rackets.'

'Rackets?' queried Salmon uneasily, 'An outfit like the Florents?'

'The Florents were involved in everything a respectable jeweller ought not to be,' the Colonel replied. 'For one thing, they were smuggling in cheaper gold from Italy and for another, I suspect doing a bit of receiving of gems of questionable origin as well, particularly from over the border. As you know, whenever there is a jewellery theft, the thieves break up the pieces at once; emeralds, diamonds, rubies, sapphires of reasonable size cannot be identified.' He turned to Salmon, 'There would have been no guarantee that some of the stones in the article you might have bought for Madame Salmon would not have had a previous home with some other attractive lady. The two girls were their couriers in all of this illicit traffic. As a matter of fact, there were originally three; Florent married one of them who actually had a German mother living in Lisbon. Ilse had no choice. The Florents simply parked their own baby with her during their absence in Lisbon. The child never left the country. When the Florents returned, they took it back from Ilse and never would have been suspected.'

'If your Captain Scoubide hadn't come to you for help,' Fairchild concluded.

'Yes. There, that little fellow—that's Captain Scoubide, just passing,' the Colonel said.

They looked and saw a thin, sallow, camera-garlanded tourist. If at one time he had been on the point of exhaustion he was recovered now. His small moustache was bristling and his shoulders were carried high. As he passed in the throng he glanced up at Colonel Roquebrun. They were not aware of any signal, but in the dark eyes of the detective Fairchild thought he had caught a glimpse of such worship as he looked upon Colonel Roquebrun as comes to few men from their fellows.

The Colonel said, 'He will probably receive the highest award from France that his rank and position will enable them to give him. Well, he's deserved it. He, too, has suffered.'

Arnold Salmon suddenly burst out, 'Hey, wait a minute!' For he was a professional of plots and in a story conference would invariably put the finger on a weak spot, or something left uncovered. 'What about that ear? Okay, so you said there were so many accidents on the roads around here, but what if no ear had been found?'

'Oh, yes, the ear. Shall we say that it was in a sense a *façon de parler*—a manner of speaking—a symbol? Captain Scoubide was on twenty-four hour call for any traffic accident happening within fifty kilometres, empowered to take over on the scene and the investigation thereafter. Any other member would have done—a finger a thumb, a toe. After we had the Florents' child it was suggested to him that there be an even exchange. He refused. The anguish that he must have caused his wife by this refusal, thinking we were bluffing, shows you the manner of man he was. And so something more drastic was required and the little box arrived and with it a note that unless the de Merseraux baby was restored alive, or if it were to be killed, he would be receiving the rest of his own child piecemeal. It worked. It was sheer coincidence that Scoubide did come across a severed ear; or justice.'

'God Almighty!' said Salmon, and seemed to collapse in his chair as though all the wind had gone out of him.

Fairchild had a large drink. His eyes were sparkling. Everything but the share of the Colonel, the Zoo Gang and the connivance of the police in the double kidnapping was publishable. He said, 'Brother, what a story!' and then, 'Shall we go to dinner where we can talk some more? Where do you suggest?'

The Colonel said, 'Just a few yards up the Croisette, *"Chez Felix"*. He is an old friend of mine and will look after us properly. He had a wonderful record in the Resistance during the war.'

For a moment Salmon turned his head and

looked at the empty table and the look on his
face was so patent that the Colonel could hardly
forbear to smile. It said so plainly, 'There went
my babe for the night', and he was almost tempted
to say to him, 'Cannes is full of them, and one is
very much like another,' but refrained. Instead he
said, 'I'm afraid, Mr Salmon, that you will have to
give up the idea of a Florent piece for Madame Salmon. The shop will be sealed for a very long time.
But if I may suggest, only a little further up the
street you will find that Van Cleef and Arpels is
offering some designs of equal originality, and
some of even more than the Florents'. We pass the
shop on the way to Felix. You can look in the window.'

Fairchild raised his hand to call the waiter to
bring the bill.

If you enjoyed *The Anderson Tapes*
this is your kind of book!

11 HARROWHOUSE

by GERALD A. BROWNE

Here is a novel in the Hitchcock tradition of
high adventure, romance, and suspense, a story
combining an ingenious *Rififi*-like theft with an
ensuing chase that moves across many of the
exotic faces of Europe. The place is 11 Harrow-
house, a dignified structure in London's posh
Mayfair district. The target is deep within its
subterranean vault—some thirteen billion dollars' worth of diamonds. J. Clyde Massey, a man
whose personal wealth runs into billions, com-
missions the heist not for love of money but
for the pleasure of revenge. For his operatives
he selects a most unlikely crew: Chesser, a diamond merchant, and his sensuously beautiful
mistress, Maren.

A DELL BOOK $1.50

If you cannot obtain copies of this title at your local bookseller, just send
the price (plus 15c per copy for handling and postage) to Dell Books, Post
Office Box 1000, Pinebrook, N. J. 07058.

HOW MANY OF THESE DELL BESTSELLERS HAVE YOU READ?